Blue Mondays

EMILY DUBBERLEY

First published in Great Britain in 2014 by Hodder & Stoughton
An Hachette UK company

1

A CIP catalogue record for this title is available from the British Library

Paperback ISBN 978 1 444 79354 3
eBook ISBN 978 1 444 79355 0

Typeset by Hewer Text UK Ltd, Edinburgh
Printed and bound by CPI Group (UK) Ltd, Croydon, CR0 4YY

Hodder & Stoughton policy is to use papers that are natural,
renewable and recyclable products and made from wood grown in
sustainable forests. The logging and manufacturing processes
are expected to conform to the environmental regulations
of the country of origin.

Hodder & Stoughton Ltd
338 Euston Road
London NW1 3BH

www.hodder.co.uk

CHAPTER 1

The laptop bag was digging painfully into Lucy's shoulder. She tried to move it but the Tube was too packed for her to reach across her body without spilling her coffee. Her other arm was pinned in position by a perfectly groomed woman wearing an immaculate cream coat – who was now also wearing a scowl directed at Lucy. Lucy smiled apologetically, wriggled her shoulders and shifted her weight from foot to foot, hoping to somehow dislodge the strap twisted directly over the soft dip of her shoulder, but to no avail. Closing her eyes, she took a deep breath and tried to think happy thoughts: only six more stops. The pain in her feet was helpfully distracting her from her shoulder; the heels she'd fallen in love with at the weekend had been gorgeous at first glance but were hellish in reality. A bit like the men she'd been dating recently. She only realised she'd sighed out loud when the man closest to her gave her a quizzical look.

Lucy yawned: getting out of bed this morning had been a struggle, and walking to the station in the rain had only added to the Monday blues. She'd laddered her tights in a fight with her umbrella – though to be fair, the umbrella came off worse. As a result, the half hour she'd spent blow-drying her hair was wasted, and hairspray was now sticking clumps of it together in rat tails. 'Because I'm worth it,' she thought, as she caught sight of herself in the Tube window.

Still, back to the happy thoughts: she'd spent the weekend working on the reports her boss, Anna, wanted and had emailed them over late last night, so all she had to do this morning was press clippings; everyone else on her floor would be in the morning meeting. Lucy knew it was a dogsbody job but she enjoyed looking through newspapers and magazines for stories that could be relevant to the business. It gave her time to ease into the week, absorbing the latest fashion, celebrity, culture and style news to update the team – even if they did seem to know it all already, through some form of hipster osmosis. Lucy tugged self-consciously at her mint-green pencil skirt, which had a daring split up the front: all the magazines said pastels were in this season, but she wasn't entirely sure the suit was flattering. She'd find out soon enough – Anna didn't hold back on giving her opinion – whether you'd asked for it or not. The carriage lurched and Lucy bit her lip as her bag shifted on her shoulder, making her muscles twinge again.

The Tube pulled into Victoria and the doors opened; commuters flowed out rapidly onto the equally packed platform. In the short space between them leaving and more people getting on, Lucy could breathe out fully without worrying she'd be invading someone's personal space. She quickly moved her bag onto the other shoulder – bliss – and tried to manoeuvre her way towards one of the now-empty seats, but the groomed woman blocked her way, seemingly oblivious to her. As Lucy tried to squeeze past, coffee clutched close to her chest, the woman's elbow knocked her and brown froth shot out the top of the cup, down Lucy's pale suit jacket. Lucy bit her lip, her face burning, and muttered an apology – though she couldn't help noticing the woman was as pristine as before, not a drop of coffee on her. The woman scowled again; then promptly took the seat Lucy had been aiming for.

Lucy edged towards the only other empty seat, but the passengers from the platform were pushing onto the train and a slim woman with a 'baby on board' badge was making a beeline for it. The woman looked at her pointedly, and Lucy stepped out of the way to allow her to sit. She grabbed the bar overhead, put her laptop bag on the floor between her feet and took a sip of coffee –lukewarm. At least the strap wasn't hurting her shoulder any more – and she only had five more stops to go. She wiggled her toes inside her shoes as she idly glanced around the carriage.

Now that the scowling woman had sat down, the passenger standing closest to her was a man holding a large picnic basket. It seemed incongruous – if he was on his way to a date, odd timing aside, he could definitely be accused of lacking attention to detail.

Although he was obviously making some effort to look smart in a white shirt and chinos, his sleeves were rolled up, his shoes had mud on them and his tousled hair suggested he'd either got caught in the rain or had forgotten to brush his hair before he left the house. Given his stubble, either was possible – though his damp shirt suggested the weather was at least partly to blame. He looked out of place next to the Sloane Square suits and Notting Hill media-types surrounding him – though that wasn't necessarily a bad thing. His shoulders were broad and his arms were strong, muscles bulging softly as he held the hamper, thighs pressing against his chinos. He didn't have the body of a gym addict, though; more the look of a man who spent a lot of active time outdoors.

As her eyes wandered, Lucy noticed a burst of sandy chest hair poking out of the top of the shirt, which clung to his body enough to show he wasn't wearing anything underneath. She knew it was ridiculous, but seeing him in nothing but a shirt with rolled-up sleeves when the men around him were all wearing jackets or coats made him appear more masculine, unfazed by such trivialities as the weather. She looked more closely, following the outline of the muscles under his shirt, his nipples hard against the damp fabric, helping Lucy paint a mental picture that made her smile properly for the first time all morning. She shifted her gaze upwards, and realised the man was looking directly at her. Her face heated for the second time in her journey – but when he shot her a broad smile, she couldn't help but smile back – though her blush deepened.

As the train approached Sloane Square, the woman in the cream coat took a mirror from her bag and checked her make-up, dabbing at an imperceptible smudge with a handkerchief before pulling out a perfume atomiser. She sprayed herself liberally, filling the air with a sweet cloying smell that made Lucy fight against retching – she was unable to stop her nose from wrinkling. She backed a little further up the carriage, away from the perfume – and towards the man with the hamper. The woman, oblivious to the effect her ablutions were having, stood up and followed Lucy towards the doors. She took hold of the rail, displaying an armful of heavily jewelled bracelets and revealing that the cream coat was, in fact, a cape. The movement only served to waft more perfume into the faces of all those around her. When the Tube doors finally opened and the woman stepped out, Lucy had never been so grateful for London air. She gulped down a couple of cold, metallic breaths through the open door.

'So do you want her seat, before you pass out from the fumes?' the man asked her.

'Sorry?'

'Well, you look like you need to sit down. Not that I blame you – as far as I'm concerned that kind of stuff should be considered a chemical weapon. Oh – too late. Sorry.' Lucy glanced over to see another man taking the seat, but she couldn't say she regretted her loss. She could tell from his expression that the smell still lingered, so standing up had its benefits. She smiled at the stranger.

'It doesn't matter – not got far to go – but thanks for the thought. Didn't you want the seat? That looks heavy.' She gestured at the basket.

'I'm used to carrying more than a hamper around the place. Anyway, I like to practise balancing.'

Lucy blinked at him, unsure what to say.

'Don't look at me like that. It's all about bending at the knees. You never know when a good sense of balance will come in handy. Why waste a fortune on Pilates lessons when London Underground is kind enough to offer the perfect core workout for free?' As if to prove his point, the man stayed upright as the train lurched into South Kensington, even though Lucy had to lean against the glass divider to stay balanced.

'Then again, don't look a gift horse in the mouth.'

The man gestured at two seats that had emptied next to them and Lucy gratefully sat down. She was tempted to ease her feet out of her shoes but wasn't entirely sure she'd be able to squeeze them back on afterwards – did pins and needles lead to swollen feet?

She put her laptop back between her feet and turned to the man, catching his scent for the first time as he leaned towards her. He smelled outdoorsy – just a whiff of fresh-cut grass, with feral, rich undertones, his cotton shirt adding a musty but not unpleasant dampness. He was clearly wearing some fresh, citrussy aftershave but it was dominated by his natural musk in a way that made Lucy's stomach flip and her mind flounder in search of a way to continue the conversation. She had never felt so turned on just from somebody's smell. Apart from anything else, it was a welcome respite from the previous olfactory assault.

'So I have to ask, what's the hamper in aid of?' she managed. 'It's hardly picnic weather.'

'That depends where you're going. Anyway, it was only a flurry of rain this morning – I think it's going to turn out lovely.'

'Positive thinking.'

'What's the point of any other kind?' he grinned. 'If you're having a shit day, why wallow? You can't change what's happening but you can change your attitude to it. Take that perfume woman – you could either see her as thoughtless and self-centred, or as a shining example of why money doesn't matter.'

'How do you mean?'

'Well, she was clearly loaded, but she must be miserable or she wouldn't have been so snotty and rude. If money doesn't make you happy, then why chase it? Here you are first thing on a Monday morning, struggling into work when I'm sure you'd much rather be in bed.' Was it Lucy's imagination, or did he linger on the word 'bed'? 'What would happen if you didn't go into work?' he continued.

'Well, Mondays aren't really a good example. It's mostly an admin day.'

He arched an eyebrow. 'So, papers don't get filed. And . . . ?'

Lucy thought for a second. What *did* it matter if she went into work or not? What did she do that was actually useful? When she first came to London to work in events, she'd wanted to help run charity fundraisers and combine fun with helping people – use glamour for good. When she'd joined BAM! Anna had told her that they took corporate social responsibility seriously but, other than doing social media for a charity event that happened to be hosted by one of Anna's favourite celebrities, Lucy had seen little evidence of that in four years. She'd always railed against the idea that people in marketing had no souls but the longer she worked at the agency, the more she suspected the stereotype was true.

'You're doing it again.'

'What?'

'Thinking too much – you look like you've got the weight of the world on your shoulders. You've spent half your journey biting your lip so you're clearly worrying about something. Perfume woman has given you the perfect excuse to throw off your shackles. You need to relax, have some fun.'

Lucy bristled at his suggestion – did she seem uptight? 'I don't think my landlord would be happy to get his rent in "fun".'

'I don't know about that,' said the man, eyes rapidly running over Lucy's body in a way that she should have found offensive but instead made her stomach flip again. 'All I'm saying is, see life as an opportunity. You've already learned something this morning.'

'What's that?'

'Other than my world-class political analysis, that bad perfume can be a conversation-starter, of course. When's the last time you talked to a stranger on the Tube?'

Lucy smiled. 'Fair point. So what's your excuse?'

'I'm not from round here,' he said, putting on a country bumpkin accent.

'So you're not used to our London ways?'

'Exactly. I'm a Cornwall boy – far friendlier than you city types.'

'My sister lives there, but I've not been to see her yet so I'll have to take your word for it,' Lucy replied.

'It's a great part of the country but it's not ideal for setting up a business. Too far from London.'

'So the anti-capitalist wants to earn money?'

The man smiled. 'Touché – but not money. Time. I spent nearly ten years working for other people before I realised that I was spending all my time building someone else's dream. So I decided to go for my own dream instead.'

'Which is?'

'Good food and an easy life.'

'You're a chef?'

He laughed. 'If you'd ever met one you'd know that's not an easy life. No – although I did go to catering college. But I soon realised the hours were ridiculous – unless you enjoy working every weekend and having a social life that fits into two hours mid-afternoon and a staff drink at midnight if you're lucky.'

'Sounds almost as bad as my job. I've worked four weekends in a row.'

'That's a lot of admin.'

'It's not just admin,' she protested. 'I get to be creative too.'

'What was the last creative thing you did?'

Lucy thought about the last campaign she worked on, a supermarket promotion for dog toothbrushes: one of the few unglamorous clients the company had, and the only one she'd been given to manage rather than just support since she'd started at BAM!. 'I came up with a campaign that led to a twenty per cent sales increase in canine oral health products.' Even as the words fell out of her mouth, she felt foolish.

'Decaying dog teeth – an important issue. If you didn't go into work, the nation's dogs would be filling up dentists' chairs. No one could get their wisdom teeth taken out. People would be grumpy because of cavities. I take it all back – clearly, you do need to work all hours or the nation will be in peril. I'll thank you the next time I get savaged by a dog with healthy teeth.'

Even though he was teasing her, the man's eyes crinkled so mischievously that Lucy couldn't take offence.

'So what's the terribly important work that you do, then? You avoided the question.'

'I didn't – I just got diverted by doggy dentistry. I run a food network.'

'On TV?' He was certainly good-looking enough to be a television presenter.

'Hell, no. I'm not really a fan of TV chefs – their egos are more important than their stomachs. No, a local food network. I work with suppliers all over the south-east to help get the best local products out to a wider audience.'

'So you're in marketing too?'

'Not really, although I do work with a lot of campaign groups – "grow your own" initiatives, food banks, that kind of thing. But there are two main sides to my business: a centralised online shop so people can buy local products from one website, and a small wholesale service to restaurants, to help push local producers – hence the hamper.'

'What's in it?'

'Where to start? Cheese, meat, jams, pickles – and something I'm hoping will pay the rent this month.'

'What's that?' asked Lucy, her stomach rumbling. She was regretting missing breakfast.

'If I tell you I'll have to kill you. But you've got an honest face, so what the hell.'

He opened the hamper and pulled out a paper bag. When he held it out Lucy peered nervously inside.

'Mushrooms?'

'Not just mushrooms. Morels. Worth about twice as much per kilo as fillet steak at the moment.'

'So why would you have to kill me for showing me mushrooms?'

'In case you follow me home and try to find my morel patch, of course. There's good money in those hills.'

The next station is High Street Kensington.

Lucy felt a pang of disappointment as the man stood up. 'This is me,' he said. 'Pleasure to meet you. Enjoy the rest of your day. And remember, hands off my mushrooms.'

Lucy's eyes followed the man, a smile still on her lips, as he put the hamper under one arm and headed through the door. The train was emptying, so she leaned over to pick up her laptop and put it on the seat next to her. As she did, she noticed a wallet where her mushrooming companion had been sitting. The doors were beeping, and starting to close. Without thinking, she grabbed the wallet, ran for the doors, laptop flapping, and just made it through before they closed and the train pulled out of the station.

Lucy scoured the platform but couldn't see the man anywhere. Surely he couldn't move that fast carrying a hamper? She followed the flow of people, looking from left to right, but it was only when she reached the top of the stairs that she saw him, heading through the ticket hall on the other side of the barriers. She was about to call him when she realised that they hadn't exchanged names. She quickly opened the wallet and rifled for a card – Ben Turner.

'Ben,' she called, but although the man paused for a second, he kept walking. Lucy fumbled for her Oyster card and waved it at the machine, striding through the ticket hall and the short parade of shops beyond it and reaching the street exit just in time to see Ben turning down a side road. She started running, cursing her shoes with every agonising step. As she reached the turning he headed inside a building towards the end of the street – Lucy was just too far behind him to call out and attract his attention. She kept running, pace slowing as she felt her left heel start to blister. Arriving at a set of glass doors, Lucy peered inside and saw a reception desk – it must be some kind of office block. She walked in.

'Excuse me, I've got something for Ben Turner – the man who just came in here. Can you let me know where I can find him?'

'Let me just check, madam.' The man behind the desk started tapping at a computer. 'Sorry. The system's crashed. I'm going to have to do a restart. I'll be right with you.' He resumed typing.

Lucy waited, increasingly aware that she was going to be late for work. Thank god for the morning meeting – no one would be out of that until noon, so as long as she was there reading magazines when it finished they'd assume she'd been there all the time. Rosie on reception was a mate and wouldn't drop her in it. Lucy's eyes roamed carelessly around the foyer as she waited, settling on the plant in the corner, the magazines laid out for visitors, the guest book. She spotted a familiar name.

'It says here that Ben Turner signed in to Babylon. That's who I need.'

'If you'd just like to sign in.'

'I'm only popping in and out.'

'Regulations, miss.'

Lucy scribbled her name onto the badge, waited as the receptionist painstakingly slotted it into a plastic holder on a lanyard, and headed for the lift.

'You'll want the seventh floor,' he called after her.

As the lift carried her upwards, Lucy wondered what the hell she was doing. Yes, the guy lost his wallet. But what was wrong with handing it in at the Tube station like anyone else? No, she had to get all heroic. Her mum was always telling her to stop trying to save everyone around her and look after herself. Then again, he was seriously gorgeous so maybe she *was* looking after herself: her mum would probably understand if she saw him.

The lift beeped and Lucy stepped into another foyer. There was a reception desk but there didn't seem to be any staff around. She headed down the corridor, past a row of coat racks, and found herself in an empty restaurant.

'Can I help you?' asked a man cleaning glasses behind the bar.

'I'm here to see Ben Turner.'

'No one called that here. Is he here for a meeting?'

'He's . . .' Lucy tried to remember. 'A food supplier.'

'Oh, guy with a hamper?'

'That's him.'

'He's with chef outside. Follow me.'

* * *

As Lucy stepped through the door, it took her a few seconds to stop staring. Moroccan lampshades and ornate trellises decorated a formal garden that spread as far as she could see, complete with gazebos and intricately laid-out flower beds. It didn't feel like she was in London any more, but some glamorous foreign retreat – or perhaps in an Arabian fairy tale. As if in homage to the view the sun broke through the clouds, shining through sheer chiffon curtains that masked off booths around the edges. She realised she'd been gaping in silence, and thanked the barman, who gestured her towards one of the covered areas and headed back inside, saying 'I'm in the bar if you need anything.'

As she walked through the elegantly designed garden and neared the covered veranda, Lucy saw a well-muscled forearm resting on the arm of a high-backed chair turned away from her, and a hamper resting on a low table.

'Ben?'

The man stood and turned. His brow furrowed.

'Maybe I was right to be fearful for my mushrooms if you're tracking me from the Tube – and you know my name.'

'You left your wallet behind,' Lucy said, holding it out.

'You have got to be kidding me. I hadn't even noticed. You're a lifesaver.'

He pulled her into a hug so spontaneous that Lucy didn't see it coming, and she stood, arms rigid, unsure of what to do.

'No worries. Well, nice seeing you again.' When he released her she turned to go, embarrassed. His scent was provoking the same response as it had on the train and it was really rather disconcerting.

Ben reached out, fingertips brushing against the back of her arm. 'Not so fast, sunshine. You've just returned my wallet. Surely you want some kind of a reward? And you haven't even told me your name.'

'It's Lucy. And someone wise once told me money doesn't buy happiness.'

'Who said I was offering money?'

Pictures of what lay under Ben's shirt sprang all too easily to mind and Lucy gave an involuntary sharp intake of breath.

'Not that – you have a dirty mind,' Ben said. 'And you're utterly transparent. I like it.'

He smiled cheekily, with such charm that Lucy couldn't feel offended.

'No, I was wondering, could I treat you to breakfast? I've got a hamper full of food, so the least I can do is feed you. I just need to quickly go through it with Stefan – the chef here – so he can place an order. He had to go back to the kitchen to check on prep but it shouldn't take long.'

'I'm already running late for work.'

'Exactly. And didn't you say you have a heady morning of filing ahead of you? How about you heed the message of perfume woman and enjoy a free breakfast in the glorious Moroccan splendour that surrounds us. Or indeed, a Tudor garden or the English countryside – both are around the corner if only you'll let yourself escape from being a wage slave for a morning. Take advantage of the sunshine while it lasts – it'll be raining again soon enough.'

Lucy was beginning to lose track of what was happening. One minute she was sitting on the Tube on the way to work. The next she was in an idyllic roof garden with a hot man who seemed to have some vaguely communist agenda. Still, breakfast did sound good. She'd only had time for a coffee, and as Ben opened his hamper and invited her to look inside, the contents looked incredibly appetising.

'I've got rustic sungrain bread, croissants, sheep's-milk yoghurt with quince and raspberry compote, goat's cheese, acorn-smoked ham, a wild strawberry jam that will blow your mind, and that's just the start. So what's it to be? A morning of admin or a breakfast of kings in a rooftop garden? I can even throw in flamingoes to sweeten the deal.'

'There are flamingoes here?'

'Lucy, would I lie to you?'

'You might.'

'I'm offended. I would *never* lie about something as important as flamingoes. So?'

Lucy looked at her phone. Nine-thirty and no missed calls. She could easily enjoy breakfast and still get into work before the meeting finished.

'Well, thank you. That would be lovely.'

'Just you wait. These will be the best things you ever put in your mouth.' said Ben, but he turned his eyes innocently towards the hamper when Lucy looked at him, trying to work out whether he was flirting with her. 'Give me a moment. I just need to go and have a quick chat with Stefan and let him know what's going on. Coffee?'

Lucy nodded, and then watched Ben's back as he walked away. The view from behind was just as good as the one from the front: strong thighs leading up to a firm arse. She noticed her fingers flexing and realised she was probably picturing it rather too vividly – though it did look eminently squeezable. She turned her attention to her phone and checked her email, gratified to see there was nothing urgent to deal with. Perhaps Mondays weren't so bad after all. She fired up Huffington Post and started reading up on the day's news.

'OK, is there anything that you haven't tried yet?'

Lucy groaned. 'No more food. Please. It's all too good to resist but if I eat another thing, I'm going to explode.'

She looked at the plate in front of her. Flaked almonds were all that remained of the buttery almond croissants they'd started with. Then came the bread, crusty and yeasty, with rich Buttercup cheese and creamy Olde Sussex, tangy Sussex Charmer and delicate herbed goat's cheese; fresh honeycomb and gooseberry conserve, rose jelly and wild strawberry jam. She'd washed it down with a pot of fresh coffee that Ben had managed to rustle up before moving on to fresh-pressed apple and pear juice, and was now enjoying a glass of elderflower champagne.

'I can't sell it yet but it always seems to help sales if I have a bottle around,' he told her.

'I can see why. It's delicious. Is it strong?'

'No more so than normal wine – though it does tend to be more lethal.'

'How come?'

'Because it goes down so easily.' Ben gestured at her glass, and Lucy realised she'd drained it without noticing.

'Top-up?'

'I shouldn't really – I don't want to turn up to work late *and* drunk.'

'So don't,' Ben said.

'You're right, I should be getting back.'

'No, I meant don't turn up to work. Throw a sickie. You were up late last night working. Say you woke up feeling awful, and take the day off.'

'To do what?'

'Whatever you want.'

'Like see flamingoes?' Lucy remembered Ben's pre-breakfast promise.

'Like see flamingoes, if that's what it's going to take to convince you. I am a man of my word.'

He reached for her hand, which was almost entirely enveloped by his. It felt comfortable, secure. He led her through a doorway covered with vines – 'These are the

Tudor gardens – my personal favourite. But you want flamingoes, so I'll give you the full tour later.'

As they walked, Lucy felt more aware of her hand than any part of her body. Ben's strong fingers pressed lightly around her own, and she wanted to entwine her fingers in his, to pull him closer – particularly when she got another whiff of his scent.

The more time she spent with him, the sexier he became. He'd kept her entertained over breakfast with stories from his cheffing days that had her laughing in a way she couldn't remember doing for years; and his passion for food was contagious. As she'd eaten her way through the hamper's contents, he'd told her how producers made the cheese extra creamy, which roses made the rose jelly so intense, and numerous other tiny secrets that made her feel more connected to the food she was eating. It tasted delicious: a far cry from the plastic-wrapped croissant she generally had for breakfast.

Ben's thumb lightly brushed against her inner wrist as he led her away from the formal gardens towards a red hump-backed bridge over a pond. Lucy could feel the flip in her stomach turning into a warmth spreading through her belly – how was it that some men could turn you on with nothing more than the brush of a finger when others could strip you naked and work through everything in the Kama Sutra without having much effect? She thought back to David's efforts: all very considered – he liked to think of himself a sexual sophisticate – but he'd never evoked the kind of arousal that Ben was inspiring now. Was it his smell? The way he seemed to look deep inside her when his eyes met hers, making her feel as if she was the most interesting – and sexy – woman alive? His body? Whatever it was, as Ben spoke, giving her idle details about the gardens – 'They're into sustainability – all the kitchen vegetable waste is used to feed the wormery.' – Lucy could feel her desire building alarmingly. 'I can't believe I'm getting horny for a man who's talking about worms,' she thought. She glanced at Ben and was distracted by his lips – full and perfectly formed. How would they feel on hers?

When they were on the bridge, Ben stopped. He dropped her hand, and touched the small of her back.

'As promised, flamingoes,' he said, pointing.

Sure enough, there were four pale pink birds standing in the rooftop lake, surrounded by a carpet of spring flowers, crocuses and anemones. One of them casually balanced one-legged while another had its beak in the water. As it lifted its head up, water sprayed from its beak, glittering in the sunlight.

'And you doubted my word.'

'They're beautiful.'

'They're not the only ones.' Ben said, casually dropping his arm around Lucy's waist. She felt heat rise in her cheeks once more – and as Ben's fingertips rested on the swell of her hip, their warmth penetrating her skin, it seemed to be rising elsewhere too. She felt uncomfortable – this wasn't like her at all. She tried to focus on the conversation.

'So why do they have flamingoes here?'

Ben shrugged. 'I'm not sure – they've had them since the '70s, I think – Stefan told me they've had some amazing parties, particularly back in the day – Jagger, Marc Bolan, Bowie – proper stars, not the reality TV types you get today. I guess the flamingoes add to the glamour. Someone once told me you could get fined £250 for throwing one off the roof though I've no idea how he'd know something like that.'

'Can't they fly?' She pictured drunken revellers chasing flamingoes around the gardens and Kensington residents finding pink birds ambling down the high street in the morning.

'They've had their wings clipped so they don't escape, so no. It's beautiful here but I can't help feeling a bit sorry for them – stuck at endless parties in central London, forced to put up with small talk all the time. I couldn't do it.'

Lucy couldn't help but be reminded of David again. He'd insisted they went to all 'the right' parties, which was OK to start with but as soon as he'd put the diamond engagement ring on her finger they'd become increasingly pressured. David seemed to assume that the ring gave him the right to tell her what to do. 'As an engaged woman, you need to dress more elegantly.' 'I don't like you drinking more than one glass of wine while we're out – it gives the wrong impression.' 'What were you doing talking to that guy so intently?' She'd found herself spending less time with friends and more with acquaintances as she tried to fit into his world. She'd tried to be the woman he'd wanted her to be but in the end she had to accept there was no way she could change enough to make him happy. It was only now, a year on, that she was starting to remember who she'd been before she met him.

Ben took his arm from around her waist and grabbed her hand again, as if sensing her change in mood.

'Enough flamingoes?'

Lucy nodded. David was the last person she wanted to think about – she'd wasted quite enough time on him already. Why let him spoil what was rapidly turning into the most romantic morning of her life?

Ben led Lucy back to the Tudor garden, his thumb absently stroking circles in her palm as they walked, making Lucy aware of a previously undiscovered erogenous zone – or at least one that had never been triggered before. Unlike the other areas, the Tudor garden felt intimate, private, divided by tall stone walls that made Lucy think of old monastery gardens.

'You should see this place in the summer,' he said, seemingly unaware of the effect he was having on her. 'It smells amazing when the lavender's coming through and the roses are in full bloom. Then again, I've always thought there's something about gardens in spring that's a bit special – when you see the first shoots starting to come through and know that everything's woken up after winter. It feels as if life's starting to happen all over again – a fresh start to the year – much more so than New Year's Eve, in my opinion.'

Lucy looked around, and sure enough, there were pale green shoots growing from the wisteria tangling on the wall, and seedlings starting to push their way through the beds. The brown leaves and twigs around them only underlined their vibrancy – new life, making itself known. 'I've never really noticed that before, but I see what you mean,' she said. 'I used to love gardening when I was a kid but now I haven't got a garden and house plants cower in fear when they see me approaching. I've been terrified of getting any more plants since I managed to kill a cactus.'

'House plants aren't the same thing as gardening. There's something about feeling your hands in the soil, planting seeds, seeing how things change from day to day – and eating food you've grown yourself. You could always start with a window box, grow some herbs, see if you can get over your fear of committing planticide. You'd be surprised how much fruit and veg you can grow indoors.'

'Maybe,' said Lucy, uncertainly. 'I don't think you realise how rubbish I am.'

He shook his head, amused. 'Maybe you're just holding back because you're scared of failure. If something doesn't grow, it doesn't matter – you can always plant other seeds. It's all a learning experience. I bet you'd enjoy it more than you think too – see it as having fun rather than something you have to get right.'

Ben gave Lucy another grin, and she felt a burst of enthusiasm. Maybe he was right.

The pair walked around the gardens in amiable silence for a while, Lucy becoming increasingly aware of her body with every step, her breathing getting heavier from Ben's casual palm stroking and her skin tingling in anticipation of his touch. Surely he must realise the effect he was having on her – and yet he still didn't make a move. When Ben showed her a 'window' cut out of the wall, and stood behind her as she peered through to admire the view over London, one arm gently resting on her shoulder, she fought her desire to pull him closer, feel his strong chest against her back, his hardness pressing into her. When he suggested they sit down on a bench to admire the view and she felt the length of his leg alongside hers, she wanted to put her hand on his thigh, feel those firm, bulging muscles for herself. When he reached up to push some leaves to one side and show her a tiny flower growing out of one of the walls, making his shirt rise up and giving her a glimpse of his defined stomach, she had to push her hands into her pockets, so great was the urge to touch him. It was a relief when he removed the temptation.

'Ever since I first came here, when Stefan started cheffing for them, I've thought the Tudor garden was the best bit. What do you think?' Ben said.

'Well, it's certainly very pretty – but the other garden's got flamingoes. That takes quite a lot of beating.'

'The Tudor gardens have their own benefits though.'

Ben led Lucy through another doorway and she realised she was standing in a completely walled garden, totally hidden from view of the building. 'So what are they?' she asked.

Ben's fingers were moving more deliberately on her wrist now, tracing patterns as he stepped in front of her and looked into her eyes. He stood there in silence, facing her, eyes intently fixed on hers as if he was trying to see her thoughts from the outside. Lucy felt uncomfortable at the depth of his scrutiny – but it also had an intimacy that made her adrenaline race and nipples stiffen against her top. Ben stepped closer and put his hand on her hip.

'Privacy. You don't strike me as a particularly public person and I'd hate to do anything to embarrass you. Are you easily embarrassed?'

Lucy felt her confidence grow as it became more obvious that Ben wanted her as much as she wanted him. She recognised the look in his eyes – but it had never made her feel like this before.

'It depends what you want to do.' She took a step towards him and looked up.

'This.' Ben tilted his head and his lips gently touched hers, warm and firm. He waited until he felt her relax under his touch before deepening the kiss, pulling her closer to him and sliding his tongue into her mouth. His lips seemed to mirror Lucy's own: she didn't feel as if she was being kissed but instead that she was part of a kiss. She moved against him unselfconsciously, feeling his hands against the small of her back, fingertips fluttering against her skin; then stroking her neck; then softly trailing down her face as he looked into her eyes before kissing her once more.

A moan escaped from Lucy's lips as Ben pulled her closer, his leg slipping between her own, creating an almost unbearable friction against her body. His hard thigh muscles were taut between Lucy's legs, exerting a delicious pressure against her clit that was proving harder and harder to ignore. Lost in the moment, Lucy rocked her pelvis against him, feeling Ben's hardness pressing ever more insistently against her. Her tongue clashed with his as she finally breathed in his scent properly, in and out, feeling her head swim at his masculine aroma – and the tempting erection pressing against her. Her breath was coming fast, small moans escaping her lips.

Ben's hands were roaming freely over Lucy's back, tangling in her hair, moving down to her buttocks, squeezing firmly as if giving her a massage, pushing her body into his as if to meld them together. As they kissed, Ben's thigh maintained its relentless contact with her body, even as he swept her back into a deep swooping kiss, his hand in the small of her back and his lips firmer, more demanding. His tongue seemed to be dancing with hers, their mouths perfectly choreographed to make

Lucy feel the kiss in every inch of her body. The way Ben dipped her only exacerbated the pressure against her and she could feel herself swelling, becoming wetter, with every flicker of his tongue.

Ben pulled her back upright to continue the kiss without skipping a beat, his thigh still in position. Lucy found herself rocking against him as they kissed, faster and faster, falling further and further into the moment until she felt a tell-tale tingling. 'No!' she thought, but it was too late. The orgasm had been building almost since the moment she'd met Ben and there was no way he was going to let her move away before it hit. Lucy kissed him hard, tongue probing his mouth eagerly, hoping to distract him from the twitches of her body as she came, muscles pulsing violently. Her pussy twitched against his thigh and she only hoped her wetness didn't show through her pale skirt. She buried her face in his shoulder, fighting off the urge to sink her teeth into him to stop herself from crying out loud at the pleasure shooting through her body; or to mark him as her own? She pulled away, gasping slightly.

Ben looked at her, pupils so large she could barely see his irises.

Lucy gazed back, face flushed, unsure of what to do next – of whether Ben realised what had happened. She focussed on making her breathing slow and steady, on trying to return to something approaching normal. 'So, I'm hoping you don't mind that I kissed you?' Ben said, hand moving to rearrange his still-hard cock, which was signposting his desire all too clearly.

Lucy smiled. 'I'm certainly glad you picked somewhere discreet.'

'Ben? Are you about?' The voice was disconcertingly near. Lucy felt an urge to make herself presentable, as if they'd been caught with their clothes off, even though the only real visual indication anyone would be able to pick up on – other than Ben's erection – was a slight flush in their cheeks and both their pupils still black with lust.

As Lucy dropped eye contact with Ben, she realised that, had it not been for the interruption, she would have continued staring into his eyes for as long as he looked back at her like that. It was as if she could see the person inside the shell – his gaze was direct, open, challenging – and there was no doubting that he desired her just as much as she desired him. She felt herself pulse again at the intent he so clearly displayed. She wanted him inside her.

Ben seemed unperturbed as he strode towards the doorway.

'Stefan. Just giving the lovely lady who found my wallet a tour. Hope you don't mind.'

'No worries, mate. Sorry it took me so long to get back to you. The new KP is proving to be about as much use as a chocolate teapot. Fucking agencies. Pardon my French.' Stefan nodded at Lucy in apology. She smiled.

'The gardens are beautiful – thanks for letting me look round.'

'Not a problem – they're open to the public anyway. Not that I could ever turn down a request from Big Ben – so how's it going, mate? Sorry I couldn't chat properly earlier – it's been the morning from hell. The veg delivery turned up an hour late so we're behind on the *mise en place* even without the numpty the agency sent.'

'Just what you need. I'm good. Set up's going well in Brighton – food festival's coming up so lots on. Garden's starting to kick in so this month's going to be hard work. Fun though.'

'How's Clare?'

Lucy saw Ben's eyes cloud over. 'Who's Clare?' she thought, a pang in her chest. Jealous after one kiss – albeit the most memorable kiss of her life? She really needed to get a grip on herself.

'Off "liberating herself" again – with the usual suspect.'

'Shit. Well, you're best off out of it. You do too much for that girl. What about your folks?'

Lucy zoned out as the pair caught up on each other's lives – keeping one ear open in case Clare's name came up again. Her mind drifted to what would have happened if Stefan hadn't interrupted them. Even though she'd climaxed hard, she still felt horny – if anything, more so than before. Ben's erection had left her in no doubt as to his desire, conjuring erotic images of what it would look like – and feel like inside her. She could feel her own wetness, and was so swollen with desire that even the pressure of her underwear against her was proving distracting. She glanced at Ben, trying to read what he was thinking, but he was casually chatting to Stefan – though he did shoot her a devilish smile when he noticed her looking at him.

'Anyway, I should get back in the kitchen – make sure the KP hasn't fucked anything else up. Can you see any flames?' asked Stefan. Ben peered in the direction of the kitchen and shook his head. 'Here's your order – love the new cheeses.' Stefan handed Ben a piece of paper. 'Delivery by Friday, yes? Give me a call if there are any problems – just after three is probably best. And let me know about that festival idea of yours – I'd love to see more details.' Stefan turned to Lucy. 'Nice to meet you, love. Come back any time – you could bring your mates down for a drink – particularly if they're as fit as you.' He winked at Lucy and moved off rapidly, before she or Ben could respond.

'Cheeky sod,' Ben laughed. 'Useless with women though – talks the talk but if one actually approaches him, he runs a mile or finds some other way to mess it up. Nice guy though.'

'He seemed it,' said Lucy. 'How do you know him?'

'We went to the same catering college – ended up getting a place together so I know he's all talk. The amount of times I saw him boasting about pulling a woman when I knew there was only one thing he'd pulled the night before – and he didn't have company.'

Lucy laughed. 'Sounds like half the guys at work. They seem to spend so much time talking *about* women that they never seem to get round to talking *to* women.'

'And you get to spend time with these people? Lucky you. So, what do you want to do for the rest of the day? I've shown you the flamingoes.'

There was no way Lucy was going to share the images that instantly popped into her mind. Her body was still sensitive after her orgasm – but she didn't want to make any rash decisions. If he'd asked her before Stefan interrupted them, she'd have done anything he wanted, but reality was starting to filter through. Part of her was beginning to feel guilty – about having an orgasm with a stranger *and* skiving off work. It was nearly eleven. If she left in the next half hour, she could still safely be at her desk by the time Anna was back in the office. After spending the entire weekend working, she didn't want to lose brownie points by being ill. She'd missed out on three promotions in the last two years, despite working late most days, and her pay packet was barely enough to cover the basics nowadays, let alone afford the sort of clothes and lifestyle she was expected to have at BAM!.

'I don't know. I'm thinking maybe I should get back to the office. I've had a lovely morning but I don't take sickies – it makes me feel so bad.'

'Did your boss feel guilty for asking you to work the weekend?'

Lucy doubted it strongly, given that Anna's last words to her had been, 'And remember, I want it double spaced.'

'I don't think so.'

'So just see it as taking back time you're owed. Why

feel guilty for taking back something that's been stolen from you?'

Lucy had to admit that the logic certainly appealed to her. And Ben's smile was as enticing as ever. That was part of the problem. If she could have an orgasm within a few hours of meeting him – even if he didn't realise it – what would happen if they spent the whole day together? The idea scared her – but also made her twitch in anticipation, her mind racing with possibilities.

'You have a point,' Lucy said. 'So what would you suggest I do with my time?'

'Well, I'm going to be going back to Brighton. I think it's exactly the kind of place you need to escape to. It's impossible not to have a good time in Brighton unless you try very hard indeed. We can walk by the sea, play Dolphin Derby on the pier; I might even show you my own roof garden – though it's not quite up to the same standards as this. But still, it'll be more fun than filing.'

Lucy was tempted – but she had reservations. She'd only met Ben a couple of hours before – should she really be considering going anywhere with a stranger? What if he had a girlfriend, or a wife? Who was Clare? What if the mud on his shoes wasn't from gardening but from burying the bodies of his victims? Even she had to admit to herself that the last one was a little fantastical – but these things happened.

She tried to pull herself together and look at the options clearly. On the one hand, she could go to work and pretend it was any normal Monday, as long as Anna didn't catch her on the way in. She could find out what Anna thought of the report and work on her promotion prospects. On the other, she could go to the seaside with the most delicious man she had ever met and possibly end up having sex that – if it was anything like the kiss – would be the best she'd ever experienced. She knew which one she wanted more – but still she felt guilty.

Ben was looking at her intently, waiting for her answer.

'OK,' she said finally, 'I'll call in sick and go with you as long as I don't get any urgent emails before the train turns up.'

Ben shook his head. 'First returning my wallet, now being all diligent and putting work before play. Don't you ever just want to say, "Fuck it," and rebel, do exactly what you want to?'

'I'm coming to the station with you aren't I?' she retorted, feeling irritated at Ben's reading of her character – though at the back of her mind, the idea of doing exactly what she wanted without thinking about anyone else did sound fun. She couldn't remember the last time she'd done it – certainly not since long before she'd been with David.

'Want to say goodbye to the flamingoes before we go?'

Lucy grinned at his childlike enthusiasm.

'Why not,' she said.

'Now that,' said Ben, 'is one of my favourite answers.'

Sitting next to him on the Tube to Victoria, Lucy still couldn't quite believe what she was doing. Anxious guilt still nagged at her even though her colleagues threw sickies all the time: it was amazing how often food poisoning cropped up after the big award dinners. But Ben was right: she had worked all weekend. Much as she liked to think that Anna would appreciate it, she hadn't given her any extra credit for working the last four weekends. Maybe it was time to get real and accept she was never going to get a promotion at BAM! no matter what she did, and would end up stuck with dog toothbrushes (or, if she was lucky, a human oral hygiene client) for the rest of her life, while her colleagues worked on the new spirit brands, make-up ranges and luxury labels.

'You're chewing your lip again,' said Ben. 'What are you thinking about?'

'Work,' Lucy admitted guiltily.

'You really do worry all the time, don't you?' he said. 'Forget about work. If you're going to skive, you may as well enjoy it.' Lucy looked around her nervously, to make sure there was no one she knew nearby who had overheard. 'I bet you were the good girl at school – always did your homework on time; never played truant. Am I right?'

Lucy nodded. 'How can you tell?'

'Because you're still the good girl at school now – not wanting to annoy your boss even though it sounds like she's been taking the piss. Not wanting to leave your colleagues in the lurch even though, from what you've said, they're not exactly your best friends. Pleasing other people rather than pleasing yourself – like bringing back my wallet even though it made you late for work – classic good girl. Unless, of course, the latter means you're a bad girl. Was it just a subtle ploy to get to my mushrooms?'

The innuendo made Lucy blush, but as Ben put his hand comfortably on her thigh, the idea of being a bad girl was far from unappealing – particularly if he was involved. She put her hand on top of his and gave it a squeeze.

'Maybe I recognised an expert skiver when I saw one and needed some tips on how to do it. What would you recommend?'

'You clearly have excellent intuition. Well, first of all, think about all the things you love but never get time to do; or the things you've always wanted to do but have never done.'

'Like what?'

'Anything. It depends on what you like, what you've done. I spent a day at a model village eating miniature food and pretending to be a giant with a load of mates once. I spent another day reverse pirating – boarding people's boats and giving them a packed lunch and a bottle of elderflower champagne. It can be anything – big or small – as long as you can do it in Brighton. Going on a rollercoaster, drinking the perfect Martini, roller skating along the seafront, catching a fish, eating a hundred penny sweets in one go, getting dressed up like old ladies and going for afternoon tea, skinny dipping in the sea, or whatever else that mind of yours can conjure up.' Ben gave her a flirtatious glance. 'It's like playing make-believe as a kid. Just think about things that would be fun. Then do them.'

Lucy reached into her bag and pulled out a pen and paper.

'What are you doing?'

'I'm making my list to work out what I want to do the most.'

Ben slapped his hand to his head. 'She even manages to turn having fun into work. Still, I suppose it's a start.' He gave Lucy's thigh another light squeeze and leaned back, giving her privacy to write. 'Tell me when you're done making your list. But I'm vetoing anything that sounds too much like work.'

By the time they got to Victoria, Lucy had made a list of ten things she wanted to do. She handed it to Ben but he gave it back. 'It's your list. We can talk about it on the train if you want but you're the one who's going to make it happen. I'm not going to do it for you. You need the skiving practice, after all.'

As she put the list back into her handbag, Lucy felt stupid: had she really thought she'd give him a list and he'd magically create some mystery tour for her? 'And as I'm skiving too, I've got a few ideas of my own to throw in. Anything you're phobic about?'

'Not really,' said Lucy, though her stomach fluttered.

'Feel the fear and do it anyway. Excellent.'

His grin only made her more anxious.

As they reached the concourse, Lucy scanned the

train times on the board, trying to stop herself from panicking about being seen by someone she knew. Ben's hand rested lightly on her shoulder blade, stroking softly as Lucy pulled out her phone and checked her emails again.

'So, how's the office looking, Little Miss Efficiency? Have they managed to lure you away from me with their demands?'

'No, nothing yet.'

Lucy thought about calling Anna and bit her lip: she wasn't the greatest of actresses and Anna wasn't particularly tolerant of sick days – particularly if it meant she had to do her own admin. But if she wasn't going in, she needed to let them know soon – otherwise Anna would call her, and be utterly unimpressed at having to do so.

Platform 16 for the 11.45 to Brighton, calling at East Croydon, Gatwick Airport and Brighton.

Ben looked at her.

'Five minutes, Lucy. Time to decide – the ticket machine is just there . . .'

Ben's fingers continued their leisurely caress of her back, focussing Lucy's attention on her still-building desire. It was rapidly becoming her driving force, as every touch of his fingertips seemed to trigger different nerve endings, all sending signals to a central location. 'Do you want to be a good girl – or do you want to have some fun?'

Ben tilted his head to one side, eyes twinkling as he waited for Lucy's response.

CHAPTER 2

Lucy checked her phone for the fifth time in as many minutes.

'There's no point skiving if you're going to spend all day working,' said Ben. 'Your boss knows you're ill. At the moment, as far as she knows, you're curled up in bed. She's not expecting you to work.'

'I don't know about that,' Lucy said.

She thought about the disapproval in Anna's voice when she'd called the office, desperately hoping there wasn't a train announcement while she was on the phone that would give her away. Luckily, Anna had been her usual brusque self.

'I would have appreciated more notice. We've got a lot on. Are you going to be fit for the Dogsbody meeting on Wednesday?'

'Should be.' Lucy had coughed. 'I think I'm just a bit run-down after working late.'

'You need to work on your time management.' The phone had clicked before Lucy could reply.

'Come on, mobile off,' said Ben. 'Take it from a skiving expert.'

Lucy grudgingly did as she was told, ignoring the ball

of anxiety that gurgled in her stomach as she put her phone into her bag.

'Now, look out the window – we're passing over water so you get to make a wish.'

Again, Lucy obeyed him – smiling at the view of Battersea Bridge with the Thames twinkling underneath it. She closed her eyes and thought hard. 'I wish that Anna won't find out about me skiving.'

When she opened her eyes, Ben was looking at her with an indulgent smile on his face.

'You shut your eyes to make a wish.'

Lucy blushed. 'My mum always told me you had to close your eyes and be quiet when you made a wish or it wouldn't come true.'

'Smart woman – easy way to keep you quiet.'

'Sorry – have I been talking too much?'

'God, you're defensive. I like you talking,' he replied. 'But have you ever been around kids? They're exhausting – they question everything. Fun in small doses, but knowing how to shut them up is the only way to stay sane.'

'You seem to know a lot about it.'

'Keen uncle, me. You?'

'I'm an auntie but I don't get to see them much – they don't live near enough.'

Lucy felt a pang of failure, like she always did when she thought about her sister's life. Hope had done everything right – husband, mortgage, kids at appropriately spaced intervals – just what Lucy had been heading for with David before it had all gone wrong. By now she'd have been married and probably pregnant – his mum had dropped enough hints about the 'patter of tiny feet'. Instead, all she had was a job she hated and a flat with a few possessions she'd collected over the years. Hardly where she thought she'd be by now – and she wasn't getting any younger.

'Are you worrying again?' Ben asked.

She shook her head and smiled. 'No, it's just . . . do you ever feel you've got everything wrong?'

'No,' he said. 'How can you tell what's right or wrong? Sure, some things can feel good and some might feel bad but in the long run you learn more from your mistakes than anything else.'

She looked at him sceptically.

'Seriously, Lucy, why over analyse everything? You only get one life and you may as well enjoy it. Sure, I've made a few fuck-ups. I could have more money or be more successful – whatever that means – but I like my life. I have my own business that I love, plenty of time to see friends and enough money for a roof over my head and food in my belly. Isn't that what life's all about?'

Lucy was reminded of something she'd seen on Facebook: 'If you do what you love, you'll never work a day in your life.'

'But how do you know what to do?' she said.

'You just go with the flow. Like this.'

Ben leaned forwards and pulled Lucy into a kiss. As

his mouth met hers all thoughts vanished from her mind, and instead she was breathing in Ben's scent, feeling his full lips moving on hers, her pulse quickening as his tongue slid inside her mouth and his fingers stroked the back of her neck, sending tingles through her body. He had an uncanny knack of making her wet in seconds – something she'd never experienced before, certainly not from just a kiss.

As the kiss deepened, Ben cupped her head in his hands, pulling Lucy closer to him, sucking her lower lip into his mouth and biting it gently. This triggered something animal in her, and she found herself biting him back, kissing him fiercely. Their tongues tangled hungrily, as if vying for control. When Ben finally pulled away, breathing heavily, Lucy sat dazed for a second before getting her bearings and leaning back in her seat.

'You are seriously beautiful,' Ben said. 'I've never seen anyone with such expressive eyes. Particularly when you're looking at me like you are now.'

'Thanks,' Lucy said, embarrassed but delighted. She couldn't remember the last time she'd been complimented. Sure, David had told her she was 'a hot slut' – but only ever during sex and, if she was entirely honest, it didn't feel like all that much of a compliment. Sure, the word occasionally turned her on when they were talking dirty but hearing him say it every time got a bit repetitive and sometimes made her feel like she was only good for one thing. Ben's words made her feel special.

'So, now you're officially playing hooky, what do you want to do today?' Ben asked.

Lucy got out her list.

'Well, it sounds stupid but I really want to get some new shoes. These ones are killing me. And I got coffee on my suit.'

'Aha – a makeover. You're in luck. I'm king of the second-hand shops – and Brighton is my castle. What else?'

'I thought it'd be nice to go for a walk on the beach, see the sea – maybe have fish and chips?'

'I can do better than that – do you like shellfish?'

'Yes – though I haven't eaten it much. It's a bit expensive.'

'How does freshly caught crab sound – on me? I know the fishmonger on the beach.'

'Brilliant.'

'What else?'

'I've never been to Brighton Pavilion but I've seen photos and it looks really pretty. Or any other touristy things you'd recommend – it'd be nice if it feels like a holiday.'

'What sort of holidays do you like?'

Lucy paused to think. It was years since she'd been away. At university, she could never afford it – and she'd been too busy working anyway. On top of her studies, volunteering for the student union entertainments team meant that there never seemed time for a holiday. Between terms there was all the event planning to do

– not to mention working to pay her rent – and once term started she had essays by day and gigs by night: she'd barely had time to get back to see her mum, let alone go away. She'd even had to give up learning to drive because she was made ents manager midway through her course of lessons and there never seemed to be a spare hour in the day to continue. Since she'd been in London, things had continued in a similar way. She was working most nights, and even at weekends Anna always seemed to have big reports that she needed last minute. Lucy didn't want to let her down. London was her big chance – she didn't have anywhere else to go.

'Come on,' Ben said teasingly. 'It's not that hard a question. Beaches or city breaks? Countryside or sea-side? Hotels or roughing it in a hammock in the middle of the rainforest?'

Lucy laughed at the idea of herself as some Bear Grylls type.

'I can't really see myself hiking through the wilderness. I suppose I like the idea of being somewhere pretty – not a city. I spend all year in London and I want something different. I miss the countryside.'

'Where did you grow up?'

'Bath – and a bit of time in a tiny village in Gloucestershire. I used to love going tadpoling, making tree-houses and dens.'

'Sounds fun.'

'It was. The kids next door and I would go for walks

along the river and catch sticklebacks, play pooh sticks and look for newts. Oh, and I used to love rock-pooling on holiday in Devon. I saw an anemone once – bright blue, with purply-red tentacles. Can we go rock-pooling in Brighton?'

'It's a bit of a hike to the nearest rock pools – hmm. Maybe that's one for another day.' Lucy felt warm at the idea that Ben was already thinking of another day. 'So, back to the list. Anything else?'

'You're the expert. I'm happy to put myself in your hands.'

'Just remember you asked for it . . .' The twinkle in Ben's eyes made Lucy's stomach flip again.

As the train pulled through Gatwick and Haywards Heath, they continued chatting amiably. Ben seemed to have a knack for drawing Lucy out of herself, and she found herself being more open than she had in a long time – and even then, only with her best friend, Jo. She was confident enough at networking events but only when she was talking business. Ben made her feel comfortable enough to talk about things she never usually got to – to share her dreams – and made her think.

At first she'd assumed she was the brighter of the two of them – farming and cheffing were vocational rather than academic – and she'd realised as their conversation progressed that she was snobbish about people having degrees. But the more Ben had talked, the more he'd made reference to things that had her struggling to keep up – describing cooking in a scientific way, talking about Maillard reactions and temperature probes. Lucy had never heard anyone talk about food in that way – except maybe Heston Blumenthal – but there was something down to earth about Ben's approach that made it easy to absorb. He was clearly passionate about food – his eyes had the same sparkle she'd seen just after he kissed her.

Just looking at Ben kept Lucy in a state of arousal that was almost unbearable – like being hungry and peering into the window of a closed cake shop. She had never wanted to feel a man inside her as much as she did now. This wasn't helped by the frequent kisses – including one in a tunnel outside Gatwick that was so arousing that Lucy shocked herself with her response. The lights had flickered off and, as Ben's lips explored her own, Lucy found her hand moving to his thigh – and, in a move quite against her nature, his cock, which pressed hard against his trousers. She'd only just managed to pull her hand away as the lights came back on – but oddly, while her heart was racing, she felt turned on rather than embarrassed – particularly when she saw the look in Ben's eyes.

'You should be careful, young lady,' he said. 'Much more of that behaviour and I'll have to drag you into the toilets. And, much as I'm about seizing the day, you deserve a lot better than suffering the train loos.'

Lucy had smiled, and felt her pussy pulse at the realisation that Ben wanted her as much as she wanted him.

'We're nearly there,' said Ben. 'See those?' He pointed at some large railway arches covered in ivy, and Lucy nodded. 'That's where the dragons live. They protect Brighton from too much normality – and obviously, they're handy in case of zombie attack.'

'Good to know,' she laughed. 'So am I too normal to get in?'

'You're anything but normal, Lucy, although you may look a little too corporate in that suit. You need something you can be relaxed in – we've got a lot of fun to have. Got your ticket?'

'Yes.' Lucy patted her coat pocket.

'Perfect.' Ben stood up as the train drew to a halt and the doors started beeping. 'Grab your stuff and prepare to bunk off in style.'

Lucy knew she was going to fall in love with Brighton as soon as she stepped off the train and looked up. The glass and iron roof gave the station an airy, open atmosphere, and she felt as if she were free to start whatever adventure she wanted. Although the station had clearly been modernised recently, the style of the architecture had a vintage feel, making her think of Brief Encounter. Or perhaps it was Ben who was making her think of *brief encounters*, striding ahead of her, glancing back to make sure that she was keeping up – and catching her clocking his bum as he did. He really was utterly delicious. She scurried to catch up with him, breathing in sharply as her shoe dug into her heel again. She was sure a blister was imminent – it had been building all morning.

'Are you OK?' said Ben.

'Fine – just can't wait to get out of these,' she said, gesturing at her shoes.

'Shouldn't take long to get to the shops but we can't have you in pain. Do you want a piggyback?'

'You'll do yourself an injury.'

'Don't be daft, Lucy. I told you, I carry round things that are far heavier than you most days at work.'

'I'm way too old for a piggyback.'

'Not in Brighton you're not,' said Ben. 'Look around you. Everyone's a big kid here. See her shoes?'

He gestured at a beautiful woman with a bright pink bob, and Lucy looked down to see she was wearing polka-dot shoes with heels in the shape of bunny rabbits.

'And him?'

Ben pointed at a man unselfconsciously juggling bananas in front of a fruit stall outside the station.

'And him?' This time it was a man dressed as a chimney sweep and clutching a unicycle.

Lucy smiled. 'It's not like London, I'll give you that.'

'So relax and stop being scared of what other people think. Do you want a piggyback or not?'

Lucy looked at Ben and took in her surroundings. By now, they'd turned down a road just behind the station and it seemed quiet enough. The only people she could see were sitting outside a pub covered in vivid graffiti, wearing clothes that made it hard for her to tell whether they were male or female: though it was clear they were a couple from the way they were holding hands. Lucy was pretty sure that anyone happy to wear neon-blue leopard-print leggings and a snakeskin jacket, and to carry a birdcage in lieu of a bag, wouldn't even blink at her having a piggyback. What the hell.

'I'd love one, thanks.'

Lucy hoiked up her skirt, hoping it didn't look too inelegant, and when Ben sank to a crouch she climbed gingerly onto his back, slipping her laptop bag strap over her body to hold it more firmly in place. He hooked his hands under her knees, and she squealed as he effortlessly sprang up, picking the picnic basket up as he did so, and started running down the hill. When they got to the pub, he stopped and put her down. Lucy wondered if he knew the people she'd been looking at and was going to make her talk to them, but he took her shoulders and turned her towards the pub.

'You said you wanted to do touristy things. Here's a bit of Brighton culture for you – the "kissing coppers" by Banksy – are you a graffiti fan?'

Lucy looked at the black and white image of two policemen kissing, discreetly framed off amid a burst of vibrant images of music legends: Bob Marley, John Peel, Amy Winehouse. It did look familiar, now she came to think of it.

'I've never really thought about it. I don't like it when people just spray their name on things – it can be a bit scary wandering through some bits of London. But this sort of thing is different. It's beautiful – brightens the place up. And I guess it sends a good message too. Love for everyone and all that.'

'Glad you approve – the dragons will be happy. I've heard that if they hear someone making homophobic comments, they instantly burn them to a crisp. That's why Brighton is so gay-friendly.'

Lucy thought about her friend Rosie, who still hadn't come out because she was terrified of being disowned by her parents.

'Sounds like more of those dragons could be a good thing.'

'I knew I liked you,' Ben said. 'Right, now you've had some culture, are you ready for shopping?'

'Definitely.'

'Then climb aboard and hold on tight. You're in for a longer ride now.'

Lucy carefully got onto his back again, swapping her laptop bag onto her other shoulder, and flung her arms around his neck, clinging tightly to him as he carried on down the steep street then turned right and piggy-backed her past a row of kitsch-looking shops. He ran easily, covering ground so quickly that she could barely take in her surroundings, his breathing impressively steady. Lucy couldn't say the same about herself. The friction of Ben's back between her thighs was doing little to abate the arousal that had been coursing through her all morning; and feeling his obvious strength as she bounced on top of him and breathed in the smell of his hair and fresh sweat was even more intoxicating than the elderflower champagne.

Ben kept jogging until they reached an impressive set of stone gates topped with a turquoise blue minaret.

'You wanted to see Brighton Pavilion. We can go inside for the tour if you want but my favourite part is the gardens because they're free. I'm not a fan of paying to see something that our ancestors' taxes paid for – although they do let locals go in for free once a year.'

'The gardens it is,' said Lucy. 'I'm happy to follow your lead.'

Ben gave Lucy a look she couldn't quite read, before shaking his head as if trying to dash away an unwanted thought.

'The gardens it is. We can cut through them to get to St James's Street, where all the best charity shops are. How are your feet?'

'Still aching – but much better for the rest.'

'Well, why don't you have a sit down, slip your shoes off and enjoy the view. I've had an idea.'

'What's that?'

'It's a surprise. You OK with me leaving you here on your own? I won't be long.'

'That's fine,' Lucy said, looking at the beautiful formal garden that surrounded her.

'Well, grab a seat – you happy sitting on the grass or would you rather have a bench?'

'Grass is good for me.' Lucy had noticed various

groups of people sitting in the gardens looking relaxed and it seemed less exposed than sitting alone on a bench. She found a patch in the sun and sat down. Ben shot her a wide grin and set off at a run again, not even seeming to notice the hamper he was carrying.

Once he had passed out of sight Lucy looked around, enjoying the view. The Pavilion was certainly impressive, with turrets and columns, intricately designed archways and ornate stone carvings but, after a while, she found her eyes being drawn to the gardens instead. Snowdrops, daffodils and primroses filled the beds, announcing the arrival of spring. Although there was still a chill in the air, the sun was shining, making everything appear extra bright, as if in technicolour. When Lucy reached into her bag to check her phone, a gust of wind blew through the trees and a scattering of almond blossom fell through the air, dropping onto a blue-dreadlocked woman underneath the trees, who laughed at the sensation of petals against her cheeks and promptly started dancing, arms wide as she twirled. Lucy dropped her phone back into her bag. People-watching was more fun than work – and anyway, if Ben caught her looking at her phone he'd tell her off for failing to skive properly.

Lucy leaned back, arms behind her, letting her eyes wander over the people, the plants, the Pavilion. She couldn't remember the last time she had simply sat down and enjoyed the view. Notting Hill was pretty enough but the trip from the Tube to work was short and her windowless office was far from inspiring. She felt herself relaxing as she breathed in the sea air – so much fresher than the polluted London atmosphere. She watched a woman with a small boy, who was playing with a ferret on a glittery lead; a group of students openly rolling a joint and passing it round; a man walking around offering bird whistles for sale. No two people were alike and somehow, that made her feel more relaxed despite her suit. In London, she knew what she had to do to fit in – even if it was hard to actually do sometimes. Here, it seemed like no one fitted in – so no one was out of place.

Lucy was just watching a man with a handlebar moustache and stripy blazer stroll across the lawn, a vintage-dressed curvy woman on each arm, when she saw Ben walking towards her with an ice cream in each hand – and now devoid of hamper.

'I had to introduce you to Boho Gelato – the best ice cream money can buy. Seb's a mate – let me leave my stuff with him so I'm free to carry your bags. So, would you rather have cherry bakewell or lemon meringue?'

'Bit different,' said Lucy. 'I'll go for the cherry bakewell, please.'

Ben handed over her ice cream and watched as she licked it. 'It's delicious,' she said.

'They've got over three hundred flavours and I haven't tasted a bad one yet. A almost got you an ice cream sandwich but I figured it might be a bit filling. So, have your feet had enough of a rest?'

She nodded.

'In that case, let's head for St James's Street and get you kitted out.'

Ben held Lucy's hand as he led her through the gardens, making her laugh with stories of people he'd met there before. 'The caricaturist was pretty special – he was clearly drunk, and hassling everyone to let him draw them. Eventually, my mate Jon gave in because it seemed like the quickest way to get rid of him – he'd been going on at us for ages. You have never seen a picture like it – it didn't even have the right colour hair and he'd given him a huge nose – even though Jon's ears are far more noticeable. Bloke tried to charge him a fiver for it – cheeky sod.'

'What did you do?'

'Told him that if any of the people sitting next to us could identify which one of us he'd drawn, we'd give him the money. Think he realised he was on to a loser but he still tried. When it was obvious no one had a clue, we legged it. Anyway, you nearly finished your ice cream?'

'Yes,' said Lucy, as she eagerly chomped down the last bit of the sugar cone.

'Great – because we're nearly there. Sussex Beacon is brilliant – got some of my best clothes here – and all the money goes to support people with HIV. So, what are you looking for?'

'Flat shoes, definitely. Other than that, I'm not sure. What are we doing?'

'You'll see – but I'd go for something comfy and warm. If you want to go to the beach, you need to prepare yourself for the wind – it can be a bit bracing. What size shoes do you wear?'

'Seven.'

'OK, I'll start searching for shoes that will fit you. Why don't you see what else you fancy?'

Lucy hadn't been in a charity shop for years. As a student, it was all she could afford and she'd regularly spent time foraging for bargains. She'd liked the feeling of wearing something that no one else was, of creating her own look. She'd tried wearing some of her vintage finds when she first got to London but David had made so many comments about her 'quirky' fashion sense and 'dressing like a student' that she'd ended up getting rid of most of them.

Maybe she'd have resisted David's style tips more if Anna hadn't made it very clear that she expected her staff to be on top of the latest fashions. 'Dress for success, Lucy – and that doesn't mean looking like a dowdy dowager. If our clients are going to believe that we are on-trend, they need to see our staff are on-trend too – *all* our staff.' Since her dressing down, Lucy had paid extra attention to the fashion pages when she was doing the clippings, and spent most of her wages on looking right for work, but she still hadn't elicited any compliments from Anna, and couldn't help thinking her boss disapproved of her fashion sense.

Lucy flicked through the rails, not sure what she was

looking for. It had been so long since she'd chosen clothes without having to think about what David or Anna would say. She looked at sequinned tops and fringe-trimmed dinner jackets, tweed suits and denim skirts. Nothing seemed quite right.

'OK, here are all the sevens. You have a choice. Leopard-print boots . . . ?' Ben saw the look on Lucy's face and hurriedly discarded them. 'Not a fan of leopard print?'

'My mum's always said it reminded her of Bet Lynch off *Coronation Street*. I know some people love it but I feel really cheap and tarty when I wear it.'

'You say that like it's a bad thing,' said Ben with a wink. 'I reckon you could rock cheap and tarty. But moving on – how about these?'

He held out a pair of grey trainers with lime-green laces.

'I'm not a big trainer fan.'

'OK, what about these?'

Ben held out a pair of dark brown leather boots with a low heel and laces up the front. Lucy smiled.

'Those are utterly gorgeous – I've always wanted a pair of Victorian-style boots.'

Ben handed them over and Lucy eagerly pulled off her painful heels and slipped into the boots. They were lined with some sort of fluffy, padded material that made her feel as if she was wearing slippers and when she looked at herself in the mirror, she knew they were the boots she had always wanted. She walked a few steps and, sure enough, they fitted perfectly. After every step she took in her 'stylish' heels being agony, the comfort almost made her cry with relief.

'OK, that's the shoes sorted. Seen anything else you like?'

'I wasn't really sure what to go for – but now I've got the shoes, I'm thinking skinny jeans – what do you think?'

'Whatever you feel happiest in – you're the one who's going to be wearing them. And it's got to be better than that suit. I don't mean to be a cock but you really don't look comfortable in it; sexy, but not comfortable.'

Lucy felt a surge of defensiveness. 'My boss doesn't care about comfort. She cares about fashion-forward.'

'Well, your boss isn't here now. Do you care about fashion-forward?'

'Not really,' Lucy admitted. 'I prefer classic stuff – I don't really understand why we have to change what we wear every three months to be taken seriously. I always thought things either suit you or they don't. My best mate despairs of me.'

'Does she work in fashion?'

'No, she's just really into it – reads all the magazines. She was so excited when I got a job in PR – thought I'd be able to get her all the high-end freebies. I don't think she was all that impressed when she realised all I could get her was dog grooming products.'

'Well, it's a bit like fashion – if you're a dog.' Ben saw the look that Lucy gave him and hurriedly backtracked.

'Not that I'm calling your best friend a dog. So, err, you want some skinny jeans.' Ben buried himself in the denim rail and soon had four pairs of jeans in his hands. 'These all look like they're about your size. Want to try them on?'

Lucy looked through. Ben had clearly been watching her closely – they were all the right size.

'Will do.' Lucy's eyes drifted to a mannequin in the window that she hadn't noticed before. It was wearing a long cream fluffy jumper, with a shawl collar that fell in a slouchy fashion.

'And the jumper?' Ben asked.

'It's beautiful – but it looks expensive.'

'Lucy, (a) it's a charity shop and (b) this is on me. You saved me from losing my wallet – the least I can do is treat you to a few clothes.'

Lucy thought about protesting, but she had to admit that the idea of having her clothes bought for her did give her a *Pretty Woman* frisson – she'd always loved the scene where Julia Roberts goes shopping, particularly the bit when she confronts the bitchy saleswoman. OK, this wasn't quite Rodeo Drive – but then she wasn't Julia Roberts.

'OK, that'd be lovely. Thanks.'

Ben asked the shop assistant to get the jumper from the window for Lucy, and she headed into the changing room to try on her new outfit. The first pair of jeans did nothing for her – why was it that some jeans could make you look amazing and others made your bum look flat and fat all at once? But as she slipped the second pair on, she knew they were perfect. The dark blue denim made her legs look long and toned, and seeing herself in skinny jeans brought back a pang of nostalgia for her student days.

She added her new boots, shimmied out of her jacket and top and slipped the jumper over her head. It felt amazing against her skin. She pulled it off and checked the label. One hundred per cent cashmere. 'Oh my God,' she thought – particularly when she realised it was only twenty pounds. She put the jumper back on, smoothing it down over her body, loving the way it hugged and skimmed in equal measure, flattering her shape. The long line fell to exactly the right point on her thigh, and the neckline gave a teasing hint of her décolletage without giving too much away. She stepped out of the changing room to show Ben, and could tell from the smile on his face that her perception of the outfit was spot on – he clearly liked what he saw.

'By Jove, I think she's got it. You look great, Lucy.'

'Thanks.'

'Do you want to wear it out, love?' asked the shop assistant. 'If you give me the tags, I can scan it through and bag up your other clothes.'

'That'd be great,' said Lucy. She reached into the back of the jeans and easily pulled off the tag. However, when she reached for the one in the back of the jumper, it proved more challenging.

'Here you go,' said the assistant, handing her a pair

of scissors. 'You might want to get your boyfriend to help you.'

Lucy blushed at hearing Ben described as her boyfriend, but he didn't correct the assistant; instead he took the scissors and reached into the back of her top to remove the tag. As he did so, his fingers brushed against her hair, which in turn stroked against her skin with a fairy-light touch.

Lucy had to hold back a shiver of pleasure. What was Ben doing to her? Even a simple brush of his fingers drove her wild. She became all too aware of how tight her new jeans were, how much they pressed against her in all the right places, and was relieved when the assistant said, 'All done, have a great day,' and handed Ben a bag full of Lucy's old clothes – if she wasn't alone with Ben soon, she thought she might explode.

The pair walked out of the shop together. Ben reached into the bag and pulled out a cream soft wool hat, trimmed with an antique-looking brooch in the shape of an ivy leaf. 'I thought you might like this too. It gets windy on the beach.'

Lucy pulled it on, relishing the warmth. 'I love it – thanks. So, where to now?'

'Well, I thought we'd head up the road a bit and join the beach at the big wheel – tick another tourist box for you. We can go on it if you want – apparently, the view is amazing.'

Lucy thought for a second. The idea of seeing Brighton

spread out underneath her from a big wheel did appeal but she'd never been on one before.

'I'm not sure. Is there anything else we can do instead? I'm not that into heights.'

'Face your fears, Lucy. But as you're already facing up to your fear of rebellion, I guess it can wait until another day. Where do you stand on dolphins? Any phobias?'

'No,' laughed Lucy. 'Are we going to be swimming with dolphins?' After seeing flamingos in central London, she wouldn't put anything past Ben.

'Not quite. But I think you'll have fun.'

Fifteen minutes later, Lucy was laughing hard as she and Ben sat in a line with other holiday makers and frantically rolled balls towards a target in an effort to make plastic dolphins race. She was surprised at how well she was doing – though not as well as Ben, whose dolphin was a full length ahead of hers.

'You said you wanted to do something touristy – no trip to Brighton is complete without a game of Dolphin Derby on the pier. Oh – you lose, sorry. The kids are always the worst – I hardly ever beat them. Another go?'

'Definitely,' Lucy said. She was out of breath from laughing so hard and couldn't remember having so much fun in years. This time, Ben romped ahead of her, with a sneaky two-handed tactic that looked random but seemed to work wonders. He was presented with a giant cuddly fish, which he presented to Lucy with a flourish. 'Ta-dah. Just what every woman wants – a fish to cuddle. And while we're on the topic of fish, are you getting hungry? We're not far from my mate's place.'

Even though Lucy felt like she'd been eating all day, there was something about the sea air that made her hungrier than she'd been in ages. 'Sounds good to me,' she said, and smiled at Ben, feeling warm as she looked into his eyes.

'Then let's go.'

As they walked back along the pier, she couldn't recall a time she'd been happier. The sun was warm on her face, though she was glad of the hat Ben had bought her – he wasn't wrong about the wind. She felt as if the Brighton breeze was blowing away her stress. She could see the sea through the cracks in the wooden boards of the pier, which made her feel as if she was walking on air; or perhaps that was more to do with the way that Ben was stroking her hand as he held it.

They reached the end of the pier and headed down a slope towards the seafront. Lucy smiled as they passed a traditional carousel, which was just slowing to a stop, with people climbing off the elaborately decorated horses.

'I've always fancied going on a carousel.'

'You mean you've never been on one? How old are you?'

'Twenty-eight – far too old for that sort of thing. I guess I've missed the boat.'

'Don't be ridiculous,' said Ben. 'You're here to have fun. Come on.'

He leapt up onto the merry-go-round and held out his hand to Lucy. She paused for a second, before taking it and joining him.

'So, horse or cock?'

Lucy was perplexed until she realised Ben was pointing at a golden painted cockerel on the carousel.

'Definitely a horse,' she said. 'It's traditional.' She picked one called Rachael, the name picked out in elaborate script. 'It's my sister's name,' she explained.

'The one in Cornwall?'

'Well remembered – but no, that's the one with kids. Rachael's my little sister. Her and Hope couldn't be more different. Hope's got the house, the perfect husband, the two beautiful kids. Rach is more of a free spirit. She's off doing a ski season at the moment. Before that she spent the summer working at festivals all over Europe. Mum worries about her, to be honest, but sometimes I think Rach is the happiest of all of us.'

'How come?'

'Well, Hope always seems shattered – two kids under four is a lot of hard work. My life hasn't exactly gone to plan. But Rach doesn't have any plans – she just does whatever she wants.'

Ben looked pensive. 'I've got a sister like that. I don't think it guarantees happiness though.' He looked as if he was going to say something else, but before he could, the carousel owner interrupted. 'The ride's about to start. Fares please.'

Lucy reached into her pocket.

'I'll get this,' said Ben.

'No, I will. You've already bought me too much.'

Lucy handed the carousel owner the fare, wedged her bag and laptop case between her and the pole and felt her stomach flip as Ben got onto her horse, sitting behind her with his arms wrapped around her waist. Her subconscious was clearly allied with her conscious mind as she realised her fingers were sliding up and down the pole, which suddenly felt terribly phallic. She focused on keeping her hands still, and tried not to let herself get too distracted by the feeling of Ben wrapped around her.

The carousel started up with a burst of Wurlitzer music, and Lucy felt a bubble of excitement as her horse started to move up and down. As the carousel turned, she admired the view: the pebbled beach, the people ambling along the esplanade, the dilapidated old pier rising out of the sea, looking like a skeleton of holidays past. As the carousel continued to turn, Lucy saw the beach from new perspectives with every repetition: the lights on the Palace Pier, classic and ostentatious in equal measure; the teenagers skateboarding down the esplanade; the twins juggling fire on the beach, making butterfly shapes in bright trails behind their bodies. Lucy gazed in wonder – she'd never seen anything like it before.

'I love the fire jugglers,' she said.

'It's called poi – not quite the same as juggling but it does look similar.' said Ben. 'Shouldn't be too long before sunset. With any luck they'll still be here – there's something magical about watching people play with fire, don't you think? And it looks so good in the dark.'

'So will we still be here at sunset?'

'If you're OK with that? I promised you a seafood feast, after all. And I've still got a few surprises up my sleeve.'

'Looking forward to it,' said Lucy – trying not to get too excited at the thought, which was particularly challenging with Ben's warm body pressing against her. He really was the most amazingly distracting man.

The carousel slowed and came to a halt. Ben got off first and gallantly held his hand out for Lucy to dismount. She felt a little discombobulated as her body adapted to standing again and stumbled, falling towards Ben, who put his arm round her and steadied her.

'Careful, now. You don't want to get an injury after your first carousel ride. So how was it?'

'Magical,' Lucy said. 'I feel like a five-year-old.'

'I told you everyone in Brighton's a kid – clearly you're adapting. So, food time?'

'Sounds good to me.'

A short walk later and Lucy was breathing in the enticing aroma of smoked fish.

'The fisherman's quarter is one of my favourite bits of Brighton,' said Ben. 'It doesn't get as much attention as the Laines or Kemptown but there's something so peaceful about sitting on a boat, looking at the sea and eating fish so fresh that you know it was swimming there this morning.'

'I guess it is a bit "circle of life",' said Lucy.

'Exactly – and I love the feeling of history. You can imagine the fishermen going out in the clinker boats, dragging their haul in – whole families living off the sea. The boats are beautiful too; such great craftsmanship.'

Lucy looked at the old-fashioned dark wooden fishing boat that sat on the pavement outside the fish shack and couldn't help but agree.

'Well, grab a seat – I'll get our food sorted,' said Ben.

Lucy clambered into the boat, worried about the view she was giving Ben in her ungainly scramble – but when she turned to look at him, he was staring at her with such admiration in his eyes that she was pretty sure his mind was on other things. He winked at her brazenly when he realised he'd been caught, and then headed into a small shack under the arches of the beach. A few minutes later he was back, two polystyrene cups somehow clasped in one hand – he really did have impressively large, manly hands – and a plate with a crab, French bread and a chunk of lemon in the other.

'I didn't think you'd want to miss out on the bouillabaisse – it's one of Jack's specialities. Great for warming you up too.'

Lucy took a sip and sure enough, the smoky

tomato-based soup made her glow from the inside – or perhaps that was the sensation of Ben's thigh, which pressed against her own as he squeezed next to her on the bench seat of the boat. She finished the soup rapidly, the sea air only enhancing the flavour. Ben handed her the plate of crab.

'I only got one between us because I thought I'd cook us dinner later and I don't want to spoil your appetite – if that's OK with you?'

Lucy felt excitement fizz up inside her. 'I'd love that.'

'Well, dig in.' Ben passed Lucy a plastic fork and she scooped out the sweet crab meat, piling it onto the bread and squeezing lemon over it.

'Oh God, this is good,' she said, as the first bite filled her mouth with fresh, saline flavours. She realised how thirsty she was just as Ben reached into a bag and pulled out a can of ginger beer.

'Thought you might want this too.'

Ben's thoughtfulness touched Lucy – he seemed to be considering her every need, from the hat that was protecting her against the increasingly biting wind to the drink, which she gratefully gulped down. She found his attentiveness refreshing – arousing. She couldn't remember the last time someone had treated her so kindly and she liked it.

Ben and Lucy sat in happy silence. The sea's calming cadence was their soundtrack, and Lucy was sure she could hear bells ringing in the background. After a while, she became curious.

'What *is* that noise,' she asked Ben.

'The tinkling sound? That's the breeze against the boat masts moored up there.' Ben pointed to some modern boats in the distance.

'It sounds magical.'

'Maybe it is. Brighton is a pretty magical place, after all.'

'It certainly is – thanks for making me skive.'

'I didn't make you skive – I just let you, Lucy. You just needed some encouragement to put yourself first for once. And if that gorgeous smile is anything to go by, it's a good thing you did – you look like a different woman from this morning. Relaxation suits you. So, you done?'

Ben gestured at the plate, now holding little more than empty crab shell and squeezed lemon wedges.

'I am – it was delicious. Thanks.'

'I've known Jack for years – couldn't have you missing out on his amazing food. So, ready for the next adventure?'

Lucy felt a pang of nervous anticipation as she answered, 'Yes.'

'Not far to go – in fact, it's just there.' Ben pointed to a sign reading 'Brighton Fishing Museum: Admission Free'.

He climbed out the boat and stood with his arms outreached to help Lucy down. Her skin was tingling, and her tight jeans were leaving her in no doubt as to the effect Ben was having on her. It felt like she'd been wanting him for years, not hours.

Lucy followed Ben into the fishing museum and found herself in a small, peaceful space. She and Ben were the only people in there, an honesty box for donations in place of any staff. The space was dominated by a vintage boat, its wooden hull shining, with a black painted rim and the words 'Sussex Maid' painted in an elegant white font at the front of the boat.

'Want to have a look inside?' Ben asked.

'We shouldn't – look at the sign – it says not to,' Lucy said.

'Ah, the good girl is back. Where's your spirit of adventure?'

Ben climbed the stairs next to the boat and deftly manoeuvred himself aboard, leaning over the edge to pull Lucy up. She followed him up the stairs, glanced around nervously, then thought 'what the hell', took his hands and felt herself being hauled upwards. She fell back onto the floor of the boat, narrowly missing a set of fishing balls in a net.

'Careful there, Lucy. We don't want to break anything – least of all you.'

Ben lay down on the floor next to her and stroked the side of her face, looking intently into her eyes before drawing her into a kiss. After all the build-up, all the waiting, Lucy fell on him eagerly. Desire fought her natural reticence and won. She pulled Ben on top of her, gratified to feel he was already hard for her. He was breathing heavily now as his lips pressed hard to hers, his tongue ever more demanding. She could feel the delicious friction of his erection against the tight seam of her jeans, and ground against him. Even though it was more public than she'd like, Lucy felt like she should do something to show Ben how much she wanted him. She reached down and started fumbling with his top trouser button, but the pressure of his cock against the fabric stretched it taut and made it hard for her to negotiate. The more she fumbled, the more aroused she became at the thought of what lay beneath – and the harder Ben became; the more she had to see him in all his glory.

Lucy was relieved when he reached down and popped the button himself, freeing himself from the confines of clothing. She eagerly wrapped her hand around his cock, partly through lust, partly because she wanted to know if the pleasures that had been hinted at underneath his clothes were matched by the naked truth. She wasn't disappointed. She gripped his firm shaft and started to slide her hand up and down, moving his foreskin over the head of his cock, which was already slick with juices. She could feel her own desire building, much as it had in the roof gardens. By now, she couldn't care less that she was in a public place, as long as she was touching Ben – and he was touching her. But as Ben pulled up her top to stroke her stomach, they heard voices.

'Here it is – I told you it was under the arches.' A gruff male voice made Lucy freeze.

Ben calmly removed his hand from her body and pressed his finger to her lips.

'Dad, I want an ice cream.'

'I want an ice cream too.'

The children's voices had a whiny quality and the second one sounded close to tears.

'In a minute. You can get some culture first – you can't spend all day in the arcades having fun.'

'Daaaad. It's boring.'

'No it's not. Look at that boat. That's what they used to go fishing in. Can you imagine being a fisherman, getting up first thing in the morning, risking your life on the seas?'

'I want to be a pop star. Fishing sounds boring. I don't like fish.'

Lucy held her breath, hoping desperately not to be caught.

'I need the loo,' came the second child's voice.

'I told you to go before we left the cafe. Hold it in. We won't be here long.'

'I can't.'

The father sighed. 'OK, but we're coming back here after. Before any ice cream. Understood?' The voices gradually quietened as the family left the museum.

'That was close,' said Lucy.

'Yes, but it was exciting, wasn't it? Feel how much your heart is racing.'

Sure enough, Lucy's heart was pounding as she lay underneath Ben, his body – and length – pressed against her. She looked up at him shyly. 'I'm not sure that's because we were interrupted.'

Ben looked back at her. 'Want to get out of here before we're disturbed again?'

'Yes please.'

Ben clambered out of the boat and helped Lucy down. They walked out the museum and onto the beach. By now, the sun was starting to set, turning the sky orange and pink, providing a stunning backdrop to the crumbling pier.

'I love the old pier,' Lucy said.

'The West Pier – yes, it's one of my favourite Brighton sights. Sad really – it was neglected for years and just when it looked like it might be restored to its former glory, there were two fires. There were rumours of foul play of course, but no one could investigate because the structure was too unsafe.'

'That's such a shame – although it's still beautiful in a Gothic way,' said Lucy.

'You should see it at low tide. A couple of times a year you can walk right underneath it. It's covered in seaweed and mussels and smells like you're living under the sea. You get dripped on a bit but it's worth it.'

The look in Ben's eyes was wistful and it was clear he had a lot of affection for the broken and battered structure.

As Lucy looked at the West Pier, she saw a swirl of birds rising from it, an epic flock wheeling and turning, forming beautiful patterns in the air.

'It's the murmuration,' Ben said. 'Hundreds of birds all flying together – it helps keep the starlings safe and warm at night. On which note, it's getting a little chilly. Shall we head back to my place? It's not far.'

'Yes please.' The response tumbled out of Lucy's mouth in seconds. She felt a little uncool for being so keen but she needed to be alone with Ben. She wanted to carry on where they'd left off in the boat – and soon.

Ten minutes later Lucy was standing outside a dilapidated-looking house.

'It's not much from the outside but it gets better,' Ben said.

Lucy believed him – so far, he hadn't let her down – but when she walked up the stairs behind Ben and followed him through the door to his top-floor flat, she couldn't hold back a gasp.

'It's amazing.'

Ben smiled warmly. 'I thought it might appeal, after seeing how much you loved the roof gardens.'

Although the flat was tiny and clearly in need of repair, with a crumbling fireplace and painted floorboards that had seen better days, it was alive with plants. One wall was entirely covered with lettuce, growing directly out of some sort of pocketed sheet. There were shelves lined with plants: plastic seaside buckets in the shape of castles filled with rosemary, thyme and mint, lending a delicate herbal aroma over the dominant, comforting smell of soil; silver tin cans pegged to strings in the windows, with tomato seedlings reaching out towards the light. Every window had a window box filled with lavender, chilli and plants Lucy struggled to recognise. There were even plants suspended directly from the ceiling with string, roots still showing.

'Those are stunning.'

'Thanks – it's a Japanese string garden – great technique. I'll show you how to do it if you want – it means you can grow things without plant pots. Took me a while to work out how to do it but it's easy when you know how. But that's not the best of it. Do you want to see the *pièce de résistance*?'

Lucy nodded and he led her towards a door in the corner that she hadn't noticed before. She followed him through, and was now in a tiny kitchen, with plastic bottles suspended sideways on the walls, filled with yet more plants. Ben opened another door and she realised it was a fire escape.

'Follow me – be careful, it can be a bit slippery.'

Lucy gingerly followed Ben up the fire escape, glad she wasn't wearing her heels. As she reached the top, she saw that Ben had been leading her to a roof terrace. As with his flat, every surface was covered with plants. A ladder propped against a wall acted as a surrogate trellis for pea shoots, and bricks painted to look like books formed small raised beds. Lucy skimmed the titles: *Heart of Darkness*, *Fear and Loathing in Las Vegas*, *Brighton Rock*. Ben was obviously well read too.

The whole garden was an homage to up-cycling. Teapots and cups had been turned into planters, as had buckets, brightly painted pallets attached to the wall for plants to grow through,, a bath and even a vintage chest of drawers. Best of all were the seats – tyres mounted on stool legs, and planted with grass for the cushion. The only things that looked new were the solar powered lights dotted around the garden – but even they were designed to blend in – albeit in a magical way: fairy lights and toadstools lit up different areas of the roof, and there was a pathway made of lit up coloured glass slabs, with sunken bottles holding lights edging raised beds and marking a route through the rooftop grotto. The whole roof seemed to be lit from above by twinkling stars too, and when Lucy looked up she saw a row of cheesegraters pinned to a washing line, with lights inside them causing the starlight effect. She never knew the mundane could be so magical. Everything took on a golden glow as Ben lit candles inside mirrored lanterns that were strung on poles throughout the garden.

'Did you do this all yourself?' asked Lucy.

'I had some mates to help me but yes, most of it was me.'

'It's so creative.'

'Not really. You can grow plants in almost anything and I hate waste. I found most of the stuff up here in skips. It's amazing what people throw away. Says a lot about our culture – what we take for granted.'

'It is sad.' Lucy thought about her colleagues at work. They complained about wearing the same dress twice;

she could only guess their reaction if she suggested skip raiding – or even charity shops.

'Yes – but it works to my favour so I'm not complaining too much. OK, are you ready for the best bit of all?'

'Go for it.'

'Close your eyes.'

Lucy did as she was told and felt herself been guided around a corner.

'Keep your eyes closed.'

She felt her lower body press against a wall of some kind.

'Open them now.'

As Lucy opened her eyes, she realised she was standing against a cast iron fence, with plants entwined around it, looking as if they'd been there for years, and fairy lights woven around it providing a slow, pulsing, surprisingly bright light. Ahead of her was a view of the sea so stunning she didn't want to close her eyes. By now, the sun had set and stars glimmered above the dark water, the moon casting its reflection over the waves. She could see flashes of light on the beach too – the fire poi twins had clearly stayed there, and were drawing intricate patterns in the air.

'Wow.'

'Just what I was thinking,' said Ben. He put his arms around her and nuzzled his lips into her neck. Lucy pressed back against him, grinding her bum against his hardening cock.

'I'm so glad you decided to skive,' Ben said. 'Have you had fun?'

'Not as much fun as I want to.' Lucy wriggled more obviously, more sensually, trying to communicate her desire. She had to touch him, feel him – possess him. The feeling was clearly mutual, and Ben's hands started to roam. His hands slid under her top, thumb brushing her pelvis in a way that sent shooting signals directly to her core. As his hands moved upwards and cupped her breasts, Lucy gasped. Her nipples were stiff in Ben's hands as he stroked them expertly, making her clit pulse with every stroke.

'Fuck, you're amazing,' Ben said, and now he was groping her more fiercely, one hand moving between her legs, as Lucy's hand fumbled behind her, grasping at his hardness. Lucy was desperate to see him, to taste him, and knew there was something she had to do. Dropping to her knees, she looked up at Ben and smiled seductively. 'Do you mind?'

'Do I hell. Do with me as you will.'

Lucy undid Ben's fly. Even though he was going commando, she still struggled to free him because he was so swollen with desire. The smell of his natural musk hit her and she eagerly breathed it in, growing hornier by the second. She *had* to taste him.

'Fuck,' Ben said as Lucy pulled him into her hand and tentatively ran her thumb over the tip of his cock, already sopping wet with pre-cum. She leaned forward and delicately licked the tip, savouring his salty taste, before taking his glans in her mouth and starting to slowly move her head back and forth, carefully sheathing her teeth with her lips. Ben gripped her shoulders, his fingers digging into her, showing his desire. Lucy could feel his shaft pulsing and growing in her mouth and had to open her lips wider to fit him in.

While she sucked the tip, Lucy's right hand moved up and down his shaft and her left one slipped into his trousers to play with his balls – a tip gleaned from one of the many sex articles she'd read when compiling magazine clippings for work. And it was clear that the move was a hit. She felt his balls tighten at her touch, and another, 'Fuck,' burst from Ben's lips. She bobbed her head up and down, speeding up her touch as she felt him stiffen further and his hips rock with desire.

As Lucy moved, her clit pressed against the seam of her jeans and now, too horny to be self-conscious, she had to move her hand down to make herself climax. A day of anticipation followed by the delicious sensation of Ben's cock in her mouth was too much to bear without coming. When Ben looked down and saw what she was doing, he grew even harder – now Lucy was almost at full yawn to fit him in her mouth.

'If you keep that up, I'm going to come,' he said, eyes fixed on Lucy's hand between her legs.

'Good,' said Lucy, pulling her head away briefly before plunging back onto his cock and trying to take him as deep into her mouth as she could. She slowly moved her head up and down, flaring her nostrils and tilting her head back to make it easier for him to slide down her throat.

'Fuck, that's good. Oh fuck, I'm coming,' Ben said, clearly surprised by the speed of his climax as he shot thick spurts of come into her mouth; Lucy felt her own orgasm start. She'd always loved sucking cock and tasting Ben's sweet-salt come, combined with her hand pressing against her stiff clit, was too much for her to hold back any longer. She eagerly swallowed down his juices as her hips bucked against her hand and she had one of the most intense orgasms of her life, muscles pulsing again and again and again.

'Fuck,' was all Ben seemed able to say.

As her orgasm subsided, Lucy became aware of the sound of the sound of the sea. It made her feel self-conscious, suddenly aware of the reality of the situation now her need for orgasm had been sated. She was on her knees on a stranger's roof terrace having just given him a blow job while masturbating.

'So . . .' she said, unsure of what she was going to say after that – but before she could continue, a phone broke the silence, making her recoil from the loud ringing from Ben's trouser pocket. He looked down at Lucy and smiled – but when he reached for the phone and saw who was calling, his face froze. Lucy could see the panic on his face as he answered.

'Clare. What do you want?'

* * *

Lucy suddenly felt very stupid indeed. She got up from her knees. So her suspicions had been right – there was someone else. She couldn't hear what the woman on the end of the phone was saying but she could pick out an angry tone.

'OK, OK, I'll be right there,' Ben said.

After all they'd done today, he was going to abandon her for another woman. She blushed angrily, and felt tears rising up, which she fought back with deep breaths.

Ben hung up the phone.

'Look, I'm really sorry; I'm going to have to go. It's not you – you're amazing – it's – there's just some stuff I need to sort urgently. I'll see you to the station, of course.'

'Don't worry about it,' Lucy said, hurt. 'I can get a cab.'

'Let me call it for you.'

The cab arrived five minutes later and it wasn't until she was sitting in the back of it, wedged in between her shopping bags and the giant furry fish that Ben had won for her that Lucy let her tears start to fall. What the hell had she done? And more to the point, how was she going to forget about Ben?

CHAPTER 3

Lucy wasn't sure whether to be pleased or upset that she hadn't got Ben's number before he'd run off to Clare. On the one hand, she wanted to call him and find out what the hell was going on. How could he be so brazen? She felt cheap and humiliated, as if she'd been judged and found lacking, and she wanted to scream at him for making her feel that way. On the other hand, she was glad she couldn't embarrass herself further with needy calls or texts – she'd never felt such desire and it was compelling.

Of course, it wasn't his fault that the phone had rung when it did – and he had called her 'amazing'. But if she was so amazing, why had he run off to another woman without even having the decency to give her an explanation? And why hadn't he asked for her number? Maybe he'd got what he wanted and, despite all the apparent romance, the thrill of the chase had gone. She'd succumbed to him too quickly and he'd taken the first escape route offered. Lucy felt her throat tighten as she swallowed down a sob, making the two grey-haired men holding hands opposite shoot her a concerned look.

She could still taste Ben in her mouth and smell him on her skin, and while it reminded her of what she had lost, she couldn't deny the arousal his scent raised in her. She would need to shower well to scrub the memory away – though part of her didn't want to forget just yet.

As the train pulled into Victoria she caught her reflection in the window, and pulled her hat down over her ears, trying to hide as much of her face as she could. As she felt the carriage slow and saw the familiar concourse, Lucy felt a renewed anxiety about running into someone from work – though she wasn't sure they'd recognise her if they did see her now. The rain had washed her make-up off first thing and the time she'd spent on the beach with Ben had given her cheeks a healthy glow, but all Lucy saw was a bedraggled, tearful mess. The cashmere jumper still skimmed her body flatteringly, but Lucy only registered the faint red mark where her neck met her shoulder – not as obvious as a love bite, just a subtle reminder of what had been. Even her comfortable boots reminded Lucy of the fun she'd had in the second-hand shop, the bliss she'd felt as she'd finally been able to remove her heels – and the adventure she'd had with Ben afterwards.

Lucy looked at the giant furry toy sitting next to her and felt ridiculous. She was a grown woman sitting alone on a train with a cuddly fish. She guessed she'd leave it behind – her flat was too small for a five-foot toy and she was sure someone else would get more joy out of it than she would. All it was to her was a reminder of Ben's rejection.

Lucy tried to keep her emotions held inside – crying on public transport was so embarrassing – but the harder she tried to bite back the hurt that was bubbling inside her, the hotter and itchier her eyelids felt and the closer her eyes came to overflowing. She felt an errant tear push its way out and roll slowly down her cheek.

'I'm just leaking,' she told herself in an effort to fight away the grief, scrunching her eyes up as if to push the tear back in. No drama required. She took three sharp intakes of breath and reached for a tissue but as she felt it softly brush against her cheek she was reminded of the touch of Ben's fingertips and an ugly sob forced its way out of her. The couple opposite shot her another concerned look.

Their attention only served to make the tears flow more and now she could feel her eyes starting to swell. She blew her nose, muttered, 'Pull yourself together,' and forced her face into a grin; she'd read in a magazine that smiling released some chemical or other that makes you feel happy. She shot the two men a grateful look as if to say, 'I'm fine, thanks for your concern, nothing to see here.' They smiled back, politely ignoring the obvious lie. The older of them reached into his jacket and took out a packet of Polos. He offered Lucy one and she took it, though the kindness made a lump rise in her throat.

Eventually the doors beeped and opened, allowing passengers to disembark. Lucy grabbed her handbag, her laptop and the carrier bag containing her coffee-stained suit and unwearable heels. She shot one last glance at the multi-coloured fish before dashing off the train, feeling the cold of the night air as it hit her tear-stained face. The smell of London was comforting now – Brighton no longer seemed like such a breath of fresh air.

As she felt in her coat pocket for her train ticket, she wished she had a teleportation machine so she could simply press a button and be tucked up in bed in her fluffy pyjamas with a hot water bottle, a cup of tea and a packet of chocolate chip cookies. Instead, she had to negotiate the Tube. In fact, fuck it, she thought recklessly: she was going to get a cab. She wasn't sure she could face taking the Underground tonight, given that was where it had all started. She wanted an easy end to the day, so she could go to sleep and pretend it had never happened.

As she thought back over the last twelve hours, Lucy smiled sadly. Flamingos, roof gardens, dolphin derby, messing around in a boat, and a garden inside a house. It had been like some sort of magical dream. But it was time to come back to reality. She'd tried skiving and it had brought her to this. Tomorrow, it was time to get back to work.

The journey back from the station had been painless enough, and the cup of builder's tea Lucy made as soon as she walked through the door worked its usual magic, even if the accompanying chocolate chip cookies were a bit stale. After watching an episode of *Sherlock*, she thought she'd relaxed enough to consider going to bed and changed into her pyjamas. However, when she topped up her hot water bottle it belched out an air bubble, squirting boiling water over her wrist. It wasn't enough to scald her but the annoyance was enough to start her tears flowing again – all she wanted was a bit of warmth and even her hot water bottle was conspiring against her.

Lucy spent half the night crying: today had been a reminder of why she should stay away from men, but she couldn't get Ben out of her head no matter how hard she tried. His kisses. The way he looked at her. She'd thought he was different. Every time she opened up she got hurt. She thought back, trying to work out if she'd done anything wrong. Maybe David was right and she brought it on herself. The thoughts circled. She considered running a bath – she was chilled to the bone – but it was late and the boiler screeched so loudly that the neighbours complained if she had a bath after 9 p.m.

Instead, she took a fresh cup of tea into the bedroom, rubbed off what was left of her makeup with the wipes she kept next to the bed for when she was feeling lazy, and climbed between the sheets. She turned on Radio 4 to drown out her thoughts and was soon immersed in a traumatic news show that planted distracting but distressing images in her head as she drifted to sleep.

When Lucy's alarm clock beeped the following morning, she felt she'd barely slept at all, having spent most of the night running away from prison officers with torture devices, who were trying to catch her because she'd been skiving off work and not contributing to society. She ran screaming, but when they finally caught up with her they all had Ben's face – and turned away in disgust, saying, 'She's not the one we want. She's of no use to us,' before throwing her into a skip full of promotional dog toothbrushes. Lucy was still shaking when she woke up, and showered in silence rather than singing along to the radio as she usually did. It was time to forget about Ben and throw herself into work.

Lucy dressed in a grey pinstriped suit. She knew Anna hated it because she'd once said, 'Woman at Debenhams, Lucy – interesting choice,' but today she couldn't face picking out anything more ambitious. She never seemed to choose the right thing anyway. 'Dress for the job you want, not the job you have,' the magazines said, but when she tried it, she either looked frumpy or try-hard. Perhaps it was time to take her colleague Caitlin up on her offer of a makeover: she had suggested it a number of times but Lucy had never really taken it seriously. She liked Caitlin, another account manager, well enough, and they'd had enough wine-fuelled after-hours meetings to be closer than just workmates; but if she was honest, Caitlin still intimidated her. Hearing her bark down the phone at suppliers who'd let her down was enough to let Lucy know she never wanted to get on Caitlin's bad side; so far, she'd been lucky enough to get away with the occasional withering look or barbed remark.

Even though they were technically on the same level, Lucy always seemed to end up doing what Caitlin said. It wasn't just her confidence. Caitlin always looked perfect. Her clothes tended to be by up-and-coming designers with a handful of catwalk names thrown in and she spent more on clothes in a month than Lucy earned in three – though Lucy had heard Caitlin's father paid her credit-card bill. Growing up with rich parents had certainly given her great taste and a commercial mind-set, thought Lucy. And Caitlin's eye for great design and her financial ambition made her great at her job. Anna said she was on a fast track, and the clients seemed to love her, so perhaps it was time for Lucy to follow in her footsteps?

By the time Lucy got into work, she was set on the idea. Every time Ben had popped into her head, she'd blotted out the thought by imagining shopping with Caitlin. She had a credit card and she'd always been careful to pay it off in full each month. What was the harm in spending a bit of money as an investment in her future? If she got a promotion off the back of it, the clothes would pay for themselves. She felt a burst of hope as she imagined herself floating into the office looking chic and in control.

Lucy's mood was dimmed when she walked into the office to see Anna sitting on her desk.

'Wow – if you look that rough today, I can see why you took yesterday off,' were Anna's first words to her. 'Still, glad you're back. Dogsbody has revised the brief. They want us to emphasise the breath-freshening qualities of the bone-stick as well as its teeth-cleansing effect. And the Gnasher financials finally came back – it's too expensive to licence. You know Dogsbody are tighter than a gnat's arse. You'll need to find an alternative. And fast. The meeting's at three tomorrow. Get on it. You could have done without losing yesterday, really.'

Anna turned her back on Lucy and started to walk towards her office. When she was half way across the floor, she turned and called, 'Oh, and Lucy, what have I told you about wearing grey? Grey suit, grey ideas. Don't let me see you in that again. You look like an accountant.'

Lucy was beginning to think that this really wasn't her week. Her face burned, and she could feel Caitlin looking at her pityingly. She couldn't meet her eye for fear of showing how upset she felt, so she fired up her computer, only realising she had caps lock on the third time it refused to log in. She jabbed at the keyboard, her computer finally booted up and she began searching for 'cartoon dogs'. Just the sort of glamorous life she'd always dreamed of. And it wasn't like this was anything other than a normal day.

* * *

By lunchtime, Lucy was starting to feel more positive again. She'd found a brilliant illustration website profiling student artists. They were cheaper than the usual agency they used, and there were some really original concepts. She liked the idea of helping people who were just starting out – and she was pretty sure that Anna would like the idea of cutting costs. She copied and pasted her favourite images into a PowerPoint document and added the artists' credits alongside them, with a URL linking to their work so Anna could flick through the rest of their portfolios.

She was feeling so good about her presentation that when Caitlin walked past she felt confident enough to ask, 'How would you feel about going shopping this lunchtime? I think I'm ready for that makeover.'

'I heard what Anna said this morning,' said Caitlin. 'I think that's a good idea. Good to see you taking some initiative. We'll do High Street Ken and I'll load the theme tune options for the Dogsbody campaign onto my iPod so you can work at the same time – that way we can make time to get your hair done too.'

'That's really kind,' Lucy said.

'Well, to be honest, darling, Anna was right. You do look a bit rough and we can't have you turning up like that to the meeting tomorrow. What's your budget?'

'I guess I could afford ' – Lucy did a quick mental calculation. If she dropped her food budget to £10 per week for the rest of the month and skipped the pub, she could probably spare – 'two hundred pounds?'

'I thought you wanted a makeover!' said Caitlin. 'You're going to need to up your budget a bit if you want to make a change – or impress clients. Would you trust someone in a two-hundred-pound outfit with a hundred-thousand-pound budget?'

Lucy's instinctive thought was 'Dogsbody don't have a hundred-thousand-pound budget,' followed rapidly by, 'What do clothes have to do with how good you are at your job?' But Caitlin was on a roll. 'Marketing is all about brand, Lucy. If you don't invest in your own brand, why should anyone trust you with theirs?'

Lucy looked at Caitlin's effortlessly elegant outfit – almost the same colour as her own suit yesterday but somehow more polished, perfectly fitted, and with no sign of a coffee stain or even a speck of lint. Caitlin commanded authority – Lucy had seen cocky twenty-something entrepreneurs and seventy-year-old captains of industry reduced to mush when Caitlin explained why they needed to double their budget to be taken seriously. They always ended up doing what she asked and never seemed to complain about the extra expenditure once they'd committed to it. Caitlin clearly got results – Lucy had seen it time and time again.

'OK, you tell me what I need and I'll get it. I've got a good credit card limit.'

'That's the spirit,' Caitlin grinned. 'Meet me at my desk at one. You'll be a whole new woman by three.'

* * *

When she walked back into the office, Lucy was conscious of her colleagues' stares. Perhaps her haircut was a bit drastic, but Caitlin had said the dramatically deep side parting was 'very Spring 2014', and would make her appear 'on-trend', so she'd brushed away her reservations and let Caitlin have her way. Lucy had found it strange hearing Caitlin bark orders at the hairdresser when it was her hair, but it also felt oddly comforting. She could sit back without thinking, and let Caitlin turn her into a woman she'd failed to become on her own. The only thing she'd baulked at was having bright colours used to 'accent' her hair – it was far too attention-seeking. And, if she was honest, it reminded her of Brighton too much.

While Lucy was having her hair cut – and listening to cheesy themes for the Dogsbody campaign – Caitlin scoured the nearby shops, pre-selecting the outfits she deemed worthy to ensure the shopping trip ran as time-efficiently as possible. Caitlin really was an impressive organiser, she thought. Once Lucy had tried on all the outfits, meekly accepting whatever she was given, Caitlin had told her which ones to buy and picked one for her to wear back to the office. 'Start as you mean to go on,' she'd counselled.

The receipts formed a thick wedge in her purse, and Lucy had to fight hard to resist the urge to tot them up in her head. She already knew how much she'd spent – too much – and bit her lip at the thought of her next credit card bill. It wasn't just the basics Caitlin had insisted she bought. 'Accessories give you away,' she'd said. 'It's all about the detail.' And so Lucy had Wolford tights and expensive shapewear to go underneath the outfits Caitlin had chosen.

And then there was the more glamorous underwear. Perhaps it was her inner 'bitch' finally coming to the surface, but Lucy was instantly drawn towards the Kiki de Montparnasse lingerie, made from calfskin leather and Chantilly lace. She couldn't resist trying it on, and when she did, closeted in a plush changing room with velvet curtains, she knew she had to own it.

The soft leather corset-style bra hugged her breasts gently, cupping and lifting them as if presenting them to be worshipped, the two sides fastening together with delicate hooks and eyes. The silk straps were fine and delicate, caressing her shoulders with a lover's touch. The corset was cropped mid-ribcage, leaving the feminine swell of her stomach exposed, modesty preserved beneath by the scrap of Chantilly lace that just covered her mons, though the back of the briefs was more revealing, lacing up in a sexy echo of the corset top.

Lucy felt sexy, powerful. She imagined what Ben would think if he could see her now and knew, no matter what, she would certainly make him hard. The thought made a pulse shoot from her stomach to her clit. He had felt incredible in her hand – warm, hard and pulsing with life. Wearing this, she would have no qualms about telling him exactly what he could do with it – once he'd explained himself for his bad behaviour of course.

As her mind drifted to Ben, Lucy realised she'd started stroking herself through the silky lace. What was she thinking? And yet, it did feel delightfully taboo – like in the gardens. She remembered the feeling when Ben's lips first met hers and decided her hand could stay exactly where it was. Or maybe . . . there. The idea of punishing him for letting her down was surprisingly appealing and she found it all too easy to picture herself forcing him onto his knees to kiss her aching pussy better and apologise for making her wait.

As Lucy's arousal built, and her mind became increasingly full of Monday's memories, she ignored the anxious side of her brain telling her she was practically in public, a curtain all that divided her from a shop full of customers, and instead took pleasure from the risk and focussed on bringing herself to hard, fast orgasm. She pictured Ben walking into the changing rooms, pushing her to the wall, groaning with desire as he discovered her wetness. She imagined him dropping to his knees, kissing her pussy, tasting her juices and sucking her clit. As she pictured him sucking it into her mouth she came – which instantly plunged her back into normality. What the hell was she doing? And why was she thinking about Ben after what he'd done? Today was supposed to be about work.

Lucy looked at herself in the mirror, eyes gleaming and body shown off to perfection. Still, any lingerie that made her feel this good had to be bought. She paid for it without looking at the numbers that flashed up on the credit card machine. She'd accepted she had to spend the money but she really didn't want to acknowledge the true cost of power.

Caitlin arrived when Lucy was just stowing her purchase away – she wanted to keep her more intimate garments to herself. The final stop was a makeup store, where Lucy was given bold brows and a bright red slash of lipstick that made her feel like she was in an eighties Robert Palmer video. Caitlin had pronounced it perfect, but as Lucy looked in the mirror she wasn't entirely sure she agreed. The person looking back at her seemed distant, almost alien, her features paled down to nothing so that her eyebrows and lips dominated her face. She felt like she was looking at a stranger – someone she'd probably be too intimidated to talk to.

Lucy wasn't entirely comfortable with the rest of her look either. The stripy shirt-dress Caitlin had chosen would have been fine but for the frill at the bottom which made it feel like an odd hybrid of girlie and gentleman's club – like she was playing fairy dress-up in one of her stepdad's shirts. The bold printed floral tie added to the confusion: even though the rest of the outfit was black and white, Lucy still found it a bit too ostentatious for comfort. Her long socks made her feel like a schoolgirl, particularly as she couldn't help but totter in her absurdly high Jimmy Choo heels. They reminded her of cages, but Caitlin had told her that the gladiator meets bondage style was 'kick-ass', and Lucy didn't have the guts to contradict her. After all, what did she know? She thought back wistfully to her comfortable brown leather boots but Caitlin had insisted, 'Heels show your ambition – aim high.'

Lucy struggled to keep her balance as she navigated her way through the office – but she did feel different than she had before lunch, and judging from the approving looks of her colleagues, perhaps Caitlin was right. As Lucy walked past his desk, Brendan – the office lad, albeit fifteen years too old and with a heavy dose of Shoreditch metrosexual thrown in – eyed her up and down. 'Looking good, Luce.' Even though he was a senior account manager, Brendan still bantered like the junior execs. Lucy narrowed her eyes at him, suspecting he was winding her up, but the eager grin suggested his compliment was genuine and his eyes lingered rather longer than was appropriate on the gap between her long socks and the hem of her skirt.

'Thanks, Brendan,' she said, but she still felt uncomfortable as she sat down in front of her computer, and tugged the skirt down her legs to cover her thighs.

Lucy threw herself into the Dogsbody presentation and before she knew it, six o'clock had rolled around and the office was starting to empty. She'd forgotten the last time a day had gone so quickly – the new illustrations she'd found had really fired her imagination – and she felt a burst of satisfaction. This only grew when Anna nodded at her as she headed out the office. 'Good to see you taking care of your appearance for once.' It might not have been the most glowing of compliments, but from Anna it was high praise indeed.

If it hadn't been for Anna's comment, Lucy would probably have gone straight home – she was still tired after yesterday's excursion – but now she was in a celebratory mood. She might be unlucky in love but she had taken the first step towards turning her work life around. When Brendan mentioned a group of them were going to the pub and asked her to join them, the idea appealed. After all, she could count it as team building and interaction – something she'd scored badly on in her last appraisal. She picked up her new handbag, ignoring the guilt that rose in her as she remembered the price tag. OK, so it was close to a month's wages but, as she joined Brendan, Caitlin and the rest of her pub-bound colleagues, she decided that perhaps it was the price she had to pay if she wanted to fit in – and get ahead.

As soon as they got to the pub, Brendan bought a round of shots for everyone. Lucy ignored her usual 'no shots' rule and downed hers along with everyone else. When someone pointed out that two large glasses of wine cost the same as a bottle, it seemed only logical to buy a bottle instead – and after only two hours, four empty bottles sat on the table between them. Caitlin was the only one of the six who was still sober – though she was sniffing rather a lot, suggesting her sobriety may have had less to do with the amount she'd drunk and more to do with self-medication. She was talking loudly about Lucy's makeover, pointing out how much better she looked than she had in that 'awful grey suit' – apparently oblivious to Lucy's embarrassment. She almost told Caitlin to shut up – and realised if she was feeling that confrontational, she should probably slow down a bit on drinking herself.

She wished Rosie had been able to come to the pub so she had someone she could talk to properly. She'd seen Caitlin like this before at parties and found her a bit too much like hard work. Brendan was nice enough but he had been chatting intently to Annabel, the new PR exec, ever since they got to the pub. She was looking up at him, clearly smitten as he regaled her with stories about the agency, but with the intrusive music and hubbub of people chatting Lucy couldn't hear enough of what he was saying to join in. That left her with Dan from the design department – who was such a hipster he made Lucy feel out of her league, though she'd done her best to be friendly, and he had complimented her on her outfit, twice – and Mike, who had seen some success as a DJ in his early twenties but peaked too early and now made viral videos for the social media department.

As the drink flowed, conversation had moved from shop talk via bitching about clients to gossiping about their most outrageous experiences.

'There was this one bird when I was on tour,' said Mike. 'She was rough as you like but I was totally fucked in Denver – hadn't got laid in three days because the schedule was so ridiculous. She was all over me in the bar and even though she was a minger, the power of beer goggles is good. I was doing her from behind in the toilets when I started to feel really ill.'

Lucy wrinkled her nose at the image Mike was conjuring and Caitlin told him to shut up, but Mike carried on regardless. 'All the pills and the booze were swirling round in me – ended up chundering all over her back. Funniest thing was that when I pulled out, she turned round and asked me why I'd stopped.'

'You are disgusting,' said Caitlin.

'I don't get the chance nowadays, mate,' Mike said. 'Can't see Cassie being best pleased if I stayed out partying and left her to deal with night feeds on her own. On which note,' he looked at his watch. 'Yep, I should be heading back. See you in the morning, pissheads.'

Lucy waved him goodbye. She liked Mike. OK, some of his stories were pretty full-on but he was always talking about his wife and their daughter, Molly. He'd shown her pictures earlier, of a woman with a blonde mass of curls holding a baby with huge eyes and a generous head of matching platinum hair. 'She's the spit of her mum at her age – absolute darling. I get her to myself every Saturday morning when Cassie goes to art class and it's my favourite bit of the week. I never realised babies could be so clever.'

It was sweet seeing a man so enthusiastic about a kid – not something Lucy had come to expect from the men in her life. Her dad had told her kids bored him, and her stepdad hadn't shown much of an interest when she was growing up. Sure, David had gone on about having children but he hadn't seemed particularly paternal – more concerned with doing things at the right time and ticking the 'responsible adult' boxes than the reality of bringing a child into the world. Seeing Mike's genuine enthusiasm for his family was refreshing.

Lucy checked her phone for the time. Eight o'clock. She really should be getting home – she was decidedly light-headed. She reached for her bag, flinching as Caitlin leaned over the table and reached for the strap, tugging on it, her red wine swilling threateningly in her glass. 'You do know this is a design classic? Of course you don't. That's why you're so lucky to have me as your style guru.' Lucy instinctively pulled her bag away: she didn't want to be rude but there was no way she wanted her bag trashed with red wine before she'd had it for a single day. 'Thanks,' she said to Caitlin, hoping she didn't sound as irritated as she felt.

Just as she was standing up to leave, Brendan returned to the table, carrying a tray of six shots.

'Drink,' he said.

Lucy hadn't noticed him go to the bar – she really was feeling rather out of it – though not so out of it she couldn't count.

'There's only five of us now, Brendan,'

'Four,' said Caitlin, standing up. 'I'm going home. Some of us have lives. I can't spend all night in the pub.

Be good.' She pulled on her coat and left the group to its drinking.

'All the more for us,' said Brendan. 'And as I'm a gentleman' – he pushed the two extra shots towards Lucy and Annabel – 'ladies first.'

Lucy really didn't want another drink but it seemed rude to decline. She swigged back the tequila and reached for a piece of lemon, sucking it gratefully to stop herself from shuddering at the alcohol hit. Annabel did the same, clinking her glass against Lucy's once she'd done so and shooting her a broad grin.

'I never knew marketing would be so much fun,' she said. Lucy smiled back politely. Annabel was full of enthusiasm and, though she hadn't worked with her yet, Lucy regularly heard her laughing with the creatives and she seemed relaxed – and a lot more confident than Lucy, if she was entirely honest with herself.

'So how you doing, Luce?' Brendan asked, squeezing next to her on the bench, even though there was plenty of space around the table. 'Having a good night?'

'Not bad,' said Lucy. 'But I should be getting back soon.'

'The night is young. You need to have some fun. What do you reckon, Annabel?'

Annabel nodded. 'Live a bit – you never come down the pub with us. And the bosses have all gone now so we can relax.'

The mention of relaxation reminded Lucy of Ben – how come everything was reminding her of him at the moment? – and she felt a hot stab of angst in her chest.

'You know what'll make this a lot more fun,' said Brendan. 'How about we invite Mandy to join us?'

'Mandy who?' Lucy's mind flicked through the people at the agency but no one sprang to mind.

'Mandy,' Brendan said. 'You know, MDMA. Don't tell me you've never met?'

Lucy had always been too intimidated to try anything harder than a spliff but she didn't want to appear uncool.

'Oh, Mandy. Of course. She's a good friend of mine.' The lie slipped out surprisingly easily.

Brendan smiled. 'I always thought you were too good to be true – that nice girl act didn't fool me. Good to find out you're human.'

He pulled out his wallet and started doing something on his lap under the table. Lucy looked down to see him holding a small clear bag full of powder and a packet of Rizlas. He pulled out a cigarette paper and tipped some of the powder into it before carefully folding the paper around its illicit contents.

He handed her the paper packet under the table. 'Depth charge this and you'll be on your way to happy land.'

'Depth charge?' Lucy thought. She wasn't quite sure what he meant and held the packet, feeling it stick to the sweat on her hands.

Brendan handed another one to Annabel, who had

moved to sit next to him, and popped one into his own mouth. Annabel rapidly swallowed what she was offered. Lucy realised that must be what he meant by and, despite her better judgement, thought, 'What the hell.'

Who said she didn't know how to have fun?

Before long, Lucy was starting to feel distinctly odd. Everything seemed more vivid than usual – the fairy lights flashing behind the bar looked brighter than before, with a glow that seemed magical. Her limbs felt heavy and she could have sworn she was melting into the bench, becoming at one with everything – although she was slightly nauseous. Her cheeks were aching from smiling though, and it was much easier to talk to Brendan and Annabel for some reason.

Now, the other two were clearly flirting, whispering in each other's ears, and Brendan's hand was casually moving up and down Annabel's thigh. She was giggling, and Lucy noticed how pretty she was. She had a pale golden tan – a benefit of growing up in Australia, Lucy figured – and a smattering of freckles over her nose, which crinkled adorably when she was thinking hard. Her green eyes were sparkling, pupils heavily dilated, and as she ran her fingers through her hair, Lucy loved the way the curls stretched out and then sprang back into place. She'd always wanted curly hair as a child – she wondered what it would be like to touch it. A purist might say that Annabel's mouth was slightly too large for her face, but on her it worked, adding a sensual quality to her girl-next-door good looks.

Lucy could see why Brendan was coming on so strong, and found herself wondering what it would be like to kiss Annabel. She'd only kissed one girl before, but she hadn't really been attracted to her – it had been at David's behest – and even though it had felt nice enough, it hadn't turned her on much. She'd often seen women she found attractive though, even masturbated about the thought of being with a woman, though she always felt a bit embarrassed afterwards, as if she'd done something wrong. Now she wondered why she'd been so hung up about it. She looked at Annabel's lips again and imagined how they'd feel against hers.

'How you doing, Luce? Coming up yet?' Brendan asked her, hand still on Annabel's thigh.

'I think so,' Lucy said. 'I feel great.'

'You look great too,' Brendan said.

'You really do – love the makeover,' said Annabel.

By now her hand was moving up Brendan's thigh too, and showing no signs of stopping. Lucy couldn't quite believe it when she saw Annabel start rubbing Brendan's obvious erection through his trousers. Despite herself, she found herself hypnotised by the circular movements of Annabel's hand.

'Like what you see?' asked Brendan.

Lucy realised with a jolt that she'd been so immersed in her thoughts that she was openly staring at Brendan's crotch. But he didn't seem to mind, and Annabel's hand hadn't stopped moving. Indeed, now she seemed to be moving more deliberately, her hand sliding up and down Brendan's cock, its outline getting clearer in his tight trousers. Lucy looked at Annabel, who was still smiling, and then at Brendan, who really was rather handsome. Without thinking, she said, 'I do. I do like it.'

Brendan shot Annabel a conspiratorial glance, and then looked back at Lucy.

'Want to join us? We were going to nip into the disabled loos, where it's a bit more private. But you know what they say – two's company, three's a party. Want to party?'

By now, Lucy was feeling more relaxed than she had in years. It was as if all the tension had melted from her body and, although she was a bit woozy, she felt happy. And horny – particularly at the thought of feeling Annabel's body pressed against her own. The body-con top Annabel was wearing pushed her breasts up in a way that made Lucy want to touch them, firm, plump flesh spilling out a little more than it should. Annabel looked at Lucy and parted her lips suggestively.

'You look so hot,' she said. 'Come and play – it'll be fun.'

Fun. There was that word again. Annabel stood up and held out her hand to Lucy. 'Come on – we'll go first and Brendan can meet us there in a bit.' Lucy eagerly took the offered hand and noticed how small Annabel's felt in her own; how different from a man's with its slender fingers and oval-shaped nails.

'Give us ten minutes, eh, Brendan? Don't want to

look too suspicious.' Again, Annabel and Brendan shared a complicit look. Annabel interlaced her fingers with Lucy's and led her towards the back of the pub, past the kitchens and along a dark corridor to the disabled toilet. Lucy followed her through the door, wobbling a little on her new heels as Annabel locked the door behind them. The toilet was clinically clean, with scented candles and mirrored surfaces making it feel as glamorous as the main bar. Lucy could see Annabel's face and body reflected all around her and she liked what she was seeing.

'Brendan will give us a knock when he gets here. But I wanted you to myself first. I've fancied you for a while, but I didn't know if you played that way?'

'I don't usually,' said Lucy, feeling giddy with confidence and possibility. 'But life's for living, right?' That was what Ben had said, anyway, she thought. And if he wasn't prepared to continue on an adventure with her, Annabel certainly seemed eager to explore.

'Good attitude,' said Annabel, and pulled Lucy into a gentle kiss. Lucy loved the way she smelled – orange blossom and cocoa butter. Her skin was so soft, and her lips felt even better than Lucy had imagined, yielding and demanding in equal measure.

Lucy couldn't resist the urge to stroke Annabel's hair any longer, and wound several of her corkscrew curls around her fingers. She heard Annabel moan as she stroked the back of her neck, pressing her pelvis hard against Lucy's and starting to grind. Lucy moved to kiss

Annabel's neck, loving how responsive she was. She tasted as good as she smelled and the way she was rocking against Lucy made her pussy pulse.

'God, you're hot,' Annabel said, hands trailing sensually over Lucy's sides and back. 'Can I touch you?' Her hands were stretched out under Lucy's breasts, brushing the undersides, and Lucy was in no doubt as to what she meant. Her nipples pressed hard against her dress, and she suddenly wanted to feel Annabel's touch more than anything.

'If I can touch you,' she said.

Annabel pulled her top off instantly, revealing breasts even more delectable than Lucy had imagined, displayed in a silky bra that showed her nipples were just as hard as Lucy's. Lucy moved her hand to them instinctively, cupping Annabel's breasts and letting her thumb run softly over the nipples, circling around them until the other girl was pushing forwards into her hands and moaning more loudly. Lucy enjoyed the heavy weight of Annabel's breasts in her hands, the way her nipples stiffened further as she stroked them.

'Pinch my nipples,' Annabel murmured, her hands now inside Lucy's dress, stroking and squeezing her breasts in a way that made Lucy feel breathless and hot. She could feel a tingle going from her nipples to her clit every time Annabel touched her – she was good! – and had the urge to feel Annabel's body rubbing against her own. She pulled her dress over her head and was rewarded with a 'Wow!' from Annabel, who promptly pulled her close, insinuating her leg between Lucy's thighs as their breasts rubbed together.

Lucy felt as if she was melting into Annabel's body, and when Annabel started kissing her way down over her breasts and stomach, she knew what was coming – her pussy got wet at the thought of it. Sure enough, Annabel worked her way down Lucy's body, her hands and lips finding erogenous zones Lucy had never encountered before, before dropping to her knees in front of her.

'You want it?' she asked, tugging the sides of Lucy's knickers.

'Yes,' Lucy said. 'Please.'

Annabel pushed her knickers down to the floor and Lucy stepped out of them. At first, Annabel just looked at her. Lucy felt exposed having a woman staring directly at her pussy – but also turned on. When Annabel moved her hand and gently parted her lips, Lucy pushed her hips forwards, hungry for more. Annabel's lips moved to her clit and she kissed it, first with her lips, only then, as Lucy moaned, letting her tongue explore it at a leisurely pace. Lucy had to hold on to the sink to keep herself upright – God, this felt good. Annabel's fingers were parting her, sliding inside her, rubbing her as she licked Lucy's pussy, making her head spin even more than it already was. All her focus was now on her clit, which was throbbing, almost burning, as Annabel's expert tongue worked its magic.

'You taste amazing,' Annabel said before plunging

her tongue into Lucy, fucking her with it as her fingers pressed against Lucy's G-spot. Lucy was lost in sensation, hands tangling in Annabel's hair, pulling her deeper, arousal overriding embarrassment: all that mattered was coming. Her hips rocked with a steady motion and she found herself freeing her hands and reaching for her own nipples, tugging and tweaking them as Annabel eagerly went down on her. She felt Annabel add another finger and, with a twist of her hand, suddenly she was pressing into Lucy in a way that sent her over the edge. She started coming hard, knees buckling as her juices covered Annabel's face. The other girl kept licking and sucking, moving her attention from Lucy's now sensitized clit to the rest of her pussy, fingers still moving back and forth until she was sure she'd milked every last bit of the orgasm from Lucy's trembling body.

'God, you make me horny,' Annabel said, as she stood up to kiss Lucy, who loved tasting herself on Annabel's lips.

'I guess I should do something about that,' said Lucy. But as she moved her hand to Annabel's pussy, there was a knock on the door.

Annabel quickly pulled her top over her head and opened the door a crack.

'Nice timing,' she said when she saw Brendan's face. He slipped inside, grinning widely as he saw Lucy's near-naked body.

'Hello, ladies.' He pulled Annabel into a kiss. 'Tastes

like you've been getting busy without me. But now I think you need some cock.'

Lucy was still floating from her orgasm but Brendan's crass words brought her crashing back down to earth. When he came over and leaned in for a kiss, he tasted of cheese and onion crisps, and the nausea she'd been fighting earlier started to rise up again. His hardness pressed against her, reminding her of Ben, and suddenly she wanted to be anywhere but in the toilet. Annabel was standing behind Brendan, kissing his neck and pressing her breasts against him, her hands running over his body, insinuating themselves between Brendan's erection and Lucy's pubic mound. But where her touch had previously made Lucy feel great, now it just seemed seedy.

She started to notice the smell of man sweat and cheese and onion, mingling with the scented candle in a way that was less than sensual. As Annabel undid Brendan's fly to release his cock, Lucy felt bile rise inside her like a tidal wave and couldn't fight it back down. She pulled away from the pair and started throwing up in the toilet, first retching frothy white foam, then emptying the contents of her stomach. Ben's words about her being too good for toilets suddenly popped into her head. She could hear Brendan say, 'For fuck's sake,' as Annabel moved to hold her hair back. Her eyes watered as she threw up again and again, cheeks burning with embarrassment. All feelings of being 'at one with the universe' were gone now; instead she felt like an idiot.

Eventually, she had thrown up all she could. Her stomach was aching and she still felt nauseous but all she could do was dry heave.

'Come on, you,' Annabel said kindly. 'Let's get you some water.'

Brendan was clearly pissed off at having his threesome dreams shattered and made no effort to hide it. As they walked out the toilets together, they passed Dan and a woman Lucy didn't recognise, clearly on their way to use the facilities. As she dabbed at her mouth with a piece of tissue, wiping away her spit, Lucy noticed Brendan make a lewd gesture using both hands, and thrusting his tongue into the side of his mouth. Annabel hit him on the arm, but from the grin Dan shot at Brendan, it was clear that he'd got Brendan's gist. As soon as she'd finished her glass of water, Lucy left the pub, feeling ashamed of herself. Throwing up had helped sober her up – but it had also brought her anxieties flooding back.

For the second time in a week, Lucy struggled to hold back her tears as she sat on public transport. The Tube had arrived mercifully quickly, but the journey had dragged. She still wasn't feeling a hundred per cent. She could smell vomit in her hair and her qualms about her new look had returned when a drunk guy had pointed her out to his friend and the pair of them had fallen about laughing. She'd sat opposite them for two stops, cheeks flaming as they whispered and pointed. Usually, she hated having to change trains twice to get home but tonight she was relieved when she reached Notting Hill and could escape their critical gaze.

The journey had felt three times longer than usual, and Lucy managed to miss her stop by nodding off. Luckily she awoke at London Bridge and just made it off the Tube train with all her bags. She was surprised to see it was still fairly early – just before ten – and as her Southwark flat wasn't that far she decided to walk and let the night air clear her head. She felt as if it was much later and knew she'd be heading to bed as soon as she got home: two days running that she just wanted to pretend had never happened.She felt mortified at being so slutty – hardly professional behaviour. OK, Annabel was very sexy and it had been kind of hot being with a woman, if she was honest with herself, but somehow Brendan had made it all seem so sleazy. And she still hadn't succeeded in getting Ben out of her head. Her mind drifted back to the way he'd looked at her in the gardens – as if he wanted to understand her to her core – and a sob escaped as she thought about what an idiot she'd been.

As she made her way through the station towards Borough High Street, Lucy's bags weighed her down. Her back ached, and her throat was sore from all the retching. She walked like a zombie, one foot in front of the other, paying little attention to her surroundings – so when she heard someone call her name, it took her a moment to register where it was coming from.

'Lucy!' The voice was louder this time. She looked up – and saw Ben standing in front of her. 'Hello. I wasn't sure it was you at first. Bit of a different look from yesterday. But I'm glad it is.'

As if by magic, Lucy's mood lifted. Ben did want to see her. He looked gorgeous, in a white T-shirt, brown leather jacket and pair of well-worn jeans that hugged his body, reminding her of what lay beneath. But she was pissed off with him, she reminded her face.

She gave Ben a stern look just as he said, 'Sorry about leaving you in the lurch yesterday. Had some personal stuff to sort then realised I'd been a dick and forgotten to get your number. Can't believe I bumped into you – what are the odds?'

'Pretty low,' said Lucy, feeling a burst of excitement at the romance of it, even though she didn't really like Ben seeing her in the state she was in. 'Unless you're a weird stalker type of course. Are you? How come you're not in Brighton?'

'Sorry to disappoint you but no, sheer fluke. Had a meeting at Borough Market about a new project I'm planning. How about you – what are you doing here?'

'I live just up the road.'

'Great area – lucky you. I've always thought that if I had to live in London, it'd be round here.'

Lucy thought about her poky flat. 'Not sure you'd say that if you saw my place. But it's more affordable than Notting Hill.'

'Notting Hill's full of wankers. And if you didn't live here, you wouldn't have met me. So, before I forget again, can I get your number?'

Lucy thought about asking him what had been going on with Clare before she gave it to him, but she didn't really feel up to any more drama. She gave it to him, and typed his number into her phone.

'I would say we should go for a drink but my train goes in twenty minutes so I haven't really got time – don't want to get stranded and the night train takes an age. How was it back at the office? Did they work out you'd been skiving?'

'No, I got away with it,' Lucy said.

'So how come you were looking so glum when I saw you. Admin overload? And why are you dressed like that – I thought you hated high fashion?'

Lucy found Ben's directness refreshing. 'Not exactly. Shall we sit down?'

They wandered to the nearest bench and Lucy filled Ben in on her day, telling the truth about the drink and drugs – something about him made her want to be honest – but omitting the assignation in the toilets. After what she'd done with him yesterday, she didn't want him to think she was easy.

'Can I be honest with you?' Ben asked, as she finished.

Lucy nodded.

'I'm sorry you've had a shit day but I do think you've been a bit of an idiot – first of all blowing money you don't have on clothes you don't like, and then letting yourself be pressured into getting wasted.'

Lucy felt a wave of anger surge up from her stomach

to her chest. 'Thanks a lot. All I'm trying to do is fit in.' Her voice was tight and shrill.

'Exactly. Why? Stop trying to *prove* yourself and just *be* yourself.'

'Easy for you to say. You don't have anyone to answer to *but* yourself.'

'Neither do you, if only you realised it. Do you really think it's your clothes holding you back at work? Or the fact that you don't get off your head with your colleagues? Come on, Lucy, you're smarter than that.'

'Oh, so I'm stupid am I? You don't know what it's like. It's not like you've ever worked in London.'

'No, but I have seen people trying desperately to fit in before and it never turns out well.'

'Are you calling me desperate?'

The alcohol remaining in her body took the edge off Lucy's usual fear of confrontation and she was rapidly regretting bumping into Ben.

'You're not listening to me.'

'Yes I am – I just don't like what you're saying.'

Platform 5 for the 22.26 to Brighton

Ben stood up at the announcement. 'Well, maybe you should think about it a bit harder. Anyway, this is me. See you around.'

As Ben walked away, part of Lucy wanted to run after him, apologise, ask if she could come back to Brighton with him. But more of her felt hurt. Rather than giving her sympathy, he'd all but blamed her for everything that had happened. He didn't understand what it was like, how much pressure she was under. And anyway, she was feeling like death and was pretty sure that if she tried running, she'd throw up again. Sod him. The last thing she needed was someone telling her how to live her life – she'd had enough of that with David. Why were some men so controlling – as if they were so perfect?

But when she got home twenty minutes later and saw herself in the mirror – eyes red, pupils dilated, wearing an outfit that, if she was entirely honest with herself, she hated – Lucy realised Ben was right. She was clearly in a state – not something she was used to – and she felt ashamed of her reflection.

She looked at the bags of clothes Caitlin had urged her to buy. All of them made her feel as ridiculous as the ensemble she was wearing now: like they were wearing her rather than the other way round. She'd return them tomorrow lunchtime. Everything except the Victoria Beckham tennis dress. It might be fashionable but unlike everything else she actually felt comfortable in it. And now Anna had noticed her, she didn't want to vanish off her radar by wearing the wrong thing.

When Lucy woke up the next morning, she was relieved to find she had escaped the hangover she'd been expecting. She'd got up a few times in the night to get water and it had clearly done the job. But when she tried to eat breakfast, her throat closed up and she was unable to swallow. She gave up on her cereal bar after she realised she'd been chewing the same mouthful for five minutes, and poured herself a smoothie. She needed to be on form for the Dogsbody meeting and her brain never worked properly when she hadn't eaten.

As she showered, she thought about Ben. She couldn't remember exactly what she'd said but she did know she'd probably overreacted: she remembered him saying, 'See you around,' which was hardly a good sign. She thought about texting him but she wasn't sure what to say – she'd call him later. But now she had to get ready for work. She pulled on her Wolford tights and slipped the tennis dress over her head: perfect – she felt professional but, unlike yesterday's outfit, it also made her feel like herself, albeit a smarter, more grown-up version of herself than she'd ever seen before. She grabbed the rest of her shopping bags, slung her laptop over her shoulder and headed off to work feeling a little muted but positive. If she could overlook whatever was happening with Clare, Ben could surely forgive her for some drunken cross words?

The Dogsbody meeting went better than Lucy could have possibly hoped. Julian, the Dogsbody MD, had loved the illustrations she'd found, and chose the designer who was her favourite too. She'd always got on well with Julian – he had a great sense of humour, and wasn't above seeing the absurdity in selling dog grooming products. Better yet, he'd had an exciting announcement. 'As you know, we've been looking for investment to take things to the next level for quite some time. Now, I'm pleased to announce that we've got funding. We can finally progress a lot of the products that we've been researching – and start investing a lot more in marketing. Over the next year we'll be launching a vitamin-enriched ice cream for dogs, an aromatherapy shampoo and conditioner range, holistic health supplements and a fashion range. Budgets are still being set but I think you'll find the figures to your liking. We'll need to move fast but I know you're more than capable of doing that.' He directed the last sentence at Lucy, who felt warm at the validation.

After the meeting Anna had pulled her to one side. 'I don't know what's going on with you at the moment but I like it. Your presentation today was clear and creative – and you showed initiative with the Gnasher issue. You're getting better at costings too. How would you feel about managing all the new Dogsbody accounts? It'll be a lot of hard work but I think you're ready for it. You don't really have enough accounts for someone of your level – though it will mean Caitlin will have to get support from one of the execs rather than you.'

Lucy had to fight to stop herself from hugging Anna but her excitement clearly showed on her face. 'Thanks so much – I'd love to.'

It was only after Anna had gone back to her office that Lucy wondered exactly how much extra work the new business would require – and whether she'd be getting paid any more for the extra workload. Still, it was a definite step up. She'd talk to Anna about the details once she'd proved she could handle the responsibility.

As Lucy walked past reception on the way back from the meeting room, Rosie gave her a worried look.

'Are you OK, Lucy?'

'Never been better,' Lucy said. 'Did you hear about the Dogsbody meeting?'

'No, but I have heard something else. What did you get up to last night?'

Lucy blushed. 'What have you heard?'

'Well, it's probably bollocks but Brendan's been telling everyone that he had a threesome with you and Annabel last night.'

'What?'

'That's what I thought – I mean, I didn't think you'd do something like that. Annabel maybe – she's worked her way through half the agency – but you . . .'

Lucy looked around to see if anyone could overhear them.

'It's kind of true,' she said in a hushed voice.

'You are kidding me?'

As Lucy filled Rosie in on the details of the night before, she felt sick. She'd known Brendan was pissed off with her but she never thought he'd gossip about it. It's not as if anything had really happened – or at least not that he knew about.

'You need to talk to Annabel,' said Rosie. 'Find out whether she knows what he's doing. If not, it's two against one. You don't need this kind of shit floating round about you – you know what this place is like.'

Lucy knew Rosie was right.

'Don't tell anyone,' she said.

'Of course not,' Rosie said. 'So, stupid gossip aside, does this mean you'll be coming out on the pull with me to Retro Bar?'

Lucy smiled. 'Annabel's lovely,' she said. 'But I don't think so – unless you need a wingwoman. There's someone else I'm interested in.'

'Damn – I know a girl who'd be perfect for you. So who's this person you're interested in – not Brendan?'

'God, no,' Lucy said. 'No one you know. Fancy going for lunch together tomorrow and I'll tell you all about him? I need to crack on.'

'Sure thing – I'll be waiting. Do you want me to spit in Brendan's coffee the next time he asks me to make him one?'

Lucy smiled. 'I couldn't possibly endorse such behaviour – particularly not now Anna's decided I'm ready for responsibility.' But as she started to walk away, she looked over her shoulder at Rosie. 'Unless you really want to, of course.'

Rosie winked at her and, although she felt mortified at the idea of being the subject of office gossip, Lucy felt a little better knowing that some form of justice would be hers.

'So, I hear Anna's given you the new Dogsbody accounts to manage,' Caitlin said when Lucy got back to her desk.

'Yes. I was a bit surprised but I'm really excited about it.'

'Don't get too excited – it's a lot of work being an account manager. On which note, can you file these for me please, and then research which social media is best for reaching thirty- to forty-year-old mums. I've got a Maternitease meeting tomorrow.'

Caitlin often asked Lucy for help on her own accounts. While it did loosely fall under Lucy's job description, Anna had made it very clear to her that managing her own accounts should take priority and Caitlin should only call on her for support if she really needed to.

'I'm really sorry but I've got a lot on myself – I've got all the new Dogsbody product lines to research.'

Caitlin looked as if Lucy had thrown a glass of water in her face. She'd never said no to her before.

'But I'll have to work late to get it done and I'm supposed to be going out for dinner with Daddy tonight.'

'Really sorry, Caitlin – I'm going to be working late too. We can always order a pizza.'

The snarl on Caitlin's face showed she wasn't best pleased at the idea. She turned on her heel and stalked away without even giving Lucy a response. Lucy wondered if she should follow her – she'd already pissed Caitlin off once today, when she'd admitted she was returning most of the clothes. 'Thanks for wasting my time,' Caitlin had hissed, obviously in a foul mood. Lucy hoped she hadn't damaged the relationship between them permanently. But as she saw Caitlin stop to talk to Brendan, she decided to get stuck into her work instead of worrying about it.

Caitlin's bad mood continued for the rest of the day and into the evening. It seemed to Lucy as if she was even typing extra-aggressively. She'd refused to eat any of the pizza Lucy had ordered and responded tersely to any questions Lucy asked. By 9 p.m., when the two of them finally finished work, Lucy was glad to get away from Caitlin's negativity.

As soon as she got out the office, Lucy picked up her phone to call Ben. She'd been fighting the urge all day but she'd spent lunchtime writing follow-up notes from the Dogsbody meeting and there hadn't been a second to spare. She didn't want to wait until she got home – she wasn't sure how late Ben stayed up and it'd be nearly ten by the time she got back. But when she dialled the number, it went straight through to voicemail. She didn't want to leave a message – she wasn't entirely sure what she was going to say – so she hung up. She'd call him tomorrow. Although she was still furious at him, she'd also been feeling increasingly embarrassed about her own behaviour as the day progressed and she wanted to fix things – not least so they could arrange to see each other again. She'd decided to ask him about Clare. Maybe there was an innocent explanation – he'd seemed pleased enough to see her, and surely he wouldn't have been if he was in love with someone else? There was only one way to find out . . .

CHAPTER 4

'The number you are calling is currently unavailable. Please try again later.'

Lucy's stomach fell. It was the second time she'd tried Ben that morning – once before she got on the Tube, and now walking from the station to work. She guessed he could have his phone switched off – it was early after all. Or maybe he was away from home – with Clare? – and had forgotten his charger. The more she'd thought about it, the guiltier she felt about getting so cross with him: she *had* been trying to be something that she wasn't, and it hadn't made her happy. He'd hit a nerve, but she wished she hadn't overreacted.

Her mind was still racing with possible scenarios – all negative – when she walked into reception.

'Morning, Lucy. You OK?' asked Rosie.

'I've been better.'

'I can tell – you've got a face like a smacked arse.'

'Cheers,' said Lucy, forcing a smile. 'It's just – oh, it's all a bit complicated. Still on for lunch?'

'Of course. Meet you here at one?'

'Will do. And then I'll fill you in.'

'Can't wait,' said Rosie. 'I want to know *all* about your mystery crush.'

Lucy felt another stab of insecurity. 'Cool. See you at one,' she said, stepping through the double doors into the office before Rosie could ask her any more questions.

'Lucy, my office, now,' said Anna, as soon as she saw her. Her jaw was fixed, as if she was grinding her teeth, and she had a hard glint in her eyes – there was no doubting that she was unimpressed. Lucy felt her chest tighten. What was wrong? Had Anna spotted something wrong with the Dogsbody proposal? She hoped she hadn't messed up the figures. Lucy scuttled into her office, and was surprised when Anna closed the door behind her. Usually she left it wide open, all the better for people to hear her 'constructive criticism'.

'Take a seat.'

Anna's voice was oddly formal. She was always terse but somehow she seemed more officious than usual.

Lucy did as she was told, feeling embarrassed as the chair leg scraped loudly against the floor. She sat rigidly, playing with the skin at the base of her fingernails as she waited for Anna to explain the reason she was there.

It seemed like an age before she spoke.

'I have something serious to discuss with you, Lucy.'

'Have I messed up the financials? I went over them three times.' Lucy's voice quavered.

'It's nothing to do with Dogsbody. It's of a rather more personal nature.'

Lucy's brow furrowed. Had Anna figured out she'd been skiving on Monday? Or had she heard about what happened with Brendan and Annabel? She wasn't sure which was worse, and thought it best to stay silent.

'I have heard some rumours floating round the office that make me very uncomfortable. I need you to shed some light on them.' Lucy tried to feign innocence.

'What rumours are those?'

'The rumours about a senior account manager offering you and another member of staff drugs. Is that right?'

Lucy's heart started pounding harder. She couldn't believe details of Tuesday night had already got back to Anna. But how much did she know? Lucy hadn't had a chance to talk to Annabel and she didn't know what Brendan had said. She wished she'd asked Rosie more about what she'd heard.

'Is this true, Lucy?'

She could feel her face going cold and her head starting to spin. Bile rose up in her throat and she gulped, trying to swallow back her fear.

'Well, Lucy?'

'What am I being accused of?' she said.

'It's not you I'm worried about. I need to know that I can trust my senior managers with staff – and that does not involve feeding junior account managers drugs. Particularly not the night before a major presentation – even though you did handle it very well.'

Lucy felt a little relief knowing her own job wasn't

at risk, but still – Brendan might have spread some gossip but she didn't want to lose him his job. She thought quickly.

'I'm not sure what happened,' she said. 'We'd been doing shots. I'm not used to it.'

Anna looked at her hard.

'Are you sure?' Lucy focused on keeping her gaze steady.

'I'm sorry – I blacked out. I remember leaving the office but after that it's a blank.'

Anna seemed sceptical. 'Well, perhaps you are suffering from stress if you need shots on a weekday to relax. Blacking out is not healthy. You need a holiday. I suggest you take some time off next week.'

'What about the Dogsbody presentation?' asked Lucy, her heart sinking.

'If you're that stressed, I don't think you should take on any new accounts for the time being,' replied Anna. 'I hadn't put the paperwork through for your promotion yet anyway. Relax, see if any memories drift back and we'll reconvene once you're feeling more yourself. Now, can you file these for me please? And scan in the clippings from Friday.'

Anna's meaning was clear. She had no choice but to take Lucy at her word but she didn't believe her for a second. Either Lucy confessed what had really happened, potentially losing Brendan his job, or she was back to being bottom of the pile with Dogsbody – and Anna.

She was shaking as she went to her desk. How the hell had it come to this? If she hadn't gone to the pub, she'd still be a senior account manager. Ben's words came back to her. 'Stop trying to prove yourself and just be yourself; desperately trying to fit in never turns out well.' If only she'd seen him on the way to the pub rather than afterwards, things could be very different. Maybe his phone wouldn't be switched off now?

Caitlin walked past to her own desk, bags under her eyes, blowing her nose then peering furtively into the tissue. She noticed Lucy looking at her and hurriedly threw it away.

'Nice outfit,' she sneered as she sat down. 'Though it looked better with the right handbag.'

Lucy had returned the bag. Luckily, it had a waiting list – Caitlin had leapfrogged it through one of Daddy's connections – so the saleswoman happily refunded her.

Without replying, Lucy turned to her computer and started logging on. Then she heard Caitlin sniff particularly loudly and inelegantly. Lucy looked over at her, startled, and took in her pale skin and tapping foot. Her manner suddenly seemed spookily familiar. Anna's talk about drugs was circling in her brain and everything clicked into place: Caitlin's sniffing on Tuesday night, her snappiness, her 'go getting' attitude. Lucy knew from experience what a cokehead looked like. Until now, she'd been too busy being intimidated by Caitlin to notice her confidence was artificially enhanced. How could she have missed it?

She noticed Anna staring at the pair of them through the window, and wondered if their boss realised the extent of the agency's drug problem.

'I had better things to spend my money on,' she said, quietly.

Caitlin glared at her, eyes flashing, but noticed Anna and clearly thought better of going on the offensive.

'As if you'd know what to buy,' she said. 'I'll be in the design studio if you need me.'

Lucy was grateful when Caitlin left. She was becoming more of a bitch with every passing day. She wondered how much coke Caitlin did – and whether she realised the effect it was having on her.

Despite the unsettling start to her day, Lucy smiled when she saw the name pop up on her phone – Jo, her best mate from university. She hadn't seen her in nearly a year – not since she'd moved to Oxford with Martin. Jo had invited her to stay in Oxford a few times, but after Lucy turned her down three times in a row because of work commitments the invitations stopped coming – though Jo often said she thought Lucy should spend less time working and more enjoying herself.

She opened the text. *How busy are you this week? Split with Martin so could do with escaping, and got meeting in London tomorrow. Fancy a house guest?* Lucy was shocked. She thought Jo and Martin were solid. What had happened? She knew now wasn't the time to ask.

So sorry. You OK? Of course you can come to stay tonight, she hurriedly texted back.

Great. Is awful being in same house with him.

Lucy could remember what it was like living with David after they'd broken up. Every time she saw him she was reminded of what he'd done – it had been one of the toughest times of her adult life. She texted back and they agreed to meet at six.

Although she was looking forward to seeing Jo, by six Lucy was wishing she'd put her off until tomorrow. She'd had to cancel lunch with Rosie after Anna had told her she needed print quotes in triplicate for all the potential Dogsbody promotional material. It was the kind of job that Lucy hated, and Anna knew it. She was clearly taking the drug issue personally. Lucy wondered why: Caitlin was a manager and she was sure Anna wasn't naïve enough to miss the signs of her drug use – Lucy couldn't believe *she* had, now the scales had fallen from her eyes – but Anna didn't seem to care about that. OK, Caitlin hadn't offered Lucy any coke but it did affect her management style in a way that was far more destructive. Then again, she did bring in a lot of money – and 'Daddy' was a useful contact for the agency. Maybe it wasn't about drugs and Anna was looking for an excuse to get rid of Brendan – but why?

At least Caitlin had been away from her desk for most of the day – probably in Dan's office again. The two of them were generally huddled together there whenever Lucy went into the studio. Come to think of it, he'd been pretty twitchy on Tuesday too. The more she thought about it, the more she wondered exactly what it was that Anna had heard. What was the story that she wanted Lucy to tell – and why? Spending the afternoon working while trying to figure out what she needed to say or do to get back in Anna's good books was distracting – and exhausting.

Rosie called Lucy on the dot of six.

'I've got Jo in reception for you. Do you want to come and meet her? She's got a lot of bags so it might be a bit of a nightmare getting through the office.'

She was still working her way through the print quotes but she found herself thinking 'fuck it'. It was becoming an increasingly common thought. 'Why bother working late when Anna's not going to treat me properly unless I tell her about Brendan, or Caitlin, or both?' Lucy shook her head as if to make the whole mess fall away.

'I'll be right through,' she said.

She shut down her computer and walked to reception at speed. The way Anna had been acting, she wouldn't be surprised if she came up with an urgent report she needed for tomorrow morning.

When she got to reception, Jo looked surprisingly cheerful.

'Hey, Luce. Thanks so much for letting me come to stay.'

'Don't be silly – it's great to see you. I just wish it was in happier circumstances.'

'Oh, I'm happy enough,' said Jo. 'I just couldn't face spending another second in the house with Martin.'

'Back to mine, then? Let me take some of that.'

Lucy picked up three of the bags that surrounded Jo, leaving her with one bag and a monster suitcase. 'You OK with the rest of it?'

'I got here from Oxford with all of it on my own, babe. I think I can handle it.' Jo's eyes lit up with warm humour, and Lucy thought how lovely it was to see her again. She might be tired but seeing Jo had given her a burst of energy – and spending an evening listening to someone else's woes would keep her mind off her own.

The pair walked to the Tube in comfortable silence. Lucy knew Jo would tell her everything in her own good time – and anyway she didn't want to make her cry in public. She'd been doing quite enough of that herself recently and she wouldn't wish it on her worst enemy, let alone her best friend. Even though Jo seemed happy, no one could be after a relationship that serious broke up – could they?

As ever, Jo looked amazing – even if her outfit was a little too 'edgy' for Lucy to even consider wearing it. But there was no chance of Jo being subsumed by her clothes – she'd been obsessed by fashion for as long as Lucy could remember and had an instinct for colour that made even the most clashing of shades somehow work on her. No matter how outrageous her get-up, the first things anyone noticed about her were her smiley eyes and warm grin, so infectious that it often attracted comment – though that was generally closely followed by a compliment about her shoes. Jo's shoe collection put Carrie Bradshaw to shame.

Today, she was wearing her 'travelling shoes' – though the heels were still higher than anything Lucy could walk in. Jo could run and even dance in heels as if they were comfy trainers. She'd tried showing Lucy how to do it: 'Heel before toe, and imagine your feet sinking into the floor evenly through four points at each corner of your foot.' – but no matter how much Lucy had practiced, she still wobbled like a five year old in her mum's shoes.

'Slow down,' Lucy said. 'I can't keep up.'

'Sorry,' said Jo. 'I got used to Martin – he always used to rush everywhere. I tried telling him that I liked looking around me when I walked, that I liked taking in my surroundings, but he didn't understand and just got pissed off with me. It was easier to just get used to walking fast.'

Lucy knew exactly what Jo meant. David had been the same – as if he liked her trotting a few paces behind him. He never stopped if she had to tie her shoelace or wanted to stop to look in a shop window – just expected her to catch up and looked irritated if she was breathless with the effort.

'There's no need to rush now,' she said. 'So, how's everything been . . . ?'

* * *

After the pair had freshened up at Lucy's flat, they headed out for cocktails. Lucy had texted her friend Elle for a recommendation – Elle knew all the best places to go – and had promptly received a choice of three. None of them had any drinks listed under fifteen pounds when Lucy looked them up online, but seeing Jo was such a rare treat and she wanted to make sure she had a good night.

Elle had invited herself along, and promised to 'bring the girls'. It wasn't really what Lucy had planned but it seemed rude to tell her she wanted time alone with Jo.

It took them a while to find the bar. It was one of those places for people 'in the know' and the door was deliberately discreet. As they walked in, Lucy warned Jo not to sit down and steered her towards the bar. When she'd checked the website earlier, there was a £100 minimum spend to sit at a table. She'd been caught by that before with Elle, the first time they went out together. Elle had been buying cocktail pitchers – a requirement of the table – and Lucy had thought it only fair to take it in turns to buy rounds. That was before she realised how expensive drinks were in London – she'd eaten potato curry for three weeks to cover the cost of the night. The cocktails hadn't even been that good.

'What's the point of making it so hard to find? Keeping the riff-raff out, I suppose,' said Jo, picking up the cocktail menu and raising her eyebrows, 'If the prices don't already do that – seventeen pounds for a cocktail? And people are knocking them back like alcopops. I mean, look at them.'

She gestured at a group of girls with matching tans and flippy hairstyles sitting at a low table with a central bottle of vodka in an ice bucket. They were ostensibly together, reeking of clique, but in reality all of them were staring at their smartphone screens.

'It's taking rubbernecking to a whole new level. I bet you they're the kind of people who used to look over your shoulder when they were talking to you at a party to see if there was anyone more interesting around. Now they show their superiority by making you compete with the whole of the internet instead – all to show how 'busy' they are and how desperately they're needed. Too busy Instagramming themselves looking cool to actually have any fun.'

As if she'd osmosed what Jo said, one of the girls grabbed the arm of the woman next to her and pulled her into the frame of a shared selfie – with obligatory Sapphic overtones.

'Look at them – trying to show how sexy they are by pretending to be into each other. I bet you they'd run a mile if they were actually confronted by muff,' said Jo.

She was openly bi and, although Lucy had never met any of her girlfriends, she had heard her rant about 'lipstick lesbians' on more than one occasion.

'They're the kind of women that get us bisexuals a bad name. Nothing more disappointing than thinking you're in with some gorgeous woman then realising the only fun you'll get is a bit of a boob grope and, if you're really lucky, the chance to go down on her. Unreciprocated, of course – and almost inevitably followed by tears, guilt and drama.'

Lucy wondered if she fitted into that category – she hadn't told Jo yet about what happened with Annabel. But she'd been thoroughly enjoying herself until Brendan turned up – if there was any drama, it was down to him. And she'd always thought it was better to give than to receive – the idea of tasting Annabel certainly wasn't a turn-off. Her pussy tingled at the memory of Annabel's tongue on her clit. She really should talk to her about things. Annabel had been kind to her and she felt a bit guilty for ignoring her since their assignation. And a little curious – particularly given that Ben seemed to have vanished from the scene.

'God, and now look at them.' The women had stood up and were twerking with each other, taking photos of themselves. 'It's like life isn't worth living unless it's on social media. Talk about an expensive way to ignore your friends.'

Lucy couldn't help but agree. She much preferred going to an old-fashioned pub and chatting with mates, maybe playing some pool, to coming to expensive cocktail bars where you couldn't hear each other over the 'sound sculpture' – more foreground music than background music. The women they were watching looked as if they came here every night – indeed, as one danced around for the camera, she accidentally knocked two drinks over and barely registered it. When the owner of the other drink pointed it out to her, she shrugged and loudly said, 'I'm sick of Mojitos anyway. I can't believe they don't have balsamic cocktails here. So last year.'

'Lucy. Over here!'

As the drink spiller moved to step into the eyeline of a waitress and clicked her fingers to attract her attention, Lucy realised with horror that Elle was at the centre of the group.

'What are you doing lurking at the bar? We've got a table. Come and join us. Bring your'— her look was pointed and exclusionary—'friend. Out of towner?' She ran her eyes over Jo's outfit – though Jo was as stylish as ever.

Jo raised an eyebrow at Lucy. 'You know them?' she said. She only looked mildly apologetic as she whispered, 'Sorry for taking the piss . . .' The 'but' lingered in the air. Jo was clearly withholding judgement until she met them properly, but her initial impression obviously hadn't been good.

Lucy couldn't blame her. She'd never really noticed it before but she'd been seeing a lot of things differently over the last few days.

'Elle's been really helpful to me,' she said. 'She's not as bad as she looks.'

But as Elle beckoned her over with one hand while fellating a bottle of champagne for another photo, she did wonder whether she was really telling Jo the truth.

She might have had some fun, drunken nights out with Elle, but the scene in front of her was all too familiar.

It reminded her of the first time she'd met Elle, after she'd blagged her way into the VIP area at one of BAM!'s launches – and *that* hadn't ended all that well, come to think of it. She'd been invited to join Elle's group when she went up to find out who they were for the database, and they'd persuaded her to stay with them and kept her topped up with champagne – at the sponsor's expense, of course. Lucy had felt uncomfortable, but didn't know what to do, so had drunk too much and tried to join in with their screeching gossip.

When Anna had caught her with an uninvited group she'd been furious – though Elle had rapidly fired off something about a fashion blog, which seemed to placate her a bit. Lucy had felt really bad about herself the next morning – so she was flattered when Elle texted inviting her to an art launch. It had been much the same there – though this time Elle had picked her brains for marketing ideas for half an hour; then passed them off to the artist as her own and picked him up as a client for her 'boutique promotion agency'. She always seemed to end up giving Elle something, come to think about it, in the hope of being accepted into the group. But through Jo's eyes, Lucy suddenly realised Elle's social scene wasn't really one she wanted to be a part of.

She looked at Jo and then back at Elle.

'Hi, Elle. I think you got the wrong idea on the phone. We're only having a quick drink so I don't really want to splash out on a table. Jo and I have a lot of catching up to do. Good to see you though. Looks like you're having fun.'

She was shaking, but felt defiant as Elle gaped at her.

'I got all the girls together for you. I thought you were up for a fun night.'

'I didn't say that, though,' said Lucy. 'Sorry for any confusion. But it's not like you need us to have a good time.'

She gestured at 'the girls' – most of whom she didn't even know beyond nodding acquaintance. Elle looked as if she was going to stamp her foot.

'But I wanted to have a good time with *you*. And I wanted to talk to you about Archie – his last launch was a flop: no one came. I think he might be losing it. Still, if you're going to be boring – enjoy time with your *friend*.' She made the word sound like an insult as she turned away from them. As they headed back to the bar, even though she was still shaking Lucy felt relief flood her body at the idea of just having a quiet drink with Jo.

'I have an idea,' said Jo. 'Forget buying a drink here – I can't be arsed to sell a kidney to get one. How about we spend the money on spirits at the supermarket instead and have a proper cocktail night back at yours?'

Lucy perked up. The idea seemed much more appealing – and affordable – than staying here. And she wasn't sure she could cope with much more of the twerking girls anyway.

'Sounds good. So what do you fancy?' asked Lucy.

'I'll take Manhattan, baby,' said Jo, laughing. 'It's a classic – basic, honest and softened by sweetness. A bit like you.'

'Aww, thanks.' Lucy grinned at the compliment. Usually they made her blush but Jo was so honest it just sounded as if she was stating fact. And Lucy couldn't disagree, now she came to think about it.

'Waitrose or Aldi?'

'Waitrose, darling,' said Jo. 'It is a celebration, after all. And anyway, they'll be more likely to have those monkey cocktail decorations – and umbrellas. We need umbrellas. And sparklers.'

Lucy imagined her flat going up in flames, but then batted the image away and said, 'And I guess you'll be wanting coconuts and glasses carved out of pineapples?'

'The girl's catching on. You are so back – there's that creativity I adore you for.'

'And we'll need some food too – I've had too much drink and not enough food in the last few days. How about we pick up some Jamaican Patties and jerk chicken on the way home? And I guess Piña Coladas could count as one of your five-a-day if they're made with crushed pineapple?'

'Good thinking, Sherlock – there's the sensible Lucy I know and love. I knew it the first time I saw you, queuing for circus skills society. You looked so preppy with your red satchel and matching Converse, though I was jealous of your legs in your skinny jeans. But you looked as if it was your first day at school, not Freshers' Week, in that blazer – ready for work, not fun. Everyone else in the queue had dreads, or at least a Smiths T-shirt. You looked like you should be in the campus prospectus. I thought you seemed interesting: that good girl must have a bad streak somewhere, I said to myself.'

'And now you know better.' Lucy laughed dryly.

'You *are* interesting. And I'm sure there's a bad streak deep down – even if you never did try fire breathing.'

'Once I heard you had to spit paraffin and you could get burns all down your throat if you got it wrong, I was too scared.'

'Feel the fear and do it anyway,' Jo said. 'How do you think I felt on the flying trapeze? My legs used to shake every time I got up on the rig – but I still did it. I knew you could do it too – but you always seemed to prefer being backstage.'

'I did. And it was different for you. You were brilliant,' said Lucy. 'You didn't look scared.'

'That's half the secret,' said Jo.

'What's the other half?'

'Knowing you'll feel fucking epic once it's done.'

Jo's grin seemed to spread across every muscle of her face, and Lucy could tell that she was speaking from the heart. The way she looked reminded Lucy of the way Ben looked when he was talking about food – or her. When would she get him out of her head?

'So are we going, or what?' asked Jo, spotting a barman approaching them.

Lucy nodded and headed out of the door, holding it open for Jo behind her.

Two hours later, they were curled up under a blanket on Lucy's sofa, giggling. They'd been unable to find cocktail accessories but had rustled up some serviceable Manhattans, deciding to leave Piña Coladas for another day. After a couple of cocktails, Jo produced a bottle of champagne out of her hold-all.

'Shall we move on to this? We were saving it for our fifth anniversary but that's never going to happen now, so I swiped it to bring with me when Martin was at Aldi.' When Lucy googled the price at Jo's behest, she baulked at the idea of drinking it.

'You should save it for a special occasion.'

'It is a special occasion. I'm with my best mate in the world, I've escaped a slow, miserable death by boredom and my business is finally starting to take off. What more could I have to celebrate? Did I tell you I've got more meetings since I split from Martin than I did in the last year of our relationship?'

'Yes,' said Lucy. 'Twice. But you can tell me again if you want. It's great to hear you sounding so positive.'

Jo was quiet for a moment, immersed in her own thoughts. When she spoke, her voice was softer than before.

'It's odd really. If he hadn't got pissed and lairy with me after we'd been to Beth's party and told me to fuck off after picking a row out of nothing, I'd still be sitting next to him playing Angry Birds on my phone to hide the fact we'd run out of things to say to each other. We had almost nothing in common, really. I don't know how we lasted so long. He'd stopped telling me what was going on in his head – or doing anything much, really. And whenever I told him my business ideas, he told me they were stupid – even though he was doing bugger-all to bring any money in.'

Jo sighed. 'I offered to help him with the website for his agency but he wasn't interested – got stroppy with me.'

Lucy nodded sympathetically. 'David always got cross with me for trying to help him with . . . stuff. He'd asked me for help, almost begged me, but he still got shitty with me and accused me of mothering him or being boring if I ever tried – it's one of the reasons we split.'

'What sort of help?' asked Jo. 'You never did really explain why you guys broke up.'

'I was embarrassed. And I didn't want to embarrass him.'

'There's no way you could embarrass him any more than he embarrassed himself after you split up. What was it, fourteen phone calls in one night?'

Lucy grimaced. 'That was a particularly bad night though. Usually it was only nine or ten.'

'One of those calls would have been enough. I almost called the police when I answered your phone that time and he thought I was you. So, what's the embarrassing secret? Has he got a tiny knob?'

Lucy paused, eyes distant as she considered what she was about to say. She breathed in deeply and looked at Jo, only half meeting her gaze.

'I wish. No, he was a recovering coke addict. When we first met, he told me he'd been clean for six months. It was only when we'd been together for a year that he admitted 'clean' meant only doing it at weekends.'

'Shit. No wonder he was always so arrogant. So what happened?'

'Well, it all started because I wanted us to do something nice together. I'd read this piece in a magazine about staycations and, as we couldn't afford a holiday, I showed it to him. He got really into the idea of getting a sex toy hamper – he'd been suggesting I get some toys for ages. And I loved the idea of turning our bedroom into a boudoir. I spent ages on it – got a new silky duvet cover, fresh flowers, scented candles, the works. He said he'd get the toys – although I had to give him my credit card because he said his wasn't working.'

'This doesn't sound like it ends well,' said Jo.

'I ran a nice bubble bath, lit some candles – even floated rose petals in it. David said he'd set up the bedroom, then came in with two Martinis and a cocktail shaker on a tray.'

'Smooth, in a James Bond sort of way. Did you see that article recently saying that he'd be deemed a sociopath if he really existed?'

'No,' said Lucy. 'But I've never really seen the appeal

of him. He's a bit too testosteroney for my liking – fancies himself so much.'

Jo laughed. 'And you just know you'd catch something – can you remember seeing him use a condom with all those women he shagged?' She shuddered. 'Anyway, go on – sorry I interrupted.'

'Well, I'm not really a big Martini fan – they're a bit strong for me but he'd made such an effort it seemed rude not to drink it. So there we were in the bath. He was drinking quickly and told me off for being so slow, so I drank it as fast as I could. It made me really drunk. Looking back, I think he knew what he was doing. When we got into the bedroom, there was a mirror with two lines of coke laid out – big ones – and a video camera set up at the end of the bed. There were toys laid out on the bedside table too – butt plugs and really big dildos and . . .' Lucy broke off, choked by the memory.

'It's OK – I get your gist. What did you do?' Jo was looking concerned now.

'Well, I told him I didn't really want to be filmed but he promised me he'd angle the camera so my face wasn't visible. He was really persuasive – gave me a massage, opened a bottle of champagne and kept topping up my glass. All the while he was talking dirty and it started to get me in the mood. By the time he suggested doing the coke, the champagne was all gone. He told me the coke would straighten me out – that there was no need to be scared: he'd look after me. He told me it'd be sexy for us to do it together.' Jo knew Lucy's attitude to drugs, and looked genuinely distressed. Lucy wondered if telling her the story had been a good idea. But Jo leaned towards her and patted her arm, reading her need for approval.

'You OK, love?'

'Yes,' said Lucy, though her voice was tight. 'Can I tell you the rest? Now I've started I want to get it all out.'

'Of course,' said Jo. 'So, you took the coke?'

Lucy nodded. 'I thought it would make him happy – he had this weird glint in his eyes and I didn't want to make him angry.'

'You poor love.'

'It really stung my nose, but afterwards I felt OK. My heart was racing but I felt really alive – as if I'd had a load of coffee but without the headache. And I felt sexy. When he said he wanted to capture me on film because I was so beautiful – his beautiful slut, he called me – it seemed like a good idea.'

'Shit.'

'The rest of the night is a bit of a blur but he got me doing things I'd never done before – and don't want to do again. The next morning, all of the toys had clearly been used – he'd left them on the floor next to the bed for me to clean up. I was really aching and I had a terrible hangover but he told me I'd been amazing, and was so affectionate. I thought I was happy – he was being much nicer to me than usual.'

'You didn't agree to it, Lucy. You know what that makes it?' Jo clearly didn't want to say the word out loud in case it made Lucy start crying again.

'I know. But at the time I didn't. It was only that night that I started to realise it wasn't right – when I got home to find David watching the video – with my face clearly visible. He had a really smug grin as he watched it. He looked really odd.'

'God.' Jo's face was stricken.

'I asked him to delete it but he said that wasn't possible. When I asked him what he meant, he told me he'd uploaded it to a porn site. He said he thought I'd like the idea of other people wanking over me – apparently, I'd told him I'd always fantasised about it the night before – and wanted to show me how sexy I was. I begged him to delete it but he told me that it turned him on – knowing that I was so hot that other men were wanking over me. He was only trying to make me happy. He even tried to get me to have sex with him as he watched it.'

'I hope you told him to fuck off.'

Lucy looked down. 'I ended up giving him a blow job. I thought it might help change his mind about taking it down – but it didn't.'

'What did you do?'

'I couldn't do anything. I emailed the site but they said they weren't responsible for uploaded content and refused to take it down. I pleaded with David but he refused. That's why I split up with him – although he thought I was making a fuss over nothing – still does. I told him the coke was turning him into someone different, if he could do that to me without caring, but he said I was being stupid. It's why he kept calling until I changed my number. I'm sure Mum's still cross with me for the break-up – I couldn't tell her the real reason, of course. She thinks I threw away a "catch".'

'I'd like to catch him,' Jo said ominously. 'I can't believe you went through all that on your own. Why didn't you tell me?'

'It was my own fault – I shouldn't have been so stupid. I got drunk. I took the coke. I said yes to being filmed – he got me on tape saying I wanted to be his hot porn slut. It's horrible.' Lucy's shoulders were starting to shake again.

'I'm so sorry you went through that, babe,' Jo said, reaching over to give Lucy a hug. Lucy felt her eyes well up at the affection. Her body was rigid but, as Jo stroked her back, she collapsed into her arms, tears suddenly flowing.

'I'm sorry,' she spluttered. Her body shook as she sobbed and sobbed.

'Shh, shh,' Jo said, stroking her hair. 'Let it out.'

She carried on running her hand soothingly over Lucy's hair, hugging her tightly with the other arm as if to squeeze the pain away. Lucy felt calmer at her scent of baby powder and vanilla. She breathed in, but crying had made her nose block up and she sniffed loudly.

'Have you got a tissue?' she asked Jo, pulling away.

The hug was nice but she was beginning to feel a bit claustrophobic.

'Here you go,' said Jo, pulling one out of her handbag – decorated with bright yellow ducks on a blue background. Despite herself, Lucy smiled at Jo's attention to detail – even her tissues were fun.

As Lucy blew her nose, Jo looked at her, face full of concern.

'You do know it wasn't your fault, Lucy? If you want to report him, I'll be there right beside you.'

'I don't want the police to know I took drugs,' said Lucy. 'And I checked – they hardly ever intervene in this kind of case. There're loads of revenge porn sites and they can't do a thing. Anyway, I just want to forget all about it. I don't ever want to see him again.'

'I'll happily drink to that,' said Jo. 'But if I bump into him can I beat the crap out of him?'

Jo had trained in martial arts since she was eight so the offer was far from frivolous.

'I don't think he was deliberately trying to upset me. He's just stubborn and doesn't like being told what to do.' But as Lucy thought about Jo clocking David on the nose, she found the corners of her mouth slowly turning upwards: he was such a sexist that being hit by a woman would really get to him. 'But if you really couldn't resist . . .'

Jo smiled. 'You know I've never been good at resisting temptation. On which note . . .' She gestured at Lucy's glass. 'We're out of champagne. How does a cup of tea and a spliff sound? I nicked a bit of Martin's stash too. It's only home-grown so it's not too strong.'

Lucy looked at Jo, eyes stinging but feeling relieved to have finally told the truth.

'It sounds good,' she said. 'I'm going to go to the loo and wash my face. I'm all snotty and disgusting. You know where everything is?'

'Yes,' said Jo, and gave Lucy another squeeze before heading for the kitchen.

As they smoked and drank tea, Jo subtly moved the conversation around to lighter topics, getting Lucy giggling about who would win in a dance-off between an owl and a penguin, after giving demonstrations of both birds' dance styles. Lucy loved Jo's sense of humour. She'd missed it, along with her down-to-earth perspective.

'You've just let yourself get tied down by other people's expectations,' Jo told her. 'I mean, I didn't want to say it at the time but David was never as good as the *idea* of David you painted when you talked about him – he really didn't match up to the paragon of charm you described. And you seemed more into when you were getting married and what your life schedule was than him – I thought you were rushing it when you got engaged but I didn't think it was my place to say anything.'

'I wish you had,' said Lucy.

'I wish I had. But let's not talk about him – unless you want to?'

'Hell no.' Lucy realised that, for the first time in as long as she could remember, she genuinely didn't want to talk about David. Now she'd shared her secret, it was as if she'd squeezed a spot – there was no longer as much pain underneath the surface, and it felt like it was starting to heal. All she really wanted to talk about was Ben – and what was going on at work. Leave the past in the past.

'There is some stuff going on that I could do with your infinite wisdom on, though.'

'I'm listening,' said Jo. 'Am I going to need tissues? Best be prepared.'

'Nothing like that,' said Lucy. 'What do you want first? Drug scandal or man troubles?'

'Shit. Man troubles, definitely,' said Jo. 'All that talk of David has put me in a bit of an "all men are bastards" mood.'

'I don't know if he's a bastard,' said Lucy. 'Well, I guess you can be the judge of that.'

She filled Jo in on recent events, from finding Ben's wallet to seeing him again at London Bridge, via the threesome in the pub toilets. By the time she was finished, Jo was looking at her, rapt.

'Sorry to make light of your woes but I'm going to have to move to London if life's that exciting. Strangers on a train? Flamingoes? Group sex on a work night? It's like you're in some kind of soap opera.'

'It's not as much fun as it sounds,' said Lucy, and told her about the complicated situation at work.

By the time she got to the end of that story, Jo was looking surprised – and quietly impressed. 'I never thought you'd end up in a situation like this, I have to admit,' she said. 'But it's easy. There's one thing you need to do that sorts the whole lot out in one go.'

'Which is?'

'Look after number one. It's not your fault Brendan gave you drugs – he knew the risks and you shouldn't suffer because of it. He was the one bragging about it after all – he brought it on himself.'

She made it sound so simple.

'OK,' said Lucy. 'But I don't want to lose him his job.'

'You won't be. He did it himself. Not. Your. Responsibility. Let go of the guilt.'

'You're right. But what about Ben?'

'Again, look after number one. And that means you stop obsessing. Focus on making yourself happy rather than expecting some man to do it. If he's interested, he'll call. If not, you had what sounds like a brilliant day, a hot snog and a fumble and nothing bad came of it other than a bit of a bruised ego. If he couldn't cope with seeing you a bit worse for wear and grumpy, you'd never have a successful relationship anyway. Martin and I spent half our time like that with each other – and that was when things were good between us.'

Lucy was a bit stung by Jo's no-nonsense summary, but realised she was right.

'I know. I just wish I hadn't messed things up. He was so hot – even the smell of him made me horny.'

'Ooh, I've had one of them. They are hard to forget,' said Jo. 'But it's just chemistry. And there are plenty of other molecules out there for you to bond with.' She looked at her watch. 'Anyway, it's getting late. I need to get to bed – got that meeting at lunchtime and I want to be on form. Wish me luck. I'll probably be gone by the time you get back from work – had a panicked text from Martin and I need to get back for some stuff he insists is urgent. If I find out he's just out of clean pants, I'm going to kill him – but you know how it is, best to keep these things amicable.'

Lucy gave Jo a hug.

'I understand. Good luck tomorrow. You use the bathroom first; I'll be through in a bit.'

'Sweet dreams.' Jo blew Lucy a kiss and then stepped into the bathroom. Lucy smiled. It had been a long night. But she was glad she'd finally been honest with Jo.

It wasn't long before Lucy was ready for bed too. She liked hearing her friend's breath as she drifted off to sleep – gentle and calming, unlike David's rattling snore. She found herself wondering whether Ben snored, which started an internal monologue as she struggled with her desires.

She'd tried his phone again when Jo was in the bathroom, but it had gone through to voicemail again. Lucy was worried she might look like a bunny boiler if Ben turned his phone on to see loads of missed calls from her, so she'd decided to give up. If he wanted to talk to her, he had her number. But still, visions of his lustful eyes as he'd looked down at her sucking his cock filled her dreams in an embarrassingly erotic way.

The next morning it took Lucy a few seconds to work out why she wasn't alone in bed. Her alarm went off and she realised someone was blocking her usual 'flop arm out and flail' approach to turning it off. As her brain woke up and she opened her eyes, she recognised the brilliant shock of ginger hair spread out on the pillow, and memories started filtering back.

She was embarrassed about getting so emotional. Talking about things had made her feel better, but she worried that she'd ruined Jo's first night in London – particularly when Jo was the one who'd just had a big break-up. Still, she had been lovely about things. The spliff and cup of tea had been just what Lucy needed, and she'd felt the tension melt out of her body. Yes, the whole episode with David had been horrible but now she was safe. Even if there were still strangers masturbating about her on some dodgy porn site, at least she'd managed to get out of the situation so David could never do anything like that to her again.

Her alarm clock went off again, jolting her out of her reverie. Lucy hit the off button and sneaked out of bed quietly, trying not to wake Jo. There was no need for her to get up early – Jo could enjoy a lie-in before her meeting. She, on the other hand, had to get to work. Hopefully Anna's mood had improved. The last thing she needed was another day like yesterday. She scribbled a note for Jo and left it next to the kettle with her spare key on top.

Help yourself to anything. Press the left hand boiler button if you need more hot water. Wi-Fi password is on the back of the router on the windowsill. Sorry if last night got a bit heavy and all about me. Good luck with the meeting. Love you xxx

Leaving her spare key on top of the note, Lucy headed to the Tube.

Caitlin was in Anna's office when Lucy arrived at work. When she came out she was scowling. Lucy wondered what Anna had said, but Caitlin clearly didn't want to talk about it. Instead, she typed loudly, her clattering fingernails on the keyboard offering a passive-aggressive 'fuck you' every time she hit the return key. Lucy was getting tired of working with someone who was always in such a vile mood.

After Lucy commented that a particular illustration was good, Caitlin snorted with derision – though she wrote down the illustrator's name when she thought Lucy wasn't looking. When Lucy offered to make her a drink, Caitlin guilt-tripped her about being too lazy to leave the office and get 'proper coffee' – though Lucy stood her ground. And when Lucy said she was going to lunch with Rosie, she sniped, 'You like having someone look up to you, don't you – even just a receptionist. Let's face it – no one else respects you.'

Lucy almost fought back, telling her that Rosie was setting up her own jewellery business and only worked at BAM! to pay the bills, but she didn't want to seem as if she was justifying Caitlin's snobbery. Instead, she stayed silent and gave Caitlin a withering look. As she walked away she realised she'd never felt so angry with Caitlin. The comment about Rosie had stung, probably, Lucy realised, because part of her did see Rosie as 'just a receptionist' – much as she'd seen Ben as 'just a farm-boy'. She'd never considered it before, but she liked being treated as superior and asked for advice by Rosie – it made her feel needed. In reality, Rosie had just as much experience as she did – she'd been running her own Etsy business for over a year and was already making a profit, though not yet enough to live on. However, she struggled to get meetings to take things to the next level.

At first, Lucy had thought it was her lack of experience or confidence – she'd relished the opportunity to share her skills, and had given Rosie a copy of *Lean In* for her birthday. But after watching Rosie in action at a networking event they'd gone to together, Lucy realised she was a natural at small talk, listened carefully and bubbled over with creative ideas – often better than Lucy's own. However, people who were perfectly nice to Lucy ignored Rosie. She'd felt awful. When she'd apologised to Rosie, feeling responsible for taking her to the event, she'd shrugged. 'I'm used to it. Racism's still alive and well even if people don't admit to it.' Lucy hadn't known what to say.

She should have invited Rosie out with Jo – she'd have been a lot nicer to her than Elle – but part of her had wanted to show Jo how far she'd come since her student days, how connected the people she knew were. Instead, she'd shown her what a shallow person she'd turned into. Today, she decided, she'd listen to Rosie rather than foisting ideas on her: help her if she asked, for sure, but also show Rosie how much she respected her. She was far from 'just a receptionist' and it was time Lucy started treating her that way.

Lucy glanced back to see Caitlin looking over, clearly furious at not getting a rise out of her – though she rapidly rearranged her features when she noticed Lucy was watching. Lucy realised she was stronger than she'd thought. Who'd have thought she could upset Caitlin? Still, she couldn't be bothered with her stroppy behaviour so she decided to find Annabel. Between brainstorming Dogsbody ideas, she could find out what she knew about the rumours.

Sadly, Annabel couldn't shed any light on Brendan's gossip: it was the first she'd heard about it and she was furious. 'He said "tour rules" applied. I'll kill him.'

Through the anger, Lucy could see the hurt in her eyes. She wondered whether Annabel's attraction to Brendan went deeper than she'd admitted.

However, once the pair started brainstorming, Lucy found herself wondering what Annabel thought about *her* rather than Brendan: they hadn't discussed what had happened between them, it didn't seem right in the office, but ideas sparked between them easily with their natural camaraderie, and Lucy had to admit to feeling a frisson of excitement. She remembered the feeling of Annabel's curls springing under her hand; the smell of her skin and her excitement. The rest of the morning passed rapidly: where Caitlin's foul temper had made time drag, Annabel's down-to-earth manner and dirty sense of humour made it fly by. Lunchtime arrived sooner than Lucy expected.

Over a glass of wine in a bar round the corner, she filled Rosie in on everything that had happened in the last week. No, five days – she could hardly believe it had only been that long since she'd met Ben. As they talked, she found herself telling her friend that she was seriously thinking of leaving BAM!.

'What's brought this on?' said Rosie. 'Surely the Brendan thing isn't that bad? Or is it a mid-life crisis – skiving, threesomes, drugs . . .'

'I'm too young for that!' said Lucy. Rosie was two years younger and always teased her about being old. 'I think it's mixture of things: the rumours, Caitlin, the situation Anna's putting me in. But I guess Ben got me started on it. There was this rich bitch on the tube when we met. He pointed out money wasn't making her happy – and we had so much fun in Brighton for almost nothing. It made me think about how much of the cash I spend goes on trying to fit in here. If I didn't have to 'look the part', I wouldn't have to earn anything like as much. Ben earns way less than me but he's got a gorgeous flat with a roof garden and sea views and spends his days working in the sunshine, foraging, seeing friends and eating nice food. He didn't sound like he was talking about work when he was telling me about his business – it sounded like fun.'

'So you want to give up your job, move to Brighton with this Ben and become a hippy?' asked Rosie.

Lucy laughed. 'Not exactly – although I don't think I want to be in marketing either. I always thought I'd have kids by thirty-five, and that's only seven years away so I need to meet someone in the next three years. I know that sounds a bit nineteen-fifties, but I've got my biological clock to think about!' She sighed. 'Maybe I'd be better off moving back to Gloucestershire and finding myself a nice farmer to settle down with. But we'll see. Anyway, enough about my problems – how's the business going?'

Rosie's face lit up as she started talking about her ideas. Lucy sat back and enjoyed listening to her friend, feeling envious of her for having a business of her own – a way out. She wondered if Jo could help Rosie out with her website, and made a mental note to find out what the best 'mate's rates' she could do would be – assuming Rosie wanted any help, of course.

Rosie's merry conversation and passion for her business put Lucy in a good mood that lasted the rest of the afternoon. Luckily, Anna was out of the office in meetings and Caitlin was in Dan's office again. Lucy worked through all the admin she'd been meaning to do but somehow never found time to – usually because Caitlin turned up with some urgent report she needed writing or research she needed doing. Now, without anyone watching over Lucy and demanding her time, she was on top of everything – though this was made easier because she only had one project to manage – and better yet, she was nearly on holiday.

Even though it had been forced on her, Lucy found herself looking forward to taking a break. She'd decided to go to see her parents for the weekend, and then visit her sister in Cornwall after that. She'd been meaning to go and meet her new nephew for ages. Apparently her niece was talking now too – the last time Lucy had seen her she'd been a baby so she was looking forward to finding out what her personality was like. Babies might be cute but there's only so much you can work out about a person from the way they bottle feed. Toddlers were much more fun.

By 5 p.m. Lucy was searching Facebook to fill the time. Kitten pictures aside, the day's only excitement had been a text from Jo saying, I got investment!!! Lucy was pleased for her friend – her business really seemed to be taking off.

Feeling cheerfully rebellious, she left half an hour early to pack as she wanted to get an early start in the morning – it took nearly four hours to get to her mum's place and there was no way she wanted to miss lunch.

Her stepdad was an amazing cook and it had been ages since she'd enjoyed a home-cooked meal.

Arriving home to her empty flat, Lucy felt a little muted. Now Jo was gone, the flat seemed far emptier than before she had arrived. Wandering into the kitchen, she saw a pack of double chocolate chip cookies sitting next to a vintage teapot, tea cup and saucer. The tea set was decorated with flowers and ivy vines and the lid was lifted by a butterfly, which looked as if it had just settled on the teapot for a tea break.

A Post-it note on the cookies read:

Saw this and thought of you – you may look like a city girl now but I know you're a country girl at heart. Let me know if you fancy swapping your place for mine! Have a cup of tea on me – thanks for being a gracious host. Will call when I'm home safe.

Jo xxx

PS: Other present on the bed

When Lucy walked into the bedroom, she smiled. Not only had her bed been covered with a fake fur throw, and star-shaped fairy lights wrapped around her bedhead, but in the centre of her bed there was a white gift box tied with a red bow. A tiny card was attached, reading:

To get you over your toy (and boy) trauma – trust me, you will fall in love. You don't need a man to be happy . . .

Inside was a box marked 'Doxy' with a picture of a large white wand-style vibrator. It looked intimidating but she was too curious not to open it. It was lighter than she thought it would be, but felt solid. Intrigued, she plugged it in, and was relieved to find the cable was long enough to easily reach her bed (unlike her laptop cable). When she turned it on she had to hurriedly shove it under the duvet to muffle the buzz; then she turned it down and put a curious hand on its tip. The head of the toy was warmer than she thought it would be, and the buzzing did feel rather nice under her hand. She guessed it would be rude not to try out a toy that Jo had spent time – and a lot of money, from the looks of it – on getting for her.

Taking her shoes off, she lay back on the bed and pressed the minus button until she was sure the toy was on its lowest setting. Then she tentatively moved it down her belly and towards her pubic mound. The vibrations felt good running through her, and her pussy swelled in anticipation. When she'd used a vibrator before, she'd found it rather ticklish, but these vibrations were more rumbling, deeper. She ran the head of the toy slowly between her legs and gasped as it ran over the head of her clit. 'Oh yes,' she thought. 'That's more like it.' Jo certainly knew her toys. But it was too intense to hold there for long.

Lucy slowly pulled the toy down between her legs, pressing it against her trousers. As she ran the toy over herself, the vibrations seemed to travel through the seam. She remembered the way Ben had felt pressed against her through her skinny jeans, and just the memory of him made her pussy slippery.

Lucy rocked her body against the toy, recalling the feeling of Ben's hands on her buttocks, his lips on her own, feeling herself ripen and swell as her pussy got wetter and plumper. As she got used to the sensations, she wanted more, and tentatively pressed the button to increase the power. Another gasp. Another memory of Ben – this time, the way she'd lost all control when he first kissed her, grinding against him without inhibition. She remembered the waves of orgasm crashing over her and wondered again whether he had realised what was going on.

The idea of him knowing – and keeping it a secret – made her feel dirty, horny, hot. Now, her body convulsed of its own accord and she was hungry for more. She pressed herself harder against the toy, tilting her pelvis, and as her arousal built she found herself driven to press the button again and again.

Her imagination was flowing freely, random memories popping into her mind – the curl of Ben's chest hair, the scent of his neck, the taste of his cock – and the toy was in control of her orgasm. She knew if she turned it up any more she'd be unable to hold back, but she was scared of coming when the buzz was so intense. There was no way her clit could cope with that kind of sensation once she was coming – but there was no way she could hold back any longer. She needed to come.

She clicked the button one more time and *whoosh*; she felt her orgasm overtake her in spasms, waves of joy rocking her body and rippling out from clit to pelvis to nipples to fingertips as she came harder even than she had with Ben. She hurriedly pulled the toy away, replacing it with her hand cupping her pussy, and then lay there, stunned, orgasm pulsing through her body, a rushing sound in her ears as she floated back down to earth.

'Wow,' she thought. 'Maybe I don't need a man after all.'

It was one of the best orgasms she'd had in years. In fact it was so good – Lucy looked at the toy lying next to her on the bed – that she really should test whether it was a fluke. Lucy picked up the toy and turned it on again: this time she certainly wasn't starting on the lowest setting.

CHAPTER 5

The next morning started with a smile – thanks to Doxy – followed by chocolate chip cookies with Lucy's breakfast coffee. Jo really was a true friend, thought Lucy, as she sat on the Tube feeling relaxed. She got out her phone to text her gratitude. *Doxy + cookies = perfect start to day. Who needs a man, indeed. Love you.*

She thought back to the way she used to feel after trying something new: with Ben it had been amazing – until he let her down – but with David she had always felt as if she was competing for some kind of prize. She'd tried all the moves out of the women's magazines and was always acquiescent to his suggestions, but no matter what she did he always wanted something more. He'd pestered her for ages to have anal sex and then, when she did, he wanted it to become a regular part of their repertoire.

She'd liked it when he massaged her first, slowly oiling her up and sliding his fingers around and inside her until she was relaxed enough for his well-lubed cock to slip inside. She liked sliding back onto it at her own pace, feeling herself open up for him, letting him enter her in the most intimate way. But as time had gone on, he had become less romantic, telling her he wanted to pound her into submission. It went from being something they both enjoyed to something Lucy dreaded him asking her to do – she didn't like it when he went fast, unless she was really drunk and feeling particularly submissive. She found herself drinking more in the evening so she could cope with his demands in bed – and the more she did, the more he wanted. Trying new things lost its appeal because she never knew where it might lead.

Now, on the other hand, she felt great. She'd had seven orgasms before she finally went to sleep, though she'd had to use the pillow to muffle the vibrations because the toy was so intense. She hadn't slept so well in years. And today the Doxy was still sitting there, and it seemed rude to ignore it. Every day should start with three orgasms, she thought – it made the morning so much more bearable.

Lucy looked at her phone to see if her thank-you message had sent but it was struggling to connect to the Wi-Fi. Casually looking through her phone contacts as she waited for the train to get to the next station, Lucy noticed Elle's name. Was she really ever going to call her? She'd rather save her time for real friends instead.

Feeling defiant, Lucy deleted the number and then scrolled through her phone on a friend cull, weeding out all the people she either didn't know or didn't like: the people who always accepted drinks from her but never seemed to return the favour, the ones she saw out of social obligation and the ones who only seemed to call her when they were going through some drama they needed her to fix. One swipe of her finger despatched David and she felt her chest lighten as the screen flashed up: 'contact deleted'.

When she got to Ben's name, Lucy paused. Her finger hovered over the screen but – no. Although she knew Jo was right, that she really should forget all about him, Lucy couldn't bring herself to get rid of his number quite yet.

After all, why had he been so keen to swap numbers if he didn't want to see her again?

The journey from Paddington to Cheltenham passed quickly, and Lucy called her mum when she arrived.

'Sorry, love. We weren't expecting you until later. I'm out with Jay at a steam fair. He needs some new part for his bike – he's found a 1942 one and a 1934 one but he needs a 1937 one – you know what he's like.'

Lucy felt a bit hurt, though she smiled at the thought of her stepdad dragging her mum to a steam fair – he always had some project on: painstakingly rebuilding old cars, bikes, even a boat once.

'Didn't you get my message? I told you what time I'd be arriving.'

'Yes, but I know how you like your lie-ins. I was sure you'd be a bit late – you usually are – so Jay had planned to do dinner instead of lunch.'

Lucy almost snapped back at her, suddenly feeling like a teenager, but breathed in deeply. It wasn't that unfair really – she *had* been late the last few times she'd been home, though because of work rather than over-sleeping.

'What time are you back?' she said.

'I'll tell him to get a move on but I can't see him taking less than a couple of hours and it's a bit of a drive. Should be in town by about four. Have you got your key? You could always get the bus; I think there's one at a quarter to one.'

Lucy realised with a lurch of her stomach that she'd hadn't brought the key. She glanced at the time on her phone.

'Shit – I forgot it. And it'll be a bit tight time-wise unless I get a cab. Don't worry – I can go for a wander in town – it's years since I've been; be nice to see it. Give me a call when you're done.'

'Will do. Love you.'

'Love you too.' Lucy hung up. It was so long since she'd been in Cheltenham she needed to remind herself of how to get into town. She picked up her hold-all and wandered back into the station in search of help.

Luckily it was pretty much a straight line, and Lucy started to recognise more of the route as familiar land-marks popped into view; Regency architecture was everywhere she looked, the elegant style reminding her of Brighton. Maybe it was because they were both spa towns. She smiled as a distant memory popped into her head – of tasting the spa waters at the Town Hall on a school trip. It was salty and disgusting but people had believed it had healing properties for years. She decided to visit it for old times' sake on her way past – it was a beautiful building and who knew, maybe the healing waters would do her good.

As she walked through Montpellier, Lucy paused to look more closely at the caryatids, female statues that stood, armless, hips at a jaunty angle and faces grave as they supported the buildings above them. She'd always thought it was a picturesque town and the statues were one of her favourite sights.

She cut through Montpellier Gardens, which almost looked fake: they were so precisely maintained. As she passed a familiar part of the park, she had a flashback to Stephen – her first love. He'd taken her to the formal garden on their second date, picking up a bottle of cava on the way. He'd found the perfect spot, hidden by a box hedge, and produced a travel chess set out of his inside pocket. They'd played a game, sipping cava from plastic cups. As the sun set, after lighting a candle to help them better see the board, he'd kissed her for the first time. Until Ben, Lucy hadn't had a kiss to match it. She smiled at the memory.

As she walked up the imposing Town Hall stairs, waves of nostalgia continued to roll over her. She'd spent most Saturdays in Cheltenham as a teenager – Andoversford only had one pub and who wants to drink where their parents do? She remembered nights in the beer gardens, and the balls she'd been to here – feeling a stab of embarrassment as she recalled going on the bouncy castle in a full-skirted dress, revealing her knickers and stocking tops when her date – Tim, was it, or Mark? Mark, that was it – had started bouncing her more vigorously than she'd expected and attracting laughter and scorn from the people watching. 'Have I ever fitted in?' she wondered. So many of her memories seemed to entail her feeling out of place or alone.

But as she thought back to the dates she'd been on in her teen years, she also remembered having fun: going for walks with Billy and his dog, avoiding the long grass for fear of adders, but sitting on the top of Leckhampton Hill, admiring the view and kissing for hours. Being driven out to the Green Dragon in Cowley by Martin; eating amazing food then snogging in the car park afterwards, usually making her late home. It all seemed so innocent compared to now.

Once inside the Town Hall, Lucy turned towards the elaborately decorated octagonal spa, topped by blue Doulton urns with gold taps that dispensed the waters. Or at least they used to. Lucy was disappointed to see that there were no cups. She walked to the box office.

'Excuse me, I was wondering if I could get a cup to try the waters?'

The smartly dressed teenager behind the counter smiled apologetically. 'You can't do that here anymore, I'm afraid. They stopped pumping it from Pittville ten years ago – that's the only place you can get it now.'

'Eight years ago,' came a voice from the office area behind her. 'Know your history, Andy.' The correction was serious but the tone was light and teasing – and familiar, thought Lucy. She tried to peer through but couldn't see where the voice came from.

'Eight years ago,' the receptionist corrected himself. 'Do you want a leaflet for Pittville?'

Lucy thought about it but she really couldn't face a walk to the other side of town.

'It's OK, thanks. But I'd love to have a look round while I'm here. Is that allowed?'

'I think so, as long as there's no one sound-checking. Stephen,' the teen called, 'have we got anyone in at the moment?'

Stephen? It couldn't be. But as the voice floated out from the back room again – 'Nothing booked in for the next hour so if you're quick it'll be fine.' – Lucy was sure it was him.

'That's not Stephen Hall is it?' she called.

The receptionist gave her a quizzical look.

'It is. Do you know him?'

'From way back. Stephen, it's Lucy Green.'

Stephen walked into the foyer and stood back from Lucy, taking her in. 'Don't you look like the city slicker? It's been a long time. What brings you back here? I'm guessing you haven't come all this way for a guided tour?'

Lucy felt her heart leap. Stephen had aged well. His body had thickened slightly, but it suited him – as did the neatly trimmed stubble. He looked grown-up in all the right ways.

'No, seeing family. I was just remembering old times – can't believe you work here now. But actually, I'd love a tour.' Lucy said. Maybe it was just nostalgia but as Stephen smiled at her, she felt a tug of desire.

'After all the years of work experience I did here I'd have been pissed off if they hadn't offered me a job. Do you remember playing chess when I was working at the Festival of Literature?'

'I was just thinking about it walking through the gardens,' said Lucy.

Now he mentioned it, she did remember the hours he'd spent working at events – it was one of the reasons she'd been inspired to join ents at university. Maybe she'd recalled it subconsciously and that was why she'd been drawn to the Town Hall. Who knew – it was a long time ago, a lot had happened since they'd dated: university, London – and Stephen getting sexier. She wondered if he was seeing anybody and felt a stab of guilt, as if she was being disloyal to Ben – but reminded herself he still hadn't called. She was a free agent who didn't owe him anything.

By the time they'd got to the end of the first corridor, Lucy was pretty sure Stephen was single. He was clearly delighted to see her and hadn't stopped complimenting her on how great she looked. It made Lucy warm inside, remembering how special he'd made her feel. She wondered what would have happened if she hadn't gone to university – maybe they'd never have split up?

Stephen opened the door to the main hall. 'Of course, you'll remember this room – but it's had a bit of a touch-up since you were last here.'

Gold columns soared from floor to ceiling and the boxes were housed under ornate arches. The ceiling was painted in duck-egg blue and white, restored to its original glory.

'I'd forgotten how beautiful it was,' she said.

'It's easy to do that,' said Stephen. 'Particularly if you don't see something for a while.' He gave Lucy a lingering look. 'So, what you up to nowadays?'

'I've got a job in London – marketing,' she said. 'But I'm not sure how much longer for. Working a few things out right now.'

'Married? Kids?'

'Not yet. You?'

'Not met the right woman yet,' Stephen said. 'Or, at least, not at the right time.' His brown eyes looked so warm but mournful that Lucy couldn't resist the urge to say, 'Come here,' and give him a hug.

As she put her arms around him, Lucy felt an odd blend of familiarity and novelty. Stephen still smelled the same as he ever had – clean, with a faint whiff of washing powder and spicy aftershave – and she fitted comfortably into his arms. But her arms didn't reach around him quite as far as they once had, his muscles were stronger and firmer than she remembered, and his stubble against her face was rough. He was the Stephen she had been in love with – but a man, not a boy. She felt a warm glow in her stomach, and it was starting to spread, the longer they held each other.

She could tell he wanted her too. Stephen seemed in no hurry to end the hug and, as Lucy snuggled in closer, enjoying the comfort of being in welcoming arms, she could feel his erection start to rise against her.

'God, it's good to see you,' he muttered in her ear, breath playing across it in a way that made her body tremble.

'You too,' said Lucy, realising she wanted nothing more than for him to kiss her. In fact, she could just make it happen herself, she thought, and pulled back, looking him in the eye before sliding her hand behind his head and pulling him to her.

She met no resistance. As soon as her lips pressed to Stephen's, he was kissing her back eagerly. His lips were firm on hers, tongue sliding between her lips instantly, as if it had been moments rather than years since they last kissed. Lucy responded to his passion, loving the way his lips moved from her mouth to her neck, going straight for the spot that he knew always made her melt, where her neck and shoulder met. As he gently nibbled the sensitive skin there, Lucy could feel her legs weakening, lust shooting through her pelvis and down to her clit. She could feel her heartbeat in her pussy.

As the intimacy built, Lucy felt herself sinking into the past: it was feeling more familiar as she remembered his taste, his smell, the way he gasped for breath in between kisses as if she'd been sucking his soul from him. He seemed to have a perfect memory of all the places she liked to be touched – or at least the ones she'd admitted to him back then.

'I don't suppose you'd be up for going somewhere a bit more private,' Stephen said, his desire now uncomfortably obvious.

'Why not,' said Lucy. She remembered saying the same to Ben, but banished him from her mind. Stephen was here; he was hot; and he was clearly more than willing. It had been ages since she'd felt a man inside her – and her body had decided it was quite long enough. She couldn't quite believe what she was doing, but it wasn't like Stephen was a stranger. It was almost as if they were just continuing where they'd left off.

Stephen led her back into the corridor and through a door into a smaller – but no less grand – room. Lucy didn't waste time looking around. Feeling Stephen hard against her had made her pussy warm and open. She pulled her knickers off and put them in her handbag, then leaned against the duck-egg blue wall, hands braced against it, legs spread, cheekily looking over her shoulder with an expression that made it very clear what she wanted. As Stephen hurriedly undid his trousers and reached into his wallet for a condom, Lucy pushed her skirt up to reveal her bum – which had always driven Stephen wild.

'I've missed you,' he said, dropping to his knees and kissing Lucy's round cheeks, hand sliding between her legs to feel her arousal. Lucy could feel his fingers rubbing her juices all over her, his thumb simultaneously circling on her clit. She'd forgotten how good he was at that. He licked, kissed and bit her, setting her skin tingling with every stroke of his tongue and nip of his teeth. She wanted him inside her before she got much wetter. She needed to feel him stretching her and the way he was going he'd slide in with no resistance at all.

'Please,' she said, pushing forward into the wall, all the better to arch her back and emphasise her curves. 'I want you inside me.'

Stephen gave her one last run of kisses that travelled from cheek to cheek before standing up, sliding the condom on and pressing himself to her entrance, slowly teasing her with his cock – but Lucy was in no mood to be patient. Reaching behind her, she grabbed his shaft at the base, positioned him so he could slide in easily and pushed back against him, sinking to his root in a single motion.

'Oh God,' said Stephen. 'Oh God.'

Lucy moved back and forth, fucking him hard, taking him deep inside her as he gripped her hips and tried to take control – but every time he tried to slow her down and take things more sensually, Lucy bucked back even harder. She liked the slight ache as she pounded him into her; all her frustrations were being worked out on Stephen's solid, familiar cock and she knew he liked it, despite his desire to give her all the pleasure he could. His groans gave him away. She could feel her pussy starting to grasp at him, muscles clenching in a way that warned her orgasm wasn't far away – but she knew it would be so much stronger with a little help.

She moved her hand to her pussy, cupping her mons and rubbing her clit as her hips tilted to ensure she took the full length of his cock with each thrust. Stephen was getting even harder, and she could feel the pulsing that indicated his own climax was near. She thought about him coming inside her, and this, combined with the friction of her fingers against her pussy, was enough to push her over the edge.

'Oh yes, oh fuck,' she said as orgasm hit, rapidly spasming in a short, sweet burst of bliss. She felt Stephen let loose and come hard and deep inside her – he always had been a gentleman, waiting for her to get there first. His pulsing cock sent more orgasmic waves through her and it was a while before either of them had the slightest inclination to move, milking their mutual orgasms for all they could get. They held each other for a while, enjoying the comforting familiarity of each other's bodies, before Stephen pulled away to dispose of the condom.

'So, I know we've probably done this all backwards, but do you fancy going out for dinner tonight?' he asked.

Lucy laughed. He'd always been funny, and the sex had been great – Stephen had always put a lot of effort into making her come, and his cock was a nice fit – but she didn't want to give him the wrong idea. In a way it had been more about old time's sake and horniness than anything more. Lucy felt a little guilty at the realisation, but from the way Stephen was smiling she didn't think he regretted it.

'I can't tonight – I've got plans with Mum and Jay,' she said. 'But I could see if you could come over for Sunday lunch – you know how much Jay usually cooks.'

'Sounds great, he does make the best Yorkshires I've ever had,' said Stephen. 'Do you want to text me when you know the score?' He scribbled down his number on the back of a flyer and handed it to Lucy.

'Will do. I'm really glad I . . . ran into you.' Lucy smiled at Stephen, genuinely pleased to have connected with him again. 'But I should get going now. I need to meet Mum soon – she hates being kept waiting.'

Stephen gave her a passionate kiss goodbye, and Lucy had no doubt round two was on offer if she wanted it, but now that she felt sated her desire for him had faded, leaving friendly affection in its wake.

She didn't like lying to Stephen – in reality, she had over two hours before she had to meet her mum – but she knew that if she stayed, he was going to get emotional. She could see it in his eyes – which was why she'd invited him to Sunday lunch with her folks rather than suggesting a drink alone. Even though she'd wanted him and it had been fun, it had also been a reminder that Ben was better. If even her first love couldn't match him, she really was in trouble.

Lucy enjoyed wandering round Cheltenham and revisiting her favourite spot, the Kit Williams fish clock in the Regent's Arcade. She even made a wish when she caught one of the bubbles it blew, on the hour, just as she had when she was a kid. By the time her mum rang at 4.15 she was feeling calm and happy: first sex, then solitude. She couldn't remember the last time she'd spent two hours wandering on her own. She decided to do it more often.

She was looking forward to seeing her family though. When the car pulled up outside the back of Regent's Arcade, and Lucy's mum leapt out of the car to give her a hug and help her with her bags, she felt a rush of warmth. Jay said, 'Hello, love,' from the driver's seat. He was a man of few words but his cheery tone made it clear he was pleased to see her.

When the car pulled into the drive Lucy's happiness only intensified at the familiar sight – she hadn't realised how much she missed it. The cottage was one of two tucked down a potholed lane off the main road. It had once looked out onto open fields, but was now surrounded by a '80s housing development, which tried to look rural, but didn't.

Stepping into the house, Lucy breathed in the familiar aroma: wood-smoke, home-cooking and a faint undertone of Imperial Leather.

'Cup of tea?' asked Jay.

'Yes please,' said Lucy, and followed him into the kitchen.

She was home.

* * *

It had been a lovely afternoon. After they'd got back, Jay had gone to the shed to work on his bike and she'd had a cup of tea and a catch-up with her mum, who'd filled Lucy in on Rachel's latest adventures – 'She Skyped me from Barcelona the other day. Apparently she met some people when she was skiing and they invited her to crew at a festival. She's preparing for some big "radical self-sufficiency" thing out in the desert. She terrifies me – going out into the middle of nowhere and having to fend for herself – taking her own water and everything. But apparently she's got a new van, is running a make-do-and-mend service to pay for petrol and is working on a Barrio – whatever that is – with a load of other people once she gets there. They've got their own kitchen, sound system – apparently she's going to be giving out free hugs, doing magic tricks and running the sound desk. I don't know where she gets the energy – but she's happy, so I'm happy . . .'

Lucy smiled at her mum's proud monologue. Sorting out her own water supply? Running a sound desk at a festival? The last time she'd spoken to her, Rach had been working on a boat in the Lake District, cooking and cleaning in exchange for board; before that she was living on a commune bus in Wales, studying taxidermy and making jewellery out of found items and then selling it at festivals to pay her way. Lucy could barely keep up with Rach's stories when she actually managed to get hold of her. She never knew what country she'd be in. Her little sister was all grown up. She felt impressed – and a little envious. 'So how about you, Mum? How's life?'

Lucy settled back as her mum started chattering again, about the news in the village, the crafting she'd been doing, the aches and pains she'd been having and what she was planting in the garden. She'd forgotten how much she loved her mum's company and enjoyed listening to the lateral stream of thoughts. Before long, her mum was urging her to 'have a bath before dinner – wash the journey away'. It was a long time since Lucy had felt so cared-for.

'So what do you reckon to the hogget?' asked Jay. 'Have you had it before?'

'No,' Lucy said. 'But it's lovely. It's so much meatier than lamb usually is.' Jay had pan fried the steaks perfectly, and the meat was rare and delicious.

'That's because it's kept alive for longer – before it turns to mutton but after lamb. Like the difference between veal and beef.'

Jay was full of fascinating facts about food.

'Want more wedges?' asked her mum. 'You're looking thin.'

'I'm fine, mum. But pass the mayo.'

Lucy dunked her wedge in the sauce and happily bit into it.

'Salad?' asked Jay, proffering the bowl filled with home-grown lettuce and sun-dried tomatoes made from last year's crop, cucumber, olives, feta and mint from the garden. This time, Lucy said yes. One thing was for sure: she wasn't going to go hungry this weekend.

After dinner, they shared a coffee in the lounge, with Jay putting fresh logs on the fire to ensure they stayed warm while he went to the pub. And, over a cup of tea and a game of Scrabble, Lucy and her mum had a proper chat. Lucy had skipped the work drama – she didn't want to worry her mum – but after two glasses of wine at dinner she hadn't been able to stop herself from mentioning Ben. She'd tried to forget about the day they'd had together, feeling increasingly distanced from the dream with every day he didn't return her call. But she needed to get it out – to share the romance with someone. Who better than her mum? If anyone would understand, it was her.

Predictably, her mum asked her why she hadn't just handed his wallet in at the Tube station, but when Lucy described Ben, her motivation was obvious: particularly as the details unfolded of picnics, roof gardens and flamingoes.

'Well, it does all sound very fairy-tale – and I guess it is harder to meet people these days. That's why I was worried about you splitting with David. I know how much you wanted to get married – I hate the idea of you being disappointed.'

'I'd have been more disappointed if I'd married him,' Lucy said, realising she didn't want to cling on to the lies anymore. 'I don't think you'd have wanted me to end up with him, if you knew why we broke up.'

She skipped the more graphic details and the cocaine, and didn't mention that the video had been posted online, but by the time Lucy had finished telling the story, her mum was still looking pale and shocked.

'The bastard. You poor love. Do you want a cup of tea?'

Tea was her mother's rescue remedy, and every cup made Lucy feel more at home. She nodded.

'I just don't understand why you didn't tell me about it before. I would have never told you to go back to him if I'd have known what he was like.'

'It's hard, Mum,' Lucy said. 'I was embarrassed.'

'You've got nothing to feel embarrassed about with me, love. I'm your mum. Nothing you could say would shock me.'

Lucy doubted that but thought it best not to correct her. Still, she was happy that her mum finally knew what David was really like. And, she realised, she felt a bit better about herself too. When she'd told Jo the story, she'd still been full of guilt and shame. Telling her mother the pared-down version, she'd realised the only person who needed be ashamed was David. He was a weak, immature control freak who put his own needs first, manipulating her into being something she wasn't to satisfy his own ego. In fact, she even felt a little sorry for him.

Thinking back, she could remember a few times when he'd opened up to her, been vulnerable, and they were some of the moments she'd loved him most. But when she'd seen what he was capable of, how little regard he had for her feelings when he'd uploaded the video, she'd realised he was mostly a shell. There was barely any genuine emotion in him and he was utterly incapable of empathising with her – hardly the basis for a great relationship. He spent so long trying to be somebody else that he'd forgotten how to be himself, replacing his personality with a checklist of ambitions and status symbols to acquire; and he'd been pushing her to do the same.

She shuddered at how close she'd come, trying to impress Elle and Caitlin. In fact Caitlin and David really were quite similar.

Again, Lucy found her mind turning to Ben, who had told her she needed others' approval too much. Maybe she was more like David than she'd realised, too: perhaps that's why things had lasted as long as they did. She felt an ache of sadness in her chest and realised she was mourning not the loss of David, but the loss of what could have been if he'd been himself. Still, the past was the past. And she was finally ready to move on.

Few things were more comforting than a hot water bottle made by your mum, thought Lucy as she snuggled into bed that night. It had been an odd day, but she felt relaxed: good sex, good food and good conversation in beautiful surroundings. What more could she want?

Her mind drifted to Stephen. It really had been good to see him – and how could she have forgotten that trick he did with his thumb? Her pussy warmed at the memory – maybe she'd been rash to mentally write him off. She moved her hand between her legs, trying to make as little noise as possible as she masturbated over the afternoon's assignation – but by the time she was coming, Ben's face had replaced Stephen's in her mind.

Sunday lunch was a civilised affair. Jay had been fine about Stephen joining them – 'Good appetite on that lad.' – and her mum was clearly pleased too. Although Lucy felt a bit better about what had happened with David now, she still had a suspicion that her mother would rather she was safely settled down.

Stephen was the perfect guest, bringing a nice bottle of red and helping with the washing up. But as she watched him, Lucy realised he really wasn't the one for her. He was kind, clever, funny – but even though he was attractive, there just wasn't the same kind of animal yearning she felt for Ben. And even if she couldn't have Ben, now she knew that feeling existed, she had to find it again.

Stephen left mid-afternoon – 'Don't want to take up all your family time.' – but when Lucy saw him out, he kissed her passionately. Lucy kissed him back, even though her heart wasn't in it – he was a nice man and she probably wouldn't see him again for a while.

'You know I still love you, Lucy,' he said, quietly.

'I know. I love you too. I think part of me always will. But I'm a very different person to the girl you went out with.'

'I know,' said Stephen. 'I like it. You seem calmer now, happier with yourself. It's sexy.'

He kissed her again, but Lucy pulled away and turned it into a hug as soon as she could.

'I know it might seem a bit random but promise me one thing, Lucy,' Stephen said, as they stood, arms around each other.

'Go on.'

'I know you're too busy with your London life to want to settle down in the sticks – but if you don't find someone by the time you're forty, remember I'm here – if you could cope with coming back to Andoversford?'

'I'm not sure I could,' said Lucy, regretfully. It was beautiful but too small – everyone knew everyone's business, though that had made for some good gossip from her mum last night. 'But who knows what the future holds? You are a very special man.'

She gave Stephen a soft kiss and waved him off as he got into his battered 2CV and drove away.

When Lucy left for her train at 8 p.m., she felt a pang at the thought of leaving her mum. It had been so nice seeing her – she was so gentle and kind and had a quirky, childlike sense of humour, particularly after a couple of glasses of wine. Lucy felt refreshed, if a little tipsy herself. Still, it wasn't like it mattered, as long as she got on the right train. She'd decided to take the sleeper from London – it was a long journey and she figured it'd be less boring if she slept for most of it – plus it made the most of her holiday. Better yet, her sleeper ticket meant she could use the first class lounge at Paddington while she was waiting – complete with free wine and magazines.

Lucy woke the next morning to a knock at the door. She stumbled out of her cosy – if snug – bed, and opened it, to be greeted by a man holding a tray of cornflakes, juice and coffee. She'd forgotten breakfast was included in her sleeper ticket.

She thanked the man, closed the door and settled down in bed with her tray, clicking the TV on and picking Wallace and Gromit – there was something comforting about watching kids' TV first thing. However, the view from the train window was so enticing that before long she flicked off the TV and admired the countryside whizzing past the window. She arrived at the station just before seven, feeling virtuous for being wide awake and breakfasted already – even if she had had to make do with a baby-wipe shower.

Her sister was parked outside, kids in tow, and soon Lucy was fending off a sticky-fingered attack as Kirsty, who was almost three, tried to braid her hair from the back seat. Jack was strapped into his chair so tightly that he couldn't move, and he grizzled in disgust – 'He's a wriggler,' Hope had said. 'And a wannabe Houdini. If I don't strap him down properly, he tries to escape – he managed to get the car door open the other day, though luckily we were only pulling out of the drive.'

'Shit,' said Lucy. 'Was he OK?'

'Fine,' said Hope. 'And, not being funny, but can you try not to swear around the kids. They pick things up so quickly and I got a right telling off for Kirsty saying W.A.N.K.E.R at nursery. She must have heard me talking to Ant.'

'How are things with you guys?'

'Good, good,' Hope said. But she changed the subject so quickly that Lucy decided to ask her again later, when the kids weren't around – and maybe after Hope had had a glass of wine. She'd always been a private person but Lucy knew how to get her to open up,

Lucy may have felt rested when she arrived, but it was only the third day of her stay and she was shattered. She'd never realised how much hard work children were – a night's babysitting was about the longest she'd spent with one before. She'd often wondered what Hope spent her time doing – she'd given up her job in HR when Jack was born. Now she realised that Hope wasn't being vague on the phone when she said, 'This and that.'

The day started with breakfast, which took well over an hour by the time Hope had persuaded Kirsty to eat what she was given – her preferences seemed to change daily – and cleaned up the food Jack threw on the floor. It continued with washing, changing nappies, cooking meals, breaking up fights, clearing up toys and answering hundreds of questions an hour.

At first Lucy had enjoyed Kirsty's demands for attention: 'Read me a story.' 'Play cars with me.' 'Can we make biscuits?' But as the novelty wore off, she realised it was relentless. Kirsty was very sweet but Lucy found herself yearning for an off switch. She felt the same about Jack. He was very smiley, but he was too heavy and wriggly to cuddle for long. He also seemed to be constantly leaking fluids, and she soon realised there was no way she could keep him pristine no matter how hard she tried.

No wonder Hope was always in bed by ten – if she wasn't woken up by the kids. Lucy was beginning to appreciate her child-free life more with every day that passed.

On Thursday Hope apologetically said she was going to be out with the kids for the day. 'I'm taking them to see their godmother, Patricia – it's been in the diary for ages. She's just got back from doing a postgrad in Amsterdam – Kirsty's been nagging me to see her for months. The last time she went, Patricia braided her hair and Kirsty was *very* impressed. The best I can manage is a messy French plait.'

'No worries. I can wander into town – it'd be nice to see more of the sights.' Lucy tried to keep the relief out of her voice. A bit of quiet time was just what she needed.

'There's a lovely spot you might like on the outskirts of town – St Keyne's Well. It's a request stop on the train.' Lucy looked puzzled. 'As in, you have to tell the driver you want the train to stop there,' Jo explained.

'Ah, OK,' said Lucy. 'What's there?'

'Well, you could go to the Magnificent Music Machine Museum,' Hope's eyes twinkled. 'It's famous for its collection of fairground organs.'

'A magnificent organ museum?' Lucy could see why Hope had been trying not to giggle. They shared the same naughty sense of humour.

'Yes,' Hope smirked. 'But I think the well will be more up your street. It's not far from the station and it's ever so pretty – and magical, if you believe the myth. According to the inscription, if a couple drinks from the well, whoever goes first will wear the trousers in the relationship. St Keyne was a bit of a feminist – blessed the well to give women a chance of getting the upper hand over their husbands. And it's really peaceful there – a nice vibe.'

Lucy smiled. 'Sounds lovely.'

As Jack started crying and Hope scurried off to tend to him, she thought a bit of peace was just what she needed.

'Just flag us down on your way back,' the guard helpfully explained when Lucy got off the train. The idea intimidated her a bit – hailing a cab was one thing, but a train? Still, it was rather charming, she thought as she wandered down the tree-lined road.

True to Hope's word, the well was only a short walk from the station. Before long, Lucy was standing at a junction in front of the pair of mossy stones her sister had told her to look out for. She walked between them, down a set of shallow steps that led her to a stone hut with prehistoric-looking plants surrounding it. A nearby plaque confirmed it was St Keyne's Well. Lucy felt nervous as she bent down to peer inside the dark chamber. There was something otherworldy about it, and it smelled damp, albeit in a pleasant, green way.

Lucy needed to crouch to get through the low doorway. At first she thought the well must have dried up but as she looked closer and her vision adjusted to the dark, she realised the water was just exceptionally clear and still. Coins glinted in the bottom, and she considered making a wish, but she'd used the last of her change getting her train ticket. She remembered what Hope had said about the water's powers. OK, it was just a myth but – she looked at her half-drunk bottle of mineral water – having the upper hand with men sounded like fun.

She tipped the remainder of the bottle out onto the grass and dipped it into the water. Stepping outside the dark space, she held it up to the light – it looked clean. If she could survive the Cheltenham waters as a kid, she was sure she could cope with it. She took a swig and was rewarded with a sweet, pure mouthful. She didn't feel any magical transformation, and laughed at herself internally. Did she really expect a thunderbolt? At least she was pretty sure she hadn't poisoned herself – it tasted fresh enough.

Lucy sat on one of the mossy boulders in quiet contemplation, enjoying the silence. She hadn't seen anyone since she'd got off the train and she didn't imagine many tourists would be out exploring, as it looked like rain. Just as she thought this, she felt a raindrop hit the back of her hand, followed by the skies opening up.

Even though it was raining the spring air was warm, and rather than diving for cover Lucy enjoyed the sensation of the water droplets exploding on her skin. As the rain hit the ground it intensified the fresh and earthy scent, and she eagerly breathed it in. It felt different to the city drizzle she'd got used to and impulsively she took off her coat to better feel the rain against her skin: there was something refreshing about it.

As her hair stuck to her face, she was reminded of the last time she'd got caught in the rain: just before she'd met Ben on the Tube. Her stomach flipped at the memory. Why hadn't he called? She was sure he wanted her as much as she wanted him – you couldn't fake lust like that, could you? Remembering the way his erection had felt against her, the way he'd looked at her as if he wanted to possess her, she felt a surge of desire.

The rain was coming down even more heavily now, making her shirt cling to her body, soaking through her thin bra. She felt wanton, knowing what she must look like, and imagined what Ben would do if he saw her. The feelings this conjured felt wrong for a holy site, but they needed to be acted on. She hadn't touched herself the whole time she'd been at her sister's – she was sleeping in the kid's room and it didn't seem appropriate – but now, all alone in the middle of nowhere, it had never felt more right.

She picked up her coat and wandered away from the well until she found a cluster of trees and bushes that provided a suitable level of cover. She couldn't believe what she was about to do, but her body knew what it wanted. There was nowhere to sit, so instead she leaned against a tree that was well hidden but gave her a good view of the road. She rubbed her hands together, blowing into them to warm them, then unbuttoned the fly of her jeans, licked her fingers and slipped her hand into her knickers.

Her pubes felt warm and soft against her fingertips and her clit was already hard. She wanted to be quick, and her body was firing on all cylinders. She rubbed the stiff nub, sliding her finger between her lips and rocking her hips to press her pubic bone against her hand. She could feel the wetness building at her entrance, and slipped just the tip of her finger inside herself, enjoying the way her jeans squeezed her hand tightly to her body.

The rain seemed to be coming down even harder than before and it splashed over her face as she leaned back, enjoying the delicious sensation of her fingers pushing against her pussy. She imagined Ben watching her, cock in hand – he'd certainly liked watching her play with herself on the roof terrace. She pictured his hands reaching for her breasts and squeezed her nipples hard, moving her left hand rapidly from one to the other. Her orgasm was building now.

She tilted her head back and opened her mouth, enjoying the feeling of the raindrops splashing into her mouth and wishing it was Ben's come instead. As she pictured him spraying over her, showing her how much he wanted her, it sent her over the edge and she felt her pussy open and gush as tremors racked her body, a flash of pleasure that was as fast as it was intense. It wasn't the longest orgasm she'd ever had but Lucy felt a thrill that she'd been so brazen – and got away with it.

She pulled her hand out of her knickers, rubbing it dry on a tissue – then picked up her bottle of water and bag, put on her jacket and headed back towards the station. The weather was showing no signs of letting up, and she was starting to get cold. It was time to hail a train.

'I can't believe you're going tomorrow and this is the first chance we've had to spend time together properly,' said Hope as she sat with Lucy having a glass of wine that evening. She'd got home after Lucy and had ordered them a Chinese as a treat. 'I'm so sorry – but you've seen what it's like.'

'No worries,' said Lucy. 'I don't know how you manage. It's never-ending. I can't believe you used to work as well – how did you cope?'

'It was a lot easier with one,' Hope said. 'And Ant's always been really good about pulling his weight when he's not working. But it just wasn't worth it child-care-wise when Jack was born – it would have cost me to go to work. Although it would be nice to get a bit of a break. If one of them's in a bad mood, it can ruin the whole day.'

'Now that I can empathise with,' said Lucy. 'There's a woman at work who's really moody and she's a nightmare to work with.'

'I guess some people never grow out of tantrums. So how's it all going there?'

Lucy considered giving Hope the edited version she'd given her mum – 'Fine, though I'm not sure I want to be in marketing for the rest of my life.' – but looking at her sister's open, trusting gaze, she didn't want to lie to her. She told Hope about the dilemma she was in – though she skipped the threesome in the toilets, just saying that Brendan had attempted to seduce her. There was such a thing as too much honesty – particularly with family.

At the end of Lucy's outpouring, Hope didn't beat about the bush. She'd worked in HR, and had clearly had to deal with similar situations.

'Brendan sounds like a sleazy predator. He got you drunk, offered you drugs when your resistance was low and tried to have his way with you. He's a senior manager. If he was just some guy you met in a bar, it'd still be assault but his being a colleague means it's sexual harassment too. He's in a lot of trouble – and your boss probably realises what a vulnerable position he's put the company in. I'd report the F.U.C.K.E.R.' Hope realised what she'd done and smiled at Lucy. 'Sorry, force of habit. I try to do it all the time so I don't have to worry about whether the kids are around or not.'

'So what should I say?' said Lucy.

'Just tell the truth. What he did was well out of order – even without the drugs.'

Lucy hadn't seen it that way before, but she knew Hope was right. It had been unacceptable – as was his office 'banter'. She remembered the way she'd felt when he'd eyed up her thighs, and shuddered. She knew what she had to do.

'But I don't want him to lose his job because of me. It doesn't seem fair.'

'He's not losing it because of you. He's losing it because of what he did. There's no need to feel guilty. You did enough of that when you were with David.'

'What do you mean?'

'Well, you were always apologising to him for something. I could never understand why you didn't tell him to eff off instead of being all meek and trying to keep him happy.'

'So you don't think I'm stupid for walking away from a chance for marriage and babies?' she said.

'I think you're well shot of him. And the whole marriage and babies thing isn't the happily ever after you think it is.'

Lucy saw her chance to get her sister to open up. 'Is everything OK with you and Ant?'

'We're having a tough time at the moment, to be honest. I want to move for the kids but he wants to stay put. I didn't think about schools when we first moved down here – let's face it, it's not like Kirsty was planned.'

Lucy had never realised that.

'We wanted somewhere quiet and easy for Ant to travel from, with enough space for me to do my art. This place was perfect – until we had to turn my studio into the kids' bedroom. Not that I get time to do any painting now anyway.' Hope looked wistful and, for the first time in years, Lucy felt sorry for her. She'd never realised how much control a small child could have over major life decisions.

Hope breathed in sharply and rubbed her eyes, clearly trying to stop herself from welling up. 'Oh, Hope, I had no idea,' said Lucy. She opened her arms, and Hope gratefully accepted the offer of a hug.

'I'm sorry,' she said, when she pulled away. 'I don't mean to moan about my life – I love Ant and the kids – but I can promise you, it's nothing to aspire to.'

Lucy remembered all the time she'd spent doing exactly that, but from the sounds of it Hope was a long way from living a fairy tale. Splitting from David really did feel like a lucky escape. Maybe it was time to start doing what she wanted instead of what she was told to.

The next morning Lucy woke up feeling more positive than she had in years. The Brendan situation was decided – everyone was saying the same to her and it was time to let go of the guilt and realise that if he lost his job it was his fault, not hers. Now there was only one person on her mind: Ben. After yesterday, she knew she had to try to see him again: if she didn't, she'd hate herself forever.

She hadn't called him while she'd been away, sticking

to her resolve, but she needed to know what was going on – and surely no one could have their phone off for a week? Nonetheless, she was shocked when she dialled the number and the phone started ringing rather than going straight to voicemail. Ben picked up after two rings.

'Lucy! I was just thinking about you . . .' He sounded genuinely excited to hear from her. 'Sorry if it's a bit crackly – I'm in a really bad reception area.'

Lucy wasn't quite sure what to say. She hadn't expected him to pick up.

'Hi. So, I was just calling to say hi.' Idiot. She felt herself blush.

'Well, hi to you too. I was about to give you a call. I'm back in Brighton tomorrow – working the food fair. Fancy escaping to the sea and coming along?'

Lucy's heart leapt. He wanted to see her.

'I might be a bit tired – I'm at my sister's at the moment.'

'Cornwall?'

'Yes. Liskeard to be precise.'

'What time are you going back?'

'Elevenish, why?'

'Getting the sleeper train from Exeter?'

'Yes,' Lucy said, wondering at the interest in Ben's voice.

'Me too – I've been at my folk's all week looking after my sister, Clare. Fancy travelling back together – assuming you're on the 11.21?'

Clare was his *sister*? Lucy was astonished. She couldn't believe she'd spent so much time worrying about her.

'Lucy? Are you still there? Would you like to?'

'I am,' she said quickly, 'and I would. I'd love to.'

'Meet you at the station at eleven?'

Lucy rapidly agreed and then hung up, beaming so much that her cheeks ached. Perhaps there was something magical about St Keyne's Well after all.

Her explosion of happiness was so intense she felt as if her stomach was dancing. It was infectious too: her sister commented that she looked glowing, and Lucy had a lovely day with her, Ant and the kids, wandering along the beach, building sandcastles and rock-pooling. All that activity was a good excuse for a long bath, once the kids had gone to bed. She wanted to look – and feel – her best for Ben. Maybe tonight was finally going to be the night.

Hope dropped Lucy off at the station just before eleven. 'Are you sure you don't want me to wait with you?' she said.

'You just want to see Ben,' Lucy teased. 'I think it's a bit soon for family introductions so I'll pass. But thanks for a brilliant week.'

'Thanks for helping out with the kids. You know, last night was the first uninterrupted bath I've had in three months?' Hope gave her a hug and Lucy could feel her gratitude. She made a mental note to visit her more often – not least as a reminder of what kids are really like.

As Lucy walked onto the station concourse she breathed in deeply. She couldn't believe she was finally going to see Ben – or that she was so excited about it. They'd only had one date – but what a date . . . Now she knew Clare was his sister, not a threat, Lucy could enjoy the memory of her time on the roof terrace once more, and she allowed herself to indulge, remembering the way he'd felt against her – the way he'd tasted. She wanted to taste him again.

Lucy looked up and down the platform and felt the corners of her mouth turn up of their own accord at the sight of Ben, standing under a shelter, rucksack and hamper at his feet.

'What is it about you and hampers?' she said. This one was even bigger than the one he'd had the day they met.

Ben's teeth gleamed as he grinned broadly. 'I can't believe you're down here. Serendipity. Thought we could celebrate with a midnight feast on the train.'

He nudged the hamper with his foot.

'If it's as tasty as your last hamper was, that sounds good to me.' Lucy wanted to feel his body pressed to hers, so she decided to give him a hug.

Ben looked down at her warmly, and Lucy could see his pupils dilate as he looked into her eyes. Breathing in that still-intoxicating aroma of his was doing dangerous things to her inhibitions and before long, she wasn't thinking anything other than how much she wanted to touch him more.

She reached her hand up to stroke Ben's cheek, revelling at the sensation of his soft stubble under her fingertips. He responded by stroking her back, squeezing her shoulders and easing out the tension along her spine with his thumb. His hands gradually moved lower, first over the small of her back and then, as Lucy reached up to kiss him, cupping her bum, squeezing it as Lucy gave him the kiss she'd been thinking about since she last saw him. She felt his erection rising – it really was gratifying, how responsive he was to her touch – and ground against him to signal her desire.

'You need to stop that or we'll miss our train,' Ben huskily murmured. 'We've got a lot of catching up to do – and don't think I've forgotten about the roof terrace. You were amazing. I've been planning what I can do to repay the favour all week.'

Lucy smiled wryly. All the time that she'd been worrying about Ben being off with another woman, he'd actually been wondering what he wanted to do to her.

'So is that why you've got the midnight feast?' she asked, innocently.

'That's the start of it, yes,' said Ben. 'As to where it goes from there – well, that's entirely up to you. Although I do have a few ideas . . .'

The train pulled into the platform, interrupting the moment briefly. But there was no way the tension was going to be properly broken until Lucy had been fully reacquainted with Ben.

'Maybe you should tell me what you've got in mind,'

Lucy said, as she swung her bag over her shoulder and opened the door to the train.

'I think that should wait until we're in a cabin,' said Ben, following her onto the train. 'I'm not sure it's something you'll want anyone else to overhear. So, what's it to be? Your place or mine?'

CHAPTER 6

Lucy was impressed by Ben's attention to detail. After they'd found her cabin, she'd excused herself to nip to the loo, and by the time she got back, it had been transformed. Ben had moved the pillows to turn one end of the bed into an approximation of a sofa. He'd covered the other end in a picnic blanket – 'I didn't think you'd want crumbs getting everywhere.' – and was sitting on it, laying out the contents of the hamper on disposable bamboo plates.

Although Ben was clearly trying to take up as little room as he could, the space was confined enough that Lucy couldn't avoid sitting close to him: not that she minded – though it would make it harder for her to keep her hands off him, particularly after what he'd said. She was a bit disappointed he wasn't waiting for her naked in bed, but it was nice to be romanced. In a way, Ben was a bit like Stephen, she thought. With the added bonus of that incredible chemistry.

As she squeezed next to him the mattress dipped and Ben leaned over to grab a plate that was in danger of tipping its contents over the blanket. His face was just a few inches away from hers and it took all her willpower not to lean forward and kiss him: but she was too worried about food ending up everywhere so she turned her attention to the plates to take her mind off her desire.

Having rescued the rainbow-coloured macaroons, Ben was adding the finishing touches to the spread. A breadboard sat in pride of place, laden with cheese, celery, biscuits and grapes. The air was pleasantly garlic-scented and made Lucy realise she was starving. She'd eaten with Hope and the kids at six but that seemed like a long time ago now. A plate was piled up with cured meats, while another was loaded with miniature pies.

'There's chicken and chorizo, venison and redcurrant, and "the Beast of Bodmin" – posh steak and veg,' said Ben, noticing her looking at them. 'From Grumpies – best pies in Cornwall. They even landed a distribution deal with Harrods a while back.'

Lucy's mouth watered at the thought of the pies and, as Ben opened another bag, wrapped in several layers of tea towels, her nostrils twitched at the smell of still-warm bread.

'Dad insisted on baking when I told him I was making a picnic,' Ben said. 'Left it until last minute so it was as fresh as possible. He always says that Cornish Splits are best served warm.'

'Cornish Splits?'

'Our equivalent to scones – kind of like a cross between a bread roll and a scone.'

'They smell delicious,' said Lucy.

'Just wait until you try Thunder and Lightning.' Lucy looked confused – though it sounded promising.

'Clotted cream and syrup on a Cornish Split,' Ben explained. 'It's messy, but so good.'

He laid out a selection of miniature jam and preserve jars as he spoke; then reached into the hamper again and pulled out a packet of serviettes.

'You've thought of everything.'

'Well, I figured you deserved a treat after I ran off on you like that. And I might have been a bit harsh when I bumped into you. I just didn't like seeing you in such a state. You reminded me of Clare.'

'So what's the story with her?' asked Lucy. She'd spent enough time worrying about the mysterious Clare – it would be good to know the truth.

Ben sighed. 'I don't really like talking about it much – it feels so disloyal. But after the last couple of weeks . . .' He sighed again, clearly wondering how much to share. 'Clare's always been the baby of the family. I didn't mind when we were little – she was ever so sweet-natured – though it did wind me up the way she'd always go to Dad for presents. But he didn't seem to mind.'

'Lucky Clare,' said Lucy.

'Dad wanted the best for her – for us. She hassled him into letting her go to a private boarding school when she was eleven – my gran had given her the Malory Towers books and I think she thought it was going to be all adventures and midnight feasts.' He grinned. 'Not that there's anything wrong with midnight feasts. But when she got back after the first term she was different. She still nagged him for money but she was much more aggressive about it – as if it was her right. Everyone else at the school was really loaded – Dad's done quite well for himself but not to the same level. She was in the same class as billionaires' daughters and actual princesses. I didn't want to see it at the time but that place turned her into a snob. She wasn't like the sister I'd grown up with.'

'I'm sorry,' said Lucy.

'You've got nothing to be sorry about,' Ben said. 'She guilt-tripped him into getting her a horse, a whole new wardrobe, a laptop – she knows how to wrap him round her little finger.'

'Did you say anything?'

'I didn't want to sound jealous. It's not that I begrudged her the money, but she was turning into someone she's not. By the time she finished school, there was no trace of the Clare I grew up with. She was just like a clone of all the other girls at school: same expensive clothes, same hairstyle, same entitled attitude. She thought the world owed her a living – and if anyone said no, she'd get all weepy and make out that everyone was against her.'

'I know the type,' said Lucy.

'Except Clare's not that type – not really,' Ben said. 'She was just trying to fit in. Not that she paid any attention when I told her that. She spent all her time with her "friends" – going to stay at their parents' country homes, though she was always too embarrassed to invite them to ours. I heard her describing it as our 'Cornish holiday pile' when one of her mates dropped her off one night. And the demands for money kept on coming. Dad did tell her she'd have to get a job or go to university but she always managed to get round him. She was still living at home doing bugger all when she was twenty-five – and expecting Mum to do all her washing. She spent most of her time riding her pony – though Mum seemed to end up mucking it out, and Clare always expected her to look after it when she was away. Which was a lot.'

'I hope you don't mind me saying but it sounds like she needs to grow up.'

'She does. She flitted from one hobby to another – said she was trying to find herself. Bikram yoga, shamanic drumming, mindful skiing – as soon as she saw some self-help trend appear in the style section, she'd be on to it. And those things don't come cheap. Not that it did her any good – she just ended up with cupboards full of clothes and equipment she'd got bored of and was just as unhappy as ever. She was always getting into trouble too – getting so drunk at overpriced clubs that she couldn't walk – or ending up in dodgy situations with creeps. She'd call me rather than Dad – didn't want to ruin his image of Daddy's little princess. I've lost track of the amount of times I had to rescue her from being pawed by some twat in a VIP bar. Even got punched a few times.'

'You're a good big brother,' said Lucy.

'She didn't think so – at least not when she was hammered. Half the time, she'd have forgotten she called me and would be slumped drunk in a corner. She'd get angry with me when I tried to take her home, tell me I was trying to ruin her fun. It wasn't a good time.'

'Doesn't sound it.'

'I almost didn't leave Cornwall because of her. I hated the idea of her being on her own. I knew she'd never let Dad see her in that state and Clare and my mother have never really got on that well – she can see through her manipulation and it's caused loads of rows between my parents. She only looked after the horse for her because she can't bear animal cruelty. But Clare told me to go – said it'd be cool having somewhere different to stay.'

'So what happened?'

'She came to see me a couple of times but she hated Brighton – said it was full of crusties. She'd go out clubbing in London instead – and still expected me to rescue her when she got into trouble. I got far too used to the late trains – and getting stuck in overpriced hotels when she made us miss the last one back. She was drunk more often than she was sober. She'd end up crying for hours. It was exhausting.'

'Shit.' Lucy didn't know what else to say.

'Anyway, earlier this year she asked Dad for money

to go on a round the world trip with her cronies. He agreed to pay for it – I think he thought it would be good for her – but said it was the last money she'd get from him: she'd have to get a job when she got back. I think the rose-tinted glasses were finally starting to come off for him.'

Lucy nodded, prompting him to continue.

'It was supposed to be an eight-stop trip. She only got as far as New York, two stops in, before the others abandoned her. She couldn't afford to go to the places they wanted to, and they said they didn't want to "slum it". She called, almost incoherently drunk and sobbing, when you were in Brighton with me. She'd lost her ticket and couldn't get home. I had to fly over to get her, and when I found her she'd been lying in bed in a shitty hotel for two days. She hadn't eaten or washed, and there were fag ends and empty bottles of wine everywhere. I've never seen her in such a state.'

Lucy could see the distress in Ben's eyes.

'What did you do?'

'Moved her to a clean hotel, to start with – nothing flash, but the place she was in was crawling with cockroaches. And then spent three days in hell while I tried to get her sober and she did everything she could to fight me. Eventually, I told her I'd leave her there if she didn't do as she was told. I think it scared her because she stopped sneaking out to get bottles of wine after that. I managed to get her eating and washing. As soon as she was in a fit state to travel, I got her a flight and took her back home. I think my folks were a bit shocked at how thin she was but she begged me not to tell them the whole story. I told them she'd fallen out with her friends and left it at that. She's promised me it won't happen again but, I don't know . . .' Ben trailed off, his eyes clouding over. 'I guess I've heard it all before. I hope it's true. I just don't know if I can trust her anymore.'

For the first time, Ben looked younger than his years: like a small boy who was about to burst into tears. Lucy could see he was feeling uncomfortable and instinctively grabbed his hand and squeezed it. He squeezed back, hard, and Lucy was sure she could feel him trembling slightly.

'Anyway, you don't want to hear all about my fucked-up family. I'm sure you'd much rather be tucking into our feast.'

Lucy could tell he wanted to drop the subject.

'So, what's on the menu?'

'The finest food Cornwall can offer,' Ben said, his tone artificially cheery. 'I'm planning a Best of British pop-up and thought I'd test out some new products at the food festival this weekend – my folks would never forgive me if I didn't include Cornwall. I've got a load of deliveries waiting for me back home but I got some extra for us – you seemed to enjoy the last hamper so I know you're a woman of taste.' Ben waved his hand towards the cheeseboard. 'So, you've got Yarg there – plain, and some rather special stuff wrapped in wild garlic leaves.' He pulled a folding knife out of his pocket, flicked the blade and cut off a sliver of the garlic one for Lucy. She popped it in her mouth and was rewarded with a creamy, delicate flavour infused with a hint of allium.

'Oh my God – that's delicious.'

'It's one of my favourites,' said Ben. 'Although the St Endellion Brie comes a close second – made in Trevarrian, about an hour up the road from Liskeard. Then there's Helford White – kind of like Reblochon, if you've ever had that?'

Lucy shook her head.

'You're in for a treat. It's award-winning. And finally' – he pointed at an orange-marbled cheese – 'There's Cornish Smuggler, more of a cheddary cheese.'

'That all sounds amazing,' said Lucy.

'I was going to get some Cornish Blue but I wasn't sure if you'd like it – and it does smell a bit. Didn't want to stink the sleeper car out.'

'Good call,' she said. She'd always been a huge cheese fan – she'd take it over chocolate any day of the week – but had never liked it blue. It just tasted mouldy to her, though she felt unsophisticated admitting it.

'Oh, and, of course, let's not forget the drink.' Ben pulled out two bottles. 'The Cornwall pinot noir is another award-winner – a rosé fizz. And this' – he waved a smaller bottle at her – 'is Gwires. You won't want too much of it but it's got to be tasted.'

'What is it?'

'A liqueur distilled from mead – honey wine. It always makes me think of ambrosia – the drink of the gods, not the rice pudding.'

He pulled a small tumbler out of the hamper and poured a small measure of the Gwires into it. Lucy took a sip nervously – spirits weren't really top of her list, particularly after the Brendan incident – but it was sweet and delicious, if potent.

'Is it strong?'

'Forty per cent. But don't worry, I promise I won't get you drunk and take advantage of you.'

'Damn,' thought Lucy, but she didn't want to look desperate so instead she said, 'It'd be hard with all this food – talk about lining your stomach.'

'So, what pie do you fancy first? We should make a start before they go cold – then the splits.'

'OK, boss. I'll go for the chicken I think.' As she bit into it, Lucy's eyes widened and she started to fan her mouth. 'It's hot,' she said.

'Sorry – did I forget to mention the chilli?' Ben said.

He cracked open the bottle of sparkling wine and poured Lucy a glass, which she gratefully took from him.

'It's lovely,' she said. 'I just wasn't expecting it – the heat came as a bit of a surprise.'

'I thought that, too,' said Ben.

It was clear that he wasn't talking about the pie. Their eyes met and she felt as if they were the only two people in the world, such was the intensity of his gaze. She felt self-conscious, worried the pie was going to leak its juices over her chin, and hurriedly popped the rest of it into her mouth.

'Delicious,' she said. 'Remind me what the other pies were again.'

The sexual tension was making her nervous: she wanted Ben but she was scared of the feelings he awakened within her. She'd never felt so attracted to anyone – and it was getting harder and harder to stay in control of her yearnings.

A little later, she said, 'That was one of the best meals I've ever had. You certainly know your food. Although you weren't wrong about the Thunder and Lightning being messy.' She licked her fingers, which were now covered in clotted cream and syrup.

'Thanks,' said Ben. As he spoke, he tidied the plates and leftovers away, putting them back in the hamper. 'It's my passion, so it really means a lot that you appreciate it. So you enjoyed stage one then?'

'Stage one?' Lucy said, her heart quickening. 'That suggests there's a stage two.'

She'd been hoping for that – after all, he could have told her he was planning a midnight feast without any risk of embarrassing her in front of other passengers.

'I have more than one passion,' said Ben. 'But we should probably let our dinner go down first. Fancy a coffee in the bar?'

Lucy nodded. The long day was beginning to catch

up with her and she could do with a burst of energy. Even though she wanted him, she was feeling sleepy and a bit bloated after their feast. A coffee sounded like just what she needed – for now, at least.

'Aren't you at least going to give me a clue?' she said.

Ben looked at her teasingly.

'Well, I guess it wouldn't be giving too much away to say you might be wearing a bit too much for stage two. But come on, coffee – I might not have the willpower to resist you for much longer.'

Lucy smiled. 'Dinner really was delicious. Thanks for putting it together. The coffee's on me.'

'If you insist,' Ben said, and headed out of the cabin, Lucy following closely behind him.

An hour later Lucy was feeling light-headed. Ben had picked up the Gwires on his way out of the cabin and, after coffee, he'd poured them both a glass and they'd sipped it slowly, chatting easily and laughing together as the train made its way through the starry night. But it wasn't the drink that was intoxicating her. Ben's flirty conversation and lingering looks made the heat rise in her belly. By the time they got back to her cabin, Lucy wasn't sure she could wait for him to touch her – her body was craving his more with every passing second.

Luckily, she didn't have long to wait. When they'd got back, he'd let her in on stage two – his other passion.

'When I was at catering college, there was a beauty

school on site. I used to chat to some of the girls and they persuaded me to go to their massage classes – they needed men to practice on.'

'I bet they did.' Lucy laughed, eyes skimming over Ben's muscular body.

'It was all above board,' said Ben. 'Other than a bit of flirting. Anyway, I found it fascinating – learning all about the way muscles interconnect; how the body works. It's pretty scientific really – not what I was expecting. I ended up signing up for a part-time course myself. So, I was wondering if you'd like a massage?'

Lucy looked at Ben, scarcely able to believe her luck. He got more perfect by the second. Her muscles were aching after days of running around after the kids, carrying Jack and sleeping on an inflatable mattress on the floor. She loved massage, but she couldn't afford it very often – it was so expensive.

'That would be amazing,' she said.

'Well, you don't want to mess up your clothes,' said Ben, reaching into his backpack and pulling out a bottle of sweet almond oil. 'So why don't you get ready for me – I'll wait outside so you have enough room. Let me know when you're done.'

Again, she was struck by his thoughtfulness. There was no way she could wriggle out of her skinny jeans elegantly and she was grateful for the privacy.

Lucy considered taking everything off but decided against it. It always took her time to feel comfortable naked with someone new, so she left her bra and knickers on and wrapped the towel around herself before letting him back in. 'You get more beautiful the more I see of you,' he said, before stroking her hair and leaning forward to tenderly kiss her. Lucy wanted to wrap her arms around him but she was worried the towel would drop: it was odd, but even though she had pleasured him in his roof garden the idea of letting him see her body up close felt far more intimate.

'Hop onto the bed then,' said Ben, sensing her discomfort and stepping away to spread out another towel. She slipped out of the one she was wrapped in, noting that he politely dipped his gaze away from her, gave it to him and did as she was told. 'And lie on your front. Put this underneath your . . . top half. It'll make it easier for you to breathe comfortably.' He passed her a pillow. Lucy smiled at his coy description. He was clearly trying to keep his mind on massage – and she suspected he was struggling as much as she was. 'And put this under your forehead.' He handed her a rolled up sweatshirt, tucking another one under her ankles. 'Don't worry, they're clean. I should have picked up the towel from my cabin, really.'

He busied himself with his phone and a few seconds later music was filling the cabin. He put the massage oil on the side, warming it in a cup of hot water he'd brought from the buffet car, and rubbed his hands together briskly. 'Don't want you getting a chill.'

Lucy was glad of the time she'd spent pampering

herself in the bath – and that she'd brought her favourite black lacy pants and matching bra with her. They covered her just enough to feel sexy rather than exposed.

Ben lay her towel over her, folding it to leave her upper back revealed but her bum and legs covered, and after first checking it was OK, gently undid her bra so it wouldn't get in the way.

'I'll be far too distracted to massage you with a view like that,' he murmured, leaning forward to drop a kiss on the back of her neck – exactly at the point that made her melt.

Lucy felt darts of pleasure shooting down from her neck to her pussy. She wasn't sure if this was going to be heaven or hell. Holding herself back from begging for more while Ben's hands roamed over her body would take every bit of her self-control. She was beginning to regret her shyness, her mind drifting to what would have happened if she had revealed herself to him fully.

'Breathe slowly and deeply – it'll help you relax. And let me know if it gets too much. I can be as hard or as gentle as you want.'

She felt Ben's hands on her back, sliding slowly and lightly up and down, distributing the sweet-smelling oil evenly over her skin. Goose pimples were rising on her arms and the hairs on the back of her neck were standing up. Ben noticed, and asked if she wanted him to find another cover for her, but Lucy knew it had nothing to do with the temperature and shook her head.

Ben repeated the gliding motion, applying more oil until she could feel her skin was slippery under his fingertips. Once he was satisfied she was suitably lubricated, he started running his hands up and down her back with long, smooth strokes, circling his palms on her lower back, first one side, then the other. Lucy's stomach flipped so hard she was sure he must have been able to feel it, and her pussy twitched in sympathy.

Now he started to softly pull and stretch her muscles, his strong hands clearly knowing exactly what they were doing as he targeted one area at a time. Lucy bit her lip to stop herself from whimpering with desire: it was as if he knew her body better than she knew it herself. His movements were deliberate but ever-changing – every time she thought she knew what he was doing, he surprised her. Deciding to stop second-guessing him and just enjoy the moment, she closed her eyes and let herself drift away on sensation.

Ben gradually increased the pressure as he identified where her knots were and started to ease them out. Lucy couldn't hold back a moan as he pressed his thumbs into a particularly sensitive spot: he seemed to know exactly where her tension was and – oh, yes – *exactly* how to work it out.

He used his knuckles to work on her, firm but sensitive, making her pussy pulse again; then worked his way up either side of her spine, massaging her shoulder blades, sliding his thumbs underneath them, making her realise just how much tension was trapped there.

As he moved to her neck, his touch became gentler and Lucy moaned as he ran his thumbs over the junction of neck and shoulders. 'I won't do your head – I'm guessing you don't want to get oil in your hair?' By now, Lucy couldn't have cared about anything other than making sure the massage never ended. She was lost in bliss and simply murmured, 'Uh-huh.'

She heard Ben move to stand at her head and was tempted to open her eyes, but her lids were getting increasingly heavy and she didn't want to move her head – not when he was doing such delicious things to her shoulders.

Ben's hands slid up her back from shoulder blade to neck, again and again; he was enjoying taking his time to make her feel good. Once every last knot had been eased out, his hands started to head south, over Lucy's lower back and towards her buttocks.

His thumbs lingered at the top of her hips, circling slowly, but when he started to push the towel lower he was stopped in his tracks by a soft snore. Lucy had succumbed to the sleep that had been threatening ever since their feast.

Lucy was awakened by a knock at the door. In her sleepy state, she assumed it must be breakfast. It was only when she wrapped the blanket around herself and opened it to see Ben that the previous night came flooding back to her. What had happened? She remembered the feast, the way the massage had made her feel.

With a stab of regret, she realised she must have fallen asleep, and Ben had refastened her bra and covered her with the blanket like a true gentlemen.

'Morning, sleepyhead. We're about half an hour from Paddington. Thought I'd give you a wake-up call. I didn't want you to think I'd abandoned you – I just hadn't got the heart to disturb you. You looked so angelic – did you know you smile in your sleep?'

Lucy self-consciously brushed her fingers through her hair, sure she must have bed-head.

'I'm so sorry. I must have been more tired from the kids than I thought.'

'I told you they were exhausting. And no worries. I wish I could have curled up with you but the bed's hardly big enough for one. Sleep well?'

'I did. And my muscles are so much less achy – thanks for the massage. But I could really do with a shower – I feel a bit oily.'

'We could always use the ones at Paddington,' Ben said, a twinkle in his eye. 'I've used them a few times – they're well looked after and pretty spacious.' Lucy felt a thrill at the thought.

'We?' she asked, playfully.

'Well, if there aren't any attendants around – it's got to be worth a go. In fact, have you got a hoodie and jeans in your bag?'

'Yes,' said Lucy.

'Then I've got an idea . . .'

*   *   *

'You are a bad influence,' Lucy whispered, trying not to giggle.

After Ben had outlined his plan, she'd changed into her baggiest jeans and a grey hoodie, scraped her hair back into a pony tail, which she tucked under the hood, and left her face make-up free. Once they got off the train, Ben went ahead of her into the men's shower, past the stern-looking attendant. Lucy loitered nearby, trying not to draw attention to herself, until she saw Ben reappear briefly and give her a wave, indicating there was no one else in the showers.

Lucy nestled into her hood, trying to hide as much of her face as possible, and walked into the showers, keeping her head down as she paid the five-pound fee, took a towel from the attendant, and headed for the only cubicle with water running. She tapped on the door, hoping desperately that Ben hadn't been mistaken about being alone, but it swung open to reveal him. She quickly stripped off and left her clothes outside the shower – keeping them as close as possible in case they were disturbed.

As soon as she stepped into the shower, Ben was kissing her. Lucy could feel his pectorals firm against her body, his soft dark-blond chest hair rubbing deliciously against her skin. Her hands slid to his thighs and she thrilled at the way they felt under her fingers.

Naked, he looked even better than he did clothed. He was well-built, his body tapering slightly from his broad shoulders to his waist. He lacked a six-pack, but she could feel that he was solid muscle. His arm under the small of her back made her weak at the knees: she felt vulnerable, but in a way that made her want to give herself to him rather than run away.

'God, it's good to feel you against me,' he murmured in her ear. 'You have the softest skin.'

Lucy could feel his desire rising against her.

'And you have the hardest cock,' she whispered back cheekily, reaching down between their bodies to wrap her hand around it. Her fingertips only just touched around his girth.

Ben gave a sharp intake of breath as she softly gripped him and started to slide her hand up and down. It moved easily; his cock was already leaking pre-cum, foreskin sliding easily over the head. Her thumb teased the underside, pressing the sensitive spot where head met shaft, and she gently pulsed her palm.

'Fuck, you're good at that,' Ben said with a moan, hands tracing her body reverentially, making Lucy shiver with desire – and, smiling, raise a finger to her lips to tell him to be quiet – she didn't want them to be disturbed. It felt as if he was worshipping her as he soaped his hands and slowly ran them down her sides, over her belly, pulling her closer to him so she could feel his chest against hers as her hand continued its steady motion, trapped between their bodies. Her pussy was crying out for attention but Ben took his time, running his palms over her back, her bum, her thighs, showing his appreciation for her with his touch in lieu of words. Lucy arched her hips towards him, pressing herself against his thigh as she stroked him. Ben's eyes were half-closed now and she could see he was fighting to hold himself back.

'Please,' she whispered, grinding against him, leaving him in no doubt that she wanted more. His hand slowly travelled down to her wet folds, and he cupped her pubic mound, testing her body's response, fingers slipping either side of her clit. It swelled between his fingers and now it was Lucy's turn to moan.

Keeping a smooth motion going with her right hand, revelling in the way he seemed to get harder with every stroke, Lucy moved her left hand on top of Ben's, positioning it to touch her in all the right ways. Her hips moved in rhythm with their hands and she could feel the pressure building, as his other hand firmly squeezed and caressed her buttocks, pulling her ever closer, making her desperate to feel him inside her. She was about to ask him if he had a condom when they heard a voice outside.

'Yeah, mate, at Paddington now. Just grabbing a quick shower and I'll be there. Meet in the foyer of the Shard, yeah?' The voice was booming, assertive. Lucy froze – though her hand continued its steady pace. She could tell Ben was close to coming and, even though she didn't want to get caught, she needed to feel his release – and her own. Ben's movements had stopped when he heard the voice but Lucy pressed his hand against her, indicating she wanted – needed – him to carry on.

Now the pair were silent. Lucy's right hand slid, faster and faster, as she pressed Ben's fingers against her most sensitive zones with the other hand. She had to bury her face in his shoulder to stop herself from crying out as she rocked against him, knowing her orgasm was imminent.

Ben's cock was starting to twitch. He slid his hand up her spine from her bum, pulled her hair to tilt her head back, and kissed her passionately. Lucy started to shake: feeling his lips on hers, his tongue eager and demanding, combined with the delicate ministrations of his other hand, was enough to tip her over the edge. She pressed his fingers against her entrance, and as her juices welled out of her and onto his hand, Ben lost control. His come shot out over her fingers and both their bellies just as Lucy exploded in orgasm, kissing him back hard to stop herself from squealing.

They stood for a moment, holding each other tightly as pleasure wracked their bodies, but the sound of another shower starting up broke the mood.

'You'd better be quick,' Ben said, pulling Lucy under the shower to kiss her and wash them both clean, and then turning it off. He opened the cubicle door and passed her her clothes and a towel. Lucy hurriedly dried off and got dressed.

'See you on the concourse,' he whispered.

Lucy headed out of the showers, hood pulled over her wet hair, and stood looking at the train times, trying to look innocent even though she was shaking from the thrill – and the orgasm.

'Excuse me, miss.'

The voice panicked her, but when Lucy looked up, she saw a young man in a T-shirt with a slogan proclaiming, 'Start the day as you mean to go on', a breakfast bar in his hand. 'I was wondering if you'd like to try our new health bar – it's got fifteen essential vitamins and nutrients.'

She smiled in relief. 'I'd love one – thanks. Could I get two, do you think? I'm just waiting for someone to get out of the shower. In fact, there he is now. Ben, fancy some breakfast?'

Ben grinned. 'Absolutely.' He glanced at what was written on the man's T-shirt. 'Now there's a motto to live by.'

They munched on the cereal bars as they walked through the station.

'So, what's your plan then?' Ben asked. 'Fancy coming to the food festival with me? I could do with your . . . assistance.' His flirty tone made it clear it was more than help he wanted from Lucy.

Lucy thought for a moment. She'd been planning on heading home to get rested for work on Monday, but it wasn't like she had much to do, at least until she got into the office. Now she knew how she was going to handle the Brendan issue, everything seemed simpler than it had before she went away.

'Why not,' she said.

'In that case, we should get going. The fair opens at ten and I've got a lot of setting up to do before then.'

'If only you had an events expert with you who was used to working on tight deadlines.' Lucy said. Ben grinned.

'You're a woman of many talents,' he said. 'And one thing's for sure – I can promise you it'll be a lot more interesting than dog toothbrushes.'

Ben wasn't lying about being on a tight deadline. He'd spent most of the train journey to Brighton on the phone, checking everything was going to be delivered on time and making sure his staff were prepared. Lucy flicked through a newspaper, enjoying hearing him in 'business mode'. He was relaxed but efficient, joking with his suppliers but keeping conversation short and to the point.

'It sounds like you've got a lot of people to manage,' she said when he put down the phone after his third call. 'Business must be going well.' Ben had looked embarrassed. 'Actually, Dad's helping me out a bit,' he'd said, but his phone had rung again before Lucy could find out any more details. Perhaps he wasn't quite as independent as she'd first thought?

When they arrived in Brighton, it was quieter than she expected.

'Hardly anyone gets up before ten here – particularly not at the weekends,' Ben said. 'But just you wait until later – almost forty thousand people came to the food festival last year. It's busy, to say the least.'

It certainly had got busy, thought Lucy, two hours

later. When they'd arrived at his stall, on a pretty lawn right next to the beach, it had been deserted but for the other stallholders setting up.

Now she could barely see the marquee opposite for the swell of people – though she could hear announcements coming over the tannoy, telling visitors about the attractions coming up later in the day. 'Don't forget to get your cakes in for the baking competition before twelve for your chance to win. But before that we've got food demonstrations from chefs at Amberley Castle, Ockenden Manor, and 64 Degrees, and cocktail making with Blackdown Sussex Spirits and Mixology Group.'

It sounded like there was a packed schedule – not to mention free samples galore.

Lucy's senses were stimulated by the delicious smells all around her: hog roast and sausages, garlic and curry. Ben's stall was laid out with cheese and smoked meat, sitting on slate tiles with their place of origin written on them in chalk. He'd delegated this task to Lucy and she was quietly proud of the end result. Jam and chutney lined the back of the table, with packets of cheese straws, macaroons and biscuits in front of them. Among the slates, more plates held pies and Scotch eggs, with smaller bowls at the front holding samples of the produce for people to taste. It all looked delicious – and from the reaction it got, it was clear Lucy wasn't the only one who thought so.

The morning passed in a rush of selling and packing, re-stocking and getting change. Lucy felt happy chatting to customers and soon picked up on Ben's sales spiel – 'This cheese has been made by the same family for three generations.' 'The Scotch eggs are made from Gloucestershire Old Spots from a farm just outside Lewes.' Every item had a story and it was clear Ben knew how to hold an audience.

'Do you want to go and look round a bit?' asked Ben at noon. 'You could probably do with a break. There's a tea-tasting challenge with some burlesquers I know; they've promised to send people over here for biscuits.'

'That'd be great,' said Lucy. Her feet were killing her: sitting down and having a nice cup of tea sounded brilliant. She headed over the road to the marquee and was soon sitting down while a pretty redhead in a figure-hugging vintage pencil dress poured her a cup of tea, and an equally glamorous brunette asked her, 'Is that Assam or Gunpowder?', and rewarded her with a macaroon when she got the answer right.

It seemed like no time before they were packing up. Ben's easy manner, generosity with samples and the tea promotion had helped the stall stay busy all day and Lucy was looking forward to finally being alone with Ben. They'd hardly had a chance to talk – though he had given her bum an affectionate squeeze, or pulled her into a quick kiss, whenever the stall was quiet enough for him to get away with it. She'd learned more about him though: that he was patient and responded well under pressure. The more she got to know him, the more she thought he was someone she could fall in love with.

After they'd cleared everything away, Ben invited his burlesque friends to the pub. 'Hope you don't mind,' he said to Lucy. 'But they sent a lot of people our way today so I'd feel rude if I didn't at least buy them a drink.'

'Not at all,' said Lucy.

She'd really enjoyed chatting to the showgirls – and they had taught her the secret of creating perfect wing-tipped eyeliner, something that had always evaded her.

Conversation flowed and one drink turned into another, with more of Ben's friends joining them as the evening progressed – he seemed to know everyone in Brighton. Lucy enjoyed herself but as the alcohol lowered her inhibitions she found it increasingly hard to keep her hands off him. Not that Ben was stopping her – after three drinks, she was pressed tightly against him on the bench seating, and his hand was discreetly tracing patterns higher and higher up her thigh. After four, her hand was doing the same to him, edging nearer and nearer to his cock.

Lucy noticed Ben's tone gradually getting more emphatic with every drink, and his hands wandering more freely, pressing up against the seam of her jeans. Part of her wanted to stop him: she was sure his friends would notice. But the drink kept her inhibitions pinned down and instead she relinquished herself to his touch, enjoying the sensations as his fingers cupped her pussy and rocked back and forth, making pleasure ripple through her body – all the while seeming to be paying attention to the pockets of conversation going on around him. Lucy tried to look as if she was listening to what was being said too, trying to hide the fact that Ben's fingers were now pressing lower – and she was stroking his shaft, using his coat as cover..

Now he was rubbing hard, almost too hard, trying to slide his thumb between the buttons of her fly and feel what lay beneath. She'd never known him be so sexually aggressive before: everything had been slow and sensual. He was demanding, and seemingly oblivious to the people around them, as he leaned over and kissed her, hard, teeth pressing into her soft lower lip. A flash of pain shot through her, rapidly followed by the sweet sensation of Ben's tongue sliding into her mouth, easing the sting and bringing her desire to the fore once again. But she was too self-conscious about the people around them to abandon herself fully to the kiss.

Lucy put her hand on top of Ben's, at her crotch, and intertwined her fingers with his, seemingly romantic but also subduing his hand into subtler stroking. She wanted him but she also wanted to be in one piece by the time he got her home.

He did look delectable though. He was more serious when he was drunk, wrinkling his eyes in deep thought and emphasising his points with strong hand gestures. He looked like a sexy lecturer, Lucy thought: there was no doubt he was in charge. The idea made her pussy muscles flicker and she imagined him putting her over one knee for a spanking. That line of thought really wasn't doing her self-control much good.

She moved his hand down her thigh, fingers still entwined, to take the heat out of the moment – at least for now. But she was looking forward to later.

Luckily, when his friends suggested staying for another drink, Ben declined. 'Another busy day at the festival tomorrow. Don't want to be too hung-over, and I'm already pretty wasted.' Lucy noticed he was slurring his words. Even though they'd been surrounded by food all day, they'd been busy serving customers – and, come to think of it, he hadn't taken a lunch break after she got back to the stall. No wonder the drink was hitting him hard.

He and Lucy said their goodbyes, but she was pretty sure the evening was far from over for the rest of the group, who had already bought another bottle of wine by the time she and Ben got to the door. She could see why he thought Brighton was such an entertaining town. Even though she was hot for Ben, part of her liked the idea of staying out with her new friends – but she was feeling quite shattered – and wasn't sure Ben needed more to drink.

'So, do you want to come back to mine?' Ben asked. 'Or do you want me to walk you to the station?'

'I'd love to come to yours,' Lucy said, excited at the thought of finally getting to explore his body at her leisure. 'But I'll have to head off first thing. I need to work out my plan of attack for Monday.'

'Monday?'

'I'm going to tell my boss about Brendan,' she said. 'I can't stand the atmosphere with Anna and I've realised it wasn't my fault.'

'You say that,' said Ben, 'but you do have to take some responsibility. If you hadn't lied, you wouldn't be in the mess you are.' He sounded really trashed, thought Lucy. She was, too, and she couldn't control the surge of anger that rose up at his words.

'What do you mean? You know I'm honest. We met because I returned your wallet. How can you call me a liar?'

'That's not the only kind of honesty. You tell little lies all the time.'

'I do not!' Now Lucy was getting really furious, but Ben didn't pick up on her tone.

'So you didn't get wasted because you were too scared to say no? You didn't pretend that you'd done ecstasy before to fit in? Come on, Lucy. You told me what happened.'

Lucy was dumbstruck, and now realised she *had* lied to Ben when she gave him the toned-down version of events. But he didn't know that. How dare he judge her?

Ben was on a roll. 'You lie to fit in, to make people like you – I've grown up seeing my sister do it. You can't bullshit me. Why are you so willing to change who you are? You let other people dictate your behaviour all the time – it's as if you like being told what to do – need it, even. You're too scared to make yourself unpopular by being yourself. Too worried that people might not like what they found. At least if you pretend to be something you're not, they're not rejecting the real you. It's how you stay in control. You spend so much time trying to prove yourself that you've forgotten how to be yourself. Far easier to let other people tell you how to live your life.'

Lucy knew her judgement was skewed after most of a bottle of wine, and perhaps she should try not to overreact to what he was saying, but the wine won the fight and she whirled on him furiously.

'You're a fine one to talk. Look at the way you've treated me – making me skive off work, leaving me hanging after the last time I came here, judging me all the time, not bothering to call me – you're the one who likes being in control. And the way you run around after your sister – you're like her dad, not her brother. Have you ever thought that maybe the reason she keeps on fucking up is because you keep coming to the rescue? Perhaps if she had to sort her own mess out, she'd realise what she's doing to herself – but why would she bother when she knows big brother Ben is going to come and save her – even if it means fucking his own life up?'

The words spilled out of Lucy's mouth before she even thought about them – Ben had wound her up and the long day and an excess of alcohol meant she was no longer in control of what she was saying. 'Have you ever thought that maybe you just like feeling superior? You're always telling me what to do – "Loosen up, Lucy." "Be yourself, Lucy." "Stop lying, Lucy." You don't know what my life's like – how can you know what's right for me better than I do? OK, I might not always stand up for myself but I've got my own reasons for that. At least I'm properly independent. Some of us don't have a rich daddy to look after us. Maybe you should focus on sorting your own shit out instead of trying to save everyone around you.'

Even as she spoke Lucy realised she'd gone too far, but in her anger all desire for Ben was gone. 'You know what, I think I will go to the station. I don't think I want to stay the night after all.'

Ben gaped at her, shocked at her outburst, but didn't say anything – just swayed slightly.

'Don't worry about walking me back,' she snapped. 'I'm a big girl – I can look after myself.'

Tears stung at her eyes as she walked away. How dare Ben call her a liar? And how dare he make her cry again?

It wasn't until she was halfway home that she stopped shaking. She'd been so excited about being alone with Ben but there was no way she wanted to go back with him after that.

But as she started to sober up, she wondered if she might have been a bit over the top. After all, it wasn't like he'd said anything that wasn't true, if she really thought about it – just like he'd been right when he'd bumped into her at London Bridge.

Her mind drifted to David. He'd definitely been in control of the relationship – inside the bedroom and out. But part of her had liked feeling protected, being told what to do. At least that way she could get things right: although that hadn't really been the way things had played out, had it? Lucy bit her lip: the more she'd tried to be what David wanted, the less he'd liked her. Maybe she should have been more honest with him? Maybe it wasn't all his fault. Maybe Ben was right.

His timing sucked – he'd been about to get lucky. Why hadn't he kept his mouth shut? But then again, why hadn't she? The answer was the same in both cases: they were drunk.

The next day, Lucy woke up feeling low. She never felt at her happiest after a night out drinking but it was compounded by what had happened with Ben. She thought about calling him but she knew he'd be busy at the food festival again all day. And anyway, she didn't think they'd be able to sort things with a quick chat on the phone. She cringed as she thought back over what she'd said – what she could remember of it. She couldn't believe her outburst – it wasn't like her at all. But at least Ben couldn't accuse her of lying. She may have been abrasive but she'd also told him what she really thought.

There was nothing she could do about it right now. Instead, she spent the day planning what she was going to say to Anna. She didn't want to mess things up again by opening her mouth without thinking first.

Lucy went to see Anna as soon as she got into work.

'Lucy – welcome back. How was your holiday? Relaxing?'

Even though the question seemed innocuous enough, Lucy knew what Anna really meant.

'Very. And you were right: taking some time off gave me a chance to think about what happened. I can remember now.' Lucy had decided it was best to play along with the lie Anna had given her.

'Really? That is good news. So . . .'

'You were right. Brendan did offer me drugs.' Lucy had decided to give as little detail as Anna let her get away with.

'What kind?'

'Ecstasy.'

'I see. And did he offer drugs to anyone else?'

Lucy didn't want to drop Annabel in it but wanted to tell the truth. 'He did. I don't want to say who but I'll ask them to come and see you if it's something they feel they can talk about.'

'I understand. Would you be prepared to put what you just told me in writing? It might be needed if there's any tribunal.' Lucy took a big breath – it was her last chance to save Brendan – but she didn't owe him anything.

'Yes, Anna. I would.'

'In that case, I don't think I need to know any more. Do you want to get on with the clippings this morning? I've got a lot of things I need to sort out. Oh, and can you come in for a meeting at 2 p.m. ? I need to go over some changes in the team with you – things are going to be structured a little differently from now on.'

'OK,' Lucy said. She wondered if it had anything to do with the promotion Anna had dangled at her, but didn't want to get her hopes up. For now, she was just glad the whole Brendan episode was over.

When she got back to her desk, her phone was ringing.

'It's Rosie. How was your holiday?'

'Up and down,' Lucy said. 'But I've told Anna about you-know-who.' Lucy didn't want anyone overhearing that she'd dropped Brendan in it – she hoped Anna would be discreet so he wouldn't know it was her.

'Can't say I'm sorry – it couldn't have happened to a nicer bloke. So have you heard the gossip? You've missed quite a week.'

'Go on.'

'I'll give you *all* the dirt at lunchtime if you're around – but, as a heads-up, Caitlin's gone.'

'You what?' Lucy hadn't seen her but had assumed she'd been in Dan's office as usual.

'Turns out her and Dan had a scam going on. Caitlin had Dan copying other people's designs for her to flog to clients. She deliberately picked young and up-and-coming designers so they wouldn't get caught. They were submitting dodgy invoices – splitting the money. That's how she could afford so much stuff – and a coke habit – turns out Daddy isn't so rich after all. In fact Daddy hasn't been around for years.'

'You are kidding,' said Lucy. 'How did Anna find out?'

'One of her clients recognised a design – her daughter's on that student site you found and it was from her portfolio. Of course, the pair of them have been sacked. Anna's still deciding whether to take legal action or just make them pay back the money they nicked.'

'Shit,' Lucy said, thinking it was pretty kind of Anna, in the circumstances.

'It looks like the client might sue on behalf of her daughter either way. But you know what that means? With Brendan gone and Caitlin gone, they're definitely short on senior managers. Play your cards right and the job could be yours – if you want it of course. Anyway, better go, someone's coming into reception.'

Rosie hung up and Lucy sat, stunned. She wouldn't have to work with Caitlin any more. She was back in Anna's good books again – or at least not in the doghouse. Not a bad start to the week.

Her mind wandered as she worked her way through the clippings. There was a lot for her to think about. Now she'd told Anna the truth, she felt better. Perhaps Ben was right – lying only led to trouble. But then again, so could telling the truth. Ben hadn't called her, after all.

Anyway, the more she'd thought about it, the more she'd realised that, however drunk she'd been, she'd meant everything she said. He *had* been controlling towards her and although she'd had fun in the roof garden and the showers, she wasn't sure that it was good for her to be with someone who bossed her around. After David, she was still too unsure of herself – though she was growing more confident by the day. She needed to learn to make her own decisions and, if she was honest with herself, she wasn't sure whether she could do that if she was with someone who wanted to be in control. Maybe she needed to be on her own for a while to work out what she really wanted – who she really was?

Should she go for a promotion – take the next step up the ladder even if she wasn't sure she wanted what was at the top? Or follow Rosie's example and set up her own business? Maybe she should give Rach a call, join her in whatever adventure she was going on? She had some big decisions to make.

It still took all the strength she had not to pick up the phone and call Ben. She didn't want his advice. She just wanted to hear his voice and know everything was OK between them.

Even if he wasn't the one for her right now, she hated the idea of never seeing him again.

CHAPTER 7

Lucy mentally relived the argument with Ben again and again over the weekend. She'd hated hearing him describe her as needy. She'd never realised how she looked from the outside, and had always thought of herself as just being nice. Relationships were about compromise, that's what all the magazines said.

But thinking about Ben's harsh words, she saw that she *had* tried to turn herself into the perfect girlfriend rather than being herself. She'd been doing it in every relationship she'd ever had: with Stephen she was the innocent being seduced – even though he was no more experienced than she was – so that he could feel 'manly'; with David, the career-minded Stepford wife, who he could wear as an accessory to make himself look good; and with Ben, the free, fearless woman she had always wanted to be.

OK, it wasn't just about fitting in with Ben – he'd recognised something within her that she'd needed to release. The passion was certainly genuine enough, but he'd got it right when he first met her. She was a good girl. Rule-breaking and public sex were at the edge of her comfort zone. She'd enjoyed their adventures, but

Ben had been holding the reins throughout. She was facing her fear but he was pushing her through it – and part of her was only being brave to please him.

For her entire life, she'd been going along with whatever was asked of her – with everyone from him to her friends and family – for fear that otherwise, she'd be rejected. She'd even nearly got married to make her mum happy. Now, she might have faced up to who she really was – but only because Ben was confronting her with a mirror and forcing her to take a good look.

She wasn't sure if she'd ever see him again: maybe her comments about his family had been too close for comfort. He might never forgive her – it wasn't like she'd been part of his life for long. Perhaps he'd decided she was more trouble than she was worth. Or maybe he was embarrassed about what he'd said and had decided to give up on her rather than apologise. She'd thought about it so much that she had a hundred different imagined scenarios – none of which ended with happily ever after.

She didn't feel very proud of herself for wanting to be liked. She guessed it wasn't that surprising, though, given her relationship with her dad. He'd made it clear he wasn't interested in being part of her life and she'd always blamed herself for his rejection of her. 'Daddy issues' were such a cliché, but she had to admit her relationship with her father had affected her life more than she'd ever realised before.

Still, even if she could see the bigger picture now, she didn't want to be the one to call Ben, particularly after he'd all but said she was incapable of running her own life. She sighed. It was just that he had a way of seeing things clearly that she could do with at the moment. It was all very well talking to Rosie and Jo but they both had their own ideas about who she was – they knew her too well to separate her from their perception of her. With Ben, it felt like he could see her potential – the woman she could be – not the woman she had been until now.

She had a lot to distract her from her worries. It seemed that barely a day went past that week without some big discovery. First, there was Jo. Lucy called her on Monday night to fill her in on the latest developments with Ben, and was surprised when a man picked up. She could hear Jo giggling in the background and wondered what was going on.

'Hello, love, how are you doing?' Jo had said when he passed her the phone.

'Not the best.' Lucy gave Jo a potted history of the week's events, and then said, 'How about you? That *was* Martin who picked up, wasn't it? You haven't got some new man while my back's been turned?'

'It was – sorry, we were having a play fight and he was messing around with my phone – but you're kind of right about me getting a new man too. Stop it!'

Lucy could hear a playful slap. 'Sorry, let me just go

into another room. Martin's proving to be a bit too much of a distraction.'

The phone went quiet for a moment before Jo picked up again. 'OK, that's better. He is such a pain. So yes, there's been a lot going on since I last saw you.' She launched into a story that left Lucy more than a little shocked. Apparently, Martin had called Jo back to Oxford because he'd almost had sex with someone else – but his body had refused to play ball. It had made him realise how much he missed Jo – and how he'd been neglecting her. Lucy was surprised at how blasé Jo was about it.

'Of course it stung – but he wasn't really with her. OK, they had a bit of a play but it's weird – I was actually more flattered than anything – the idea that his body would only work for me. And jealous – I realised how much I still saw him as 'mine'. But apparently she got pretty abusive when he made his excuses and left so I don't have to worry about any repeat performances. Or lack of performances . . .'

'So where are you now with him?'

'Well, we talked all night and for the first time in ages, it felt like he was himself. And we've been having more really great chats ever since. He admitted that when his business didn't take off, he felt like a failure – and depressed – which he'd never admitted to me before.'

'Sounds hard,' said Lucy.

'It all seems much easier now we've talked about it. Martin's apologised for the way he treated me – said he didn't want to talk to anyone, even me, because he was embarrassed about the way he felt – didn't want me to see him as less of a man. He's started on anti-depressants. It'll take another week for them to kick in, apparently, but he already seems happier than he did. I think that knowing he's doing something to solve the problem has shifted something in him. He's even unplugged his games consoles and started jogging – only round the block, but it's more than he's done in ages.'

'That *is* a change,' said Lucy.

'It's early days but now he's talking to me – and doing something with his life – I'm seeing why I fell in love with him again. To be honest, our sex life had been going through a slump for ages but since last week, it's been back with a vengeance: we're in the honeymoon period all over again. He can barely keep his hands off me.' Jo giggled. 'It really is like having a new man. She paused for a moment, and spoke in a more muted tone. 'I just feel bad I never noticed he was depressed before – all the signs were there: sitting around doing nothing, cutting himself off from people who love him, staying in bed for half the day, smoking and drinking. I just didn't want to see them. I made it all about me rather than looking at things from his perspective – I was so busy trying to make my business work that I didn't have time to think about him.'

Lucy thought for a second. Part of her had doubts about Martin and Jo – surely things couldn't change that much in such a short time? Then again, she'd had enough overnight changes herself recently to believe it could happen – and it was up to Jo to do what was right for her.

Then there was Rosie. When Lucy got into work on Wednesday, Rosie waved a copy of the Evening Standard at her – with the style page open, featuring one of the necklaces she'd designed. 'It came out yesterday evening. All those late nights finally paid off.' Rosie laughed, excited. 'I thought it was odd that the site was so much busier than usual – I was getting orders through all night, which never usually happens; I could hear my phone beeping in the other room and I had to get up and put it on silent in the end. I checked the web logs to see what was going on and saw the traffic coming from the Standard site. I managed to find a few the Tube cleaners hadn't recycled on my way in – Mum and Dad are going to want copies. Want to have a read?' She thrust a copy at Lucy, who smiled as she read the glowing description of her friend's work – apparently a 'must buy' item for the new season.

Things only got better for Rosie after the article came out. All through Wednesday her orders steadily increased, and after Kate Moss was pictured wearing one of her necklaces in *Metro* on Thursday she had a call from a major buyer.

'This could be just what I've been looking for to take me to the next level,' she told Lucy over lunch. 'But I've hardly got any time to make jewellery what with dealing with all the press interest. I don't suppose you fancy giving me a hand?'

Lucy felt excited at the prospect. 'I'd love to help – just let me know what you need.'

'To be honest, as well as dealing with the press, there's a lot of PA things I don't have time to do – would you mind doing filing and stuff? As work, not a favour? I can't pay you a lot, and I can only afford a few hours a week but I wouldn't want you doing it for free. It wouldn't feel right. If you can help me keep the interest going, I might even be able to leave this place soon and spend all my time on my business – who knows, I might be able to offer you a proper job.'

Lucy loved the idea, and once it was clear Rosie wouldn't let her help out unpaid – no matter how much she tried to insist – they agreed a rate that, while well below what she earned at the agency, fitted Rosie's budget and gave Lucy a bit of extra cash – something to put towards her dreams, even if she hadn't quite figured out what they were yet.

That night Lucy bumped into Elle at the launch of a new diamond-filtered vodka. She looked sheepish when Lucy first spotted her while she was standing in line to get a goodie bag. Lucy wondered if she felt bad about their last encounter – maybe she'd realised quite how awful she'd been? But as Lucy had given her a polite nod hello, Elle had made a big fuss out of working her way through the queue towards her, glancing over her shoulder, clearly keeping an eye out for someone.

'I just want you to know what happened wasn't my fault,' she said when she reached Lucy, after the obligatory double cheek-kiss. 'I didn't even know who he was.'

Lucy looked blank. One of the problems with Elle assuming the world revolved around her was that she expected everyone else to know what was going on in her life.

'I'm sorry, Elle. I don't follow.'

'Me and David. When I met him I had no idea he was your ex. He was just a hottie at a launch.' Lucy's eyes widened – what exactly was Elle saying? 'Things happened so quickly. When I found out I felt dreadful – though I really don't understand why you let him go. But I don't want to think it'll affect our friendship – or our business relationship. He's the first man I've met who I think really understands me.'

Elle spoke in a rush, as if scared to let Lucy get a word in, and was now blinking at her expectantly. 'You are OK with it, aren't you? I've never felt like this before about a man.' She was looking around nervously and kept glancing towards one particular group of people. With a jolt, Lucy saw that Elle was keeping an eye on someone familiar – David.

Lucy had always expected to feel a pang at the idea of her ex-fiancé being with someone new, even though things had ended messily, but, as she processed the information, all she could think was how perfect Elle and David would be together. They were both impressed by the same things; and both so egotistical that she could imagine them staring into each other's eyes to admire their own reflections. The fact that one of Elle's major concerns was that their business relationship wouldn't be affected told her a lot.

'Don't worry,' she said to Elle. 'I can promise you that it won't affect our relationship at all.' She smiled inwardly, knowing she had been entirely honest and certain Elle wouldn't question her response.

Elle clapped, saying, 'Fabulous. I told David you'd be fine with it – he seemed to think you had some grudge against him and would kick up a fuss. I didn't want things to be weird between us but he really is something special – and he's been ever so useful for my business – knows everyone. Lucky for me that he got fired, really – they really didn't appreciate him. Still, it seems like any idiot can try to run a company nowadays.'

Lucy hadn't known David was out of work, and briefly wondered what he'd done to lose his job before suddenly deciding that she didn't really care. She didn't need to know what was going on in his life – she'd dedicated enough of her time to him already. Now he was Elle's problem . . . 'I might even make him my partner,' Elle said. 'I mean, he's very connected – spends half his time hanging out with bankers.'

Lucy noticed an avaricious glint in her eye and wondered how much of Elle wanted David for himself and how much of it was about how useful he was to her. Perhaps that was just what he needed?

She made her excuses as soon as she'd collected her goodie bag. As she left she noticed Elle blowing David a kiss and saw him smile back at her in a way he clearly thought was suave but actually made him look creepy. 'The more things change, the more they stay the same,' she thought. Now, more than ever before, she realised she was truly free of David's hold over her. 'David and Elle,' she thought. 'Perhaps everyone gets what they deserve in the end.'

Things had been changing at work too. Anna had started giving her more responsibility as soon as she'd come clean about Brendan, and Lucy was becoming increasingly confident that a promotion was imminent. However, she didn't feel particularly enthusiastic about it. Now the carrot Anna was waving at her was one she didn't really want, her desire to prove herself was fading.

The office was a certainly a lot better without Caitlin and Brendan around, and she'd been spending more time with Annabel, who was full of great ideas – and fun – but Lucy's heart just wasn't in convincing people to buy dog grooming products. Or even beauty products for humans: she couldn't understand what half of them were supposed to do and most of them seemed to be advertised by convincing women they were ugly in some new way. She didn't need to save the world, but she liked the idea of at least putting a bit more joy into it – of doing something she believed in.

She'd realised this when indulging in an *Orange is the New Black* marathon on Monday night, in an effort to take her mind off Ben. In that moment, she decided that she wasn't going to do overtime any more. She'd been trapped in a cage of her own making for long enough. Now it was time to do what *she* wanted, and that didn't include long nights in the office.

She'd decided to be as dedicated in her mission to find fun as she had been to work – not least because it provided her with a distraction from thinking about Ben. There were only so many times she could go over the same thing in her head and it was emotionally exhausting. Deciding to start as she meant to go on, she went to the corner shop, picked up all the listings magazines she could find and spent the night filling her diary with new things to try and do over the coming month: open lectures, art launches, comedy recordings, walking tours, mixology demonstrations – it was amazing how many free things there were to do when you looked for them.

As the week progressed, Lucy found it easier than she'd expected to leave work on time, particularly with so many exciting plans. She'd never seen before how much of Caitlin's workload she'd taken on, and now that she was only responsible for her own workload she didn't need to stay late. It seemed clear now it had been partly down to her own hard work that Caitlin had had such a great reputation. Perhaps Lucy had been better than she'd thought all along, and Caitlin's superiority had come from insecurity rather than talent?

Still, she'd learned from Caitlin too. OK, her makeover wasn't the greatest success but it *had* helped Anna notice her. She'd been offered a promotion after one lunchtime of shopping when over a year of working late had failed. It had taught her a lot, too. Even though she'd thought it was what she wanted, seeing how easy it was to fit in by wearing the 'right' clothes had been one of the things that had made her recognise how disillusioned she was with marketing: it was just so shallow.

She'd fallen into her job – it seemed to fit with her English degree and events background well enough, and the lifestyle had looked glamorous from the outside. She'd wanted to make her parents proud with regular promotions, but of course her mum just wanted her to be happy and would be proud of her whatever she did. Lucy knew that now, after their conversation about David, and wondered why she'd doubted it before.

She didn't want to waste any more time on other people's dreams. Work filled a lot of time – she only had one life and she didn't want to spend a third of it doing something that left her feeling empty inside. She wanted to feel the same passion for work as Ben did – or Rosie, or Jo. If only she could figure out what made her feel that excited – other than Ben, of course. Lucy had been trapped in her false ambitions for a long time. She needed to work out what she really wanted to do with her life. What made her feel good?

Without Caitlin around, Lucy needed someone new to bounce ideas around with – particularly with her increased responsibilities – and she found herself calling on Annabel. She might not have been in the industry for long but she was incredibly savvy with social media and Lucy found herself learning lots – while teaching Annabel too.

The more they chatted, the more Lucy discovered how much they had in common: they liked the same books, were addicted to the same box sets and both enjoyed crafting, though Annabel preferred crochet whereas Lucy felt more comfortable knitting. Annabel had been travelling before she started at BAM! and as she told stories of the places she'd been, the way she'd worked her way around the world at bars and fruit farms, taking photos in clubs or simply trading work for a roof over her head, Lucy was impressed by her pragmatism as well as her sense of adventure: and more than a little curious about exploring the world for herself.

Lucy had tried to keep her mind on the job but she found it sexy spending time with someone so enthusiastic and bubbling with ideas. Was she bisexual? Lucy hardly felt the bi-curious label fitted her any more – she knew what it was like to be with a woman. But she was automatically more drawn to men than women – and her attraction to Annabel had more to do with her personality than her gender. OK, she'd originally been drawn to Annabel's curves – and curls – but now the reason she wanted to get to know her better was because Annabel was funny, clever and a good listener. All the things that she found attractive in men.

Whatever the right label was, Lucy felt like they had unfinished business. With all the fuss about Brendan, she'd paid Annabel less attention than she should have done. She at least needed Annabel to know she'd enjoyed the experience, even if it had just been an intoxicated moment of lust.

Lucy needed to talk to Annabel about the Brendan situation anyway – let her know what Anna had said. It was great justification for getting together outside the office. What happened from then depended on what Annabel wanted to happen – but Lucy didn't see anything wrong with providing a situation that was conducive to her own desires.

She wanted to be a long way from the prying eyes of their colleagues, particularly as Brendan still came into their work local to get drunk with his ex-colleagues. There was a place she remembered reading about near Embankment Tube, Gordon's – an old bar that hadn't been changed for over a hundred years. She'd seen some photos of it – all dusty brick walls and dark candlelit booths – that looked perfect for a clandestine meeting. They could also get food there. After her last experience with Annabel, she didn't want to end up getting too drunk with her; particularly as they had more of a working relationship now. She mentioned it to Annabel and was gratified – and a little excited – when she said she could make it after work on Friday. 'I've heard about that place – oldest wine bar in London, isn't it? I do like taking in a bit of culture. And it'll be nice to get away from this place.'

And so it was that the pair came to be sitting opposite each other, tucked away in one of the darkest corners of Gordon's, out of the sight of other customers. It was a quiet night, possibly due to the rain. A wine bottle dripping with wax held a candle giving flickering light that made Annabel look particularly beautiful, Lucy thought. But she had to focus on work. She ran through the drug situation with Anna quickly, and gave Annabel time to think while she went to the bar to order a bottle of wine and jug of water.

When she got back, Annabel looked up at her.

'I'm going to talk to Anna about Brendan. He really has been a wanker.'

She spilled out a story that made Lucy glad Brendan had lost his job. Apparently he was married – something he kept quiet in the office. Lucy hadn't known, despite working with him for years. He'd hit on Annabel as soon as she started at the company, without telling her about his wife. He'd done everything he could to impress her – buying her presents, leaving her sweet notes in her desk drawer. She'd only found out about his wife after she'd started to fall for him.

'I know it was wrong but he said they hadn't had sex for ages – said she never tried anything new and I was so exciting. It's one of the reasons we'd been talking about threesomes and doing Mandy together – I knew his wife would never do something like that and I wanted to show him why he should be with me instead. Sorry – I guess I used you a bit. I did think you were sexy though – still do.'

Lucy felt pleased that Annabel had been open with her. She didn't feel used – she'd learned a lot from the night with Brendan and Annabel too. It hadn't just been about her bowing to peer pressure. OK, the drink had affected her judgement but she'd wanted Annabel – had been curious about what it would be like to properly be with a woman, ever since the unsatisfactory threesome with David. They'd given her the perfect excuse to experiment.

She'd wanted to see what the fuss was about drugs too: she didn't want her experience with David to be the first thing that sprang to mind when the topic came up. She wanted to replace the memory with something less traumatic, more exciting – and to a degree it had worked, even if it was tainted by the subsequent fallout.

Although Annabel really didn't seem remotely traumatised, as her questioning hand on Lucy's thigh clearly indicated.

'I don't regret what happened with us, you know. I just feel stupid for falling for the same old married-man bullshit again. When you told me he'd been bragging about what we'd done it showed me that Brendan didn't care about me. He just wanted some young woman to help him live out a mid-life crisis. And that isn't going to be me. Women are much sexier anyway.' Annabel moved her fingertips slightly upwards. Lucy put her hand on top of Annabel's, a flirtatious smile playing around the corner of her lips. She felt seductive – or was she being seduced? As Annabel moved her other hand to Lucy's face and ran her fingers from cheekbone to clavicle, it was hard to tell who was in control.

'Just to be clear, I don't want a relationship or anything,' Annabel said. 'But you turn me on.'

Lucy thought for a second. Did she really want to do this? What about work? Ben?

Annabel licked her full lips, making them glisten, and Lucy's desire overpowered her doubts.

She looked into Annabel's eyes and moved her chair closer, wanting to be as near as she could before she leaned forward to kiss her. Annabel's lips parted as soon as she felt Lucy's mouth meet hers and her tongue flickered out, sliding over and then between Lucy's lips.

Annabel's breath was coming faster now and Lucy knew she had to touch her – feel her pussy swelling and wetness building, smell her scent. She slid her hand under Annabel's hemline and up her thigh aggressively, but stopped as she reached the edge of her knickers.

'Do you want this?' she whispered, pulling back from the kiss a little.

Annabel nodded, murmured ,'Oh, yes,' and draped

her coat over her lap to give Lucy more room to manoeuvre in privacy.

Lucy let her fingers roam, teasing at first, just underneath her knicker elastic, running up and down until Annabel gave a frustrated whimper and pushed herself forward into Lucy's hands. At this, she increased her efforts, pulling Annabel's knickers to one side and rubbing three fingers over her slit, feeling that she was already wet. She moved carefully, softly, caressing Annabel's clit and pubic mound, running up and down her labia and edging slowly towards her entrance, only sliding a finger inside when Annabel pushed her hips forwards again.

Lucy let her thumb slide up to rub Annabel's full clitoris as her finger circled inside her vagina, pushing deeper, finding the sensitive areas that swelled to her touch. Annabel was rocking along with her movement, trying to be discreet but unable to hide the arousal building inside her.

Taking a quick glance over her shoulder to check they were still unobserved, and feeling reassured they were still out of anyone's eye-shot, Lucy moved her fingers from Annabel's pussy and brought them to her own lips, tasting the sticky juices. If she was really honest, the fact they were in public was a turn-on. Not that she wanted to get caught, but there was certainly something sexy about getting away with doing exactly what she wanted – and Annabel wanted too, if her flushed cheeks and dilated pupils were anything to go by.

She wished she could bend down, savour Annabel's sweet taste directly from the source, but there was such a thing as going too far – and she knew she was only moments away from making her come with her fingers. She licked them and said, 'You're delicious,' before moving them back down to Annabel's pussy, sliding two fingers inside her now, and spreading them apart slightly as her fingertips found her G-spot.

Lucy's thumb kept up its steady movement on Annabel's clit, well lubricated with her saliva, and the dual pleasure was soon making Annabel press against her hand, muscles clamping ever more tightly around Lucy's fingers.

Lucy grabbed Annabel's hair and pulled it back, kissing her deeply, and was rewarded with a rush of juices shooting down her wrist. She kept her hand still, holding it in place until she was sure Annabel was sated.

As Annabel sighed, 'God, thank you,' Lucy brought her hand back and tasted her climax. But when Annabel started moving her own hand up Lucy's thigh, sliding towards her centre, Lucy lightly gripped her wrist.

'Don't worry about me. You've already given me enough pleasure by letting me touch you.'

It was true, but there was more to it than that. Although she'd spent time fantasising about what she and Annabel could get up to if they were together again, now Lucy felt as if the situation was balanced – not because she'd owed Annabel anything after their previous encounter but because it had been interrupted. After experiencing the bliss of feeling Annabel's release, she was satisfied – and felt slightly guilty.

In another world, she could imagine herself taking things a lot further with Annabel. But in this universe Lucy wasn't available. It would feel like cheating on Ben. She might be able to give pleasure to other people, but until she knew once and for all that there was no chance of her and Ben being together, she didn't want to give herself to anyone but him – it seemed like a breach of their intimacy. She knew it was stupid but she couldn't help the way that she felt.

Lucy couldn't deny how beautiful Annabel looked, eyes glistening and skin still pink after her orgasm. But she was relieved that she wasn't looking for a relationship: it made everything so much easier. And meant she wouldn't feel bad about reliving the experience on her own with her toy later.

Yes, being on her own was what she needed right now. But in the meantime, 'Fancy something to eat?' she asked Annabel, reaching for a menu from the centre of the table. 'The platters they do here are supposed to be amazing. And I am feeling rather hungry all of a sudden.'

'Sounds good to me,' said Annabel. 'So tell me, if we talk about work do we get to expense it?'

Lucy smiled. 'Do you know, I think we've already got a lot of valuable work done tonight – we should definitely expense it. And buy the clients we're entertaining an after-dinner whisky perhaps?'

'I like your style,' said Annabel.

After Lucy's Friday night with Annabel, she spent the weekend alone, thinking about her way forward. She felt as if she was in limbo. She wasn't happy where she was – but she didn't know where she wanted to go either. All she knew was that she had to work it out for herself.

Monday morning rolled around all too soon for Lucy. It was now eight days since she'd seen Ben, and she still couldn't get him out of her head. She saw more clearly than ever how important he had become to her. Although desire had been there from day one, after their midnight feast on the sleeper train and spending the day working together she'd felt a real intimacy between them: created through shared meals, adventures and, of course, the amazing sex. She might not have felt him inside her but there was no way she could describe what they'd done as anything other than sex – and some of the best of her life. She'd felt so connected to him, as if she was part of him – even the massage he'd given her was more intimate than some of the half-hearted proddings she'd experienced in the past. She felt a tug from her heart to her pussy at the memory of Ben's touch.

She'd changed in so many ways since she'd met him, and now Lucy felt as if she was being more true to herself than she'd ever been before. But Ben hadn't seen the whole story. He'd taken the most critical possible view of her when, in reality, the truth was more complex.

Which is why it was taking her a while to work out exactly what she should do, how she really felt about the events of the last few weeks and what, if anything, she would say to Ben if they ever spoke again. She'd spent all week fighting the urge to phone him – get on a train to Brighton, even, but she knew it wasn't right for her to do so. If she saw him, even though she was desperate to make things right between them and take things to the next level if she could, she knew she'd end up asking him for advice.

She'd admitted that to herself now, though it had taken her a few days of contemplation to accept it.

Somehow, since she'd met Ben, she'd come to value his opinion. With hindsight, she could see how he'd been gently steering her way, encouraging her to relax, think about what she wanted and live her life, rather than just existing. For the first time ever, she knew she didn't need to put on an act to be liked.

Some might say he was controlling, but she was sure he had the best intentions: his manipulation had benefited her far more than him, after all. He'd shown her the joy to be had in putting her own needs first, helping her see that she was living a life that no longer fitted. He'd helped her accept who she really was – and recognise the mistakes she'd been making. She'd faced up to things she should have confronted a long time ago, and in doing so lost the guilt she'd been carrying round for so long, weighing her down and holding her back.

Even though they'd only met a few times, each time was a memory: of laughter, play and passion. She replayed their encounters in her mind. The romantic adventures, the small kindnesses Ben had shown her, the way his body felt pressed against her – and the way he'd touched her. She wanted to keep the memories alive, even though it hurt to think they might be all she had of Ben now, if he couldn't see past his harsh judgement of her.

Yes, Lucy thought, she might have been trying to fit in with other people, but she'd also been following her dream – even if it was one she now knew she didn't want to make come true. She might have made some mistakes but she'd learned from every one of them. And hadn't Ben told her she should live life for the moment? That's what she'd been doing since she met him. Life had certainly been more fun: assignations in showers, boats and star-lit gardens. A smiled flitted over her lips, vanishing rapidly as she remembered she might never see him again.

As she logged on to her computer, Lucy turned off her mobile. She had a lot of work to be getting on with, and she could feel her willpower crumbling. If her phone was off, it would make it harder for her to call Ben.

She turned it back on when she got home, and when it rang at 10 p.m. she felt a flash of worry. Was someone hurt? She didn't usually get calls at this time. Picking it up, she saw Ben's name and answered it rapidly.

'Hello?'

'Lucy, hi. Is it too late for you? Sorry, I only noticed the time after I'd pressed the button.'

'It's fine, Ben. I was just about to have a bath. Long time no hear.' Lucy's voice came out sounding a little brittle, but she couldn't deny to herself that she was happy to hear from him.

'I know. I'm sorry. There's been a lot going on. But you were right. And I'm sorry.'

'What do you mean?'

'After we saw each other last week, I was furious with you. All I've ever tried to do is look after Clare and there you were telling me it was my fault she was such a mess.'

'I'm sorry: I was drunk,' said Lucy, tempted to correct him and point out it was nine days but worried she'd sound desperate.

'Not as drunk as I was. Family trait, I guess.' Ben laughed wryly. 'So, Clare ended up getting back to her old tricks. She'd only been at my folks' for four days when she decided she was bored and wanted to go out partying. And she really went for it.'

'Is she OK?' Lucy asked.

'Kind of – although she hates me right now. She ended up getting into one of her usual messes – arrested for being drunk and disorderly – not for the first time. She called me, trying to get me to bail her out.'

'Shit.'

'She wanted me to get the train up. I told her I didn't have that kind of time to spare – she knows how much work I've got on at the moment. I told her I couldn't.'

'How did she take that?'

'Not well – told me I might be golden boy to Mum and Dad but I was the worst brother in the world. She really let rip. Even told me it was my fault she got sent away to boarding school – not that she was making much sense. She didn't have long on the phone. She was shouting at me when we got cut off.'

'So what did you do?' asked Lucy. She couldn't believe Ben had actually stood up to Clare.

'I was going to call Dad, tell him what was going on and get him to bail her out, but then I remembered what you'd said. I knew she'd end up yelling at me if I got the family involved and as she was locked up, she was safe enough. I thought a night in the cells might be good for her – make her face up to what she was doing to herself. So I left her to it. It wasn't the easiest night's sleep I've ever had but it's not like the local police station is the scariest place in the world to be. Though I don't think Clare particularly wants to go back there.'

'Have you spoken to her since then?'

'No, she's refused to speak to me since she came out. Mum told me. She's been a bit of a legend, really – the police called her the next day and she sorted everything out. Hasn't told Dad about it yet. Mum called me after she'd picked Clare up – I think she let slip I knew more about what she'd been going through than I'd been letting on. And she made Clare a deal – she'd keep everything from Dad if Clare really focussed on sorting herself out. Clare's so terrified of spoiling Dad's image of her it's one of the few things that scares her. Mum's made her start clearing through her old stuff too, selling it on eBay to cover her rent, until she can sort herself out with some work. Mum said Clare was a bit sulky about it but she's doing as she's told, for now at least. And she says she thinks Clare will give me a call soon. Apparently, she's been talking about me quite a lot – she thought Mum and Dad wanted me more than her and that's why they sent her away to school. Mum set her straight, of course, but it's horrible to think she's felt that way for so long. And if it hadn't been for you, we might never have found out. I guess that's why I'm calling – to say thank you. And to see if you'd like to meet up? I know we haven't had the greatest of starts but what you said made so much sense. I just hadn't been able to see it before. I'm sorry I got so cross – you helped me see things in a whole new way.'

'I feel the same,' admitted Lucy. 'I was furious when you told me I was trying to please everyone but myself, that I was a liar. But you were right. I thought I was following my dream but in reality I was just trying to show that I was doing "adulthood" in the right way. You've made me want to be myself.'

'That's what I like about you, Lucy. So would you like to meet?'

There was only one possible answer she could give.

First thing on Tuesday morning, Lucy emailed Anna asking if she could book some time off the following week. She decided she needed a proper break, where she didn't have to worry about anything: and she wanted to give her social life the attention it deserved, particularly now she'd found so many fun things to do.

Even though she'd only just been away, it had hardly been of her own volition. The end of the holiday year was coming soon too, and she didn't want to end up losing it like she had last year. Days didn't carry forward and when she asked about pay in lieu, Anna always brushed it away. Lucy knew money was tight at the agency – particularly after losing two senior staff in rapid succession – but the least she deserved was a holiday on her own terms, when she wanted to take it. She was pleasantly surprised to receive an approval form in her inbox later that day.

Ben had suggested meeting in Borough Market. His pop-up plans were progressing, and Borough was a key part of it. As it was near Lucy's flat, it was convenient for her too. She called him on Thursday night to confirm the details, and they arranged to meet on Saturday morning at Roast, where Ben proposed treating her to breakfast.

'It seems to be something you like doing,' said Lucy.

'But you're very good at it so I'm not going to complain. What time?'

They agreed on eleven, so they could both start the day with a lie-in.

'I've got next week off to sort my head out,' she told him. 'May as well start with a good night's sleep.'

'What are you going to do?'

'Whatever feels right. Starting with meeting you at Borough Market. If it's OK with you, I'd rather we didn't plan anything beyond breakfast,' she said. 'I'd prefer to just go with the flow.' She knew she wanted to have an adventure with Ben – but this time, she wanted him to be free-falling as much as she was. This week was all about seeing what happened when she abandoned control and did what felt right.

'What's happened to the Lucy I first met?' Ben laughed. 'No lists? Fine by me though. See you at eleven on Saturday – and after breakfast, who knows . . .'

Lucy remembered the way he said that as she drifted off to sleep that night. She had to use her Doxy to give herself respite from the craving that was getting stronger every day: the taste of Ben had been enough to convince her that she wanted to sample more.

She enjoyed the anticipation, feeling a quiet excitement underlying everything she did the next day. Several people commented she was walking with more of a bounce in her step than usual, but Lucy simply smiled and kept the reason for her happiness to herself.

* * *

Lucy had never seen a breakfast like it. Sitting in the relaxing surroundings of Roast, she could see why Ben had chosen it. They proudly promoted British produce and the menu made it hard to choose just one thing. Ben had told her to order whatever she wanted, and Lucy had done exactly that.

She was sipping on monkey-picked tea – the rarest in the world according to the menu – while Ben had opted for a pot of organic roast coffee that wafted its delicious aroma temptingly in her direction.

Lucy's plate held perfectly scrambled eggs topped with smoked trout, a glass of Buck's Fizz making her feel decadent. The smell from Ben's plate was making her mouth water, too. It was loaded with more meat than she'd ever imagined seeing on a breakfast plate: bacon and sausages, black pudding and haggis, and a golden potato scone topped by two perfectly cooked fried eggs. A grilled mushroom and tomato tried in vain to make the plate look healthy but the Scottish breakfast was undoubtedly a love story to pork.

'Would you like to try some?' Ben asked, putting together a forkful without waiting for her answer. Lucy leaned forwards and opened her mouth, looking him in the eye as he slid the fork between her lips. She groaned at the heavenly explosion of salt, fat and spice, perfectly undercut by the sliver of tomato.

She nodded appreciatively, eyes half-closed, and happily accepted a second forkful, loving the potato scone, dripping with egg yolk. But she declined a third taster – her scrambled eggs were deliciously creamy, and the trout was perfectly smoky. She wanted to enjoy it – and she didn't want to get egg yolk down her cashmere top.

She'd thought it only apt to wear the jumper Ben had bought her – though she'd teamed it with a flippy tweed skirt, along with the Victorian boots. The weather was looking up, and the way the skirt moved around her thighs as she walked made her feel playful – as did the brown fishnet tights she was wearing over sheer skin-toned tights, a trick she'd learned from Ben's burlesque friends. She'd felt like a small child on Christmas Eve ever since their breakfast had been arranged. It felt as if it was a first date – which it was, really. They hadn't planned anything together before, Ben's midnight feast aside. The day spread out ahead of them like a treat.

After breakfast, Ben suggested a breakfast cocktail, in the form of an Earl Grey Martini. It was hedonistic, thought Lucy. But her breakfast had been filling, and the idea of doing the crossword with Ben while sipping a cocktail had a certain appeal. She wasn't sure which she preferred between her Earl Grey cocktail or the Espresso Martini Ben opted for, but it was a thoroughly civilised start to the day.

Pleasantly floaty, their breakfast warming them from within, they wandered around the stalls of Borough Market. Lucy was glad she'd eaten because otherwise she'd have been torn as to where to look, what to choose. The stalls held the contents for the picnic of her dreams.

Dried salami and rounds of cheese, roast vegetables and loaves of rustic bread; Danish pastries glistening with apricots, raspberry-swirled meringues, and trays of sweet and savoury titbits; Turkish Delight and succulent barbecued meats; aromatic pies and fantastical fruit: everywhere she looked offered Lucy a feast for the senses and it didn't take long before she was tempted into trying some of the wonders that surrounded her. She'd thought she'd never be able to eat again after her breakfast but they'd drunk their Martinis at a leisurely pace so it was a while since she'd eaten now, and the delicious smells were too much to resist.

Ben encouraged her, and soon they were arguing over which cheese was the creamiest, which terrine would be the best one to eat with walnut bread and which kind of syrup would be best for drizzling over each other's bodies.

The breakfast Martinis had made both of them a little flirtier than usual and, as a result, it hadn't just been Lucy's taste buds that had been tingling. Feeling Ben's arm around her as they wandered, the way his hands playfully squeezed her given the slightest chance, made Lucy want him more. She enjoyed his company, and found herself laughing more than she had with anyone else before – his sense of humour was a perfect mesh with hers – but there was only so long she could look without touching.

He was at his best surrounded by food: his eyes shone with passion and there was no way she could help being carried along with him. She willingly opened her mouth for every tempting morsel he proffered, even tasting oysters for the first time. She'd always been squeamish about them before, but when Ben bought her one, squeezed lemon over it and held it up to her lips saying, 'Swallow it down in one,' she didn't want to refuse him and was pleasantly surprised by the fresh taste of the sea exploding over her tongue. Ben was clearly delighted with her obvious pleasure. She could understand his enthusiasm about Borough Market – the food was genuinely exciting and she relished the diversity of flavours as they decided what to have for their lunch.

Lucy had come up with the idea of a picnic after teasing Ben about his lack of hamper. 'I thought it was your man bag. I can't believe you've left it at home when you knew we were coming here.'

'You told me not to plan anything beyond breakfast though,' said Ben. 'I was just doing as I was told.'

Lucy looked at Ben to see if he was teasing but, though his eyes twinkled, the respect in them was clear to see.

'I appreciate that,' she said. 'Now, what sort of thing do you fancy for our picnic? Some sort of platter, or would you rather grab something hot nearer the time?'

'I'm all for grabbing something hot,' said Ben, giving Lucy a lingering glance. 'But I need to work up a bit of an appetite first . . .' The flirtation was clear in his voice. 'Fancy a walk down to the river? It's not far from here.'

Lucy liked the idea of wandering along to the South Bank – she often stood and looked at the Thames, taking in the view. There was something relaxing about staring into water, letting your thoughts drift with the current. The idea of enjoying the view with Ben made her even happier – particularly because there were a lot of quiet alleyways along the way.

And suddenly she knew exactly what she wanted to be doing. 'Sounds good to me,' she said, and they started working their way through the market, still stopping for the occasional nibble but moving with intent. It was as if Ben could sense her desire and as they turned down a quiet road, he grabbed her hand, pulled her into a doorway and spun her into a kiss. It was hard and passionate, but tender, making Lucy's knees weak.

She moved her arms around his neck and leaned back against the door frame for support as he slid his hands under her buttocks, lifting her off the floor and pressing her against him. Lucy jumped up and wrapped her legs around him, needing to feel him closer as the kiss became more passionate and his cock became harder, pressing temptingly against her. Her pelvis ground against his and his shaft rubbed deliciously against her clit.

Ben's hands squeezed her bum hard, cupping and parting her cheeks under her skirt, making her feel as if he wanted to rip her tights off there and then, and was only holding back because she hadn't given him the signal.

Lucy had no such qualms. She'd been waiting for long enough: it was time. She reached for his fly and undid the first button. It was difficult to get at, and he had to help her, but once it was released all four buttons popped open at once and Ben's cock was revealed – he was going commando. Lucy felt her pussy warm at the thought – and knew that she had to have him now. There was no time to think about it. She wanted him inside her.

Until now, she'd been worried about exactly how things would pan out when they took things further: OK, he'd seen her naked, and they'd come together, but that was different. In her experience, men were happy enough to stick around until they got to 'last base' – but most lost interest afterwards. It was one of the reasons she'd put up with David for so long: at least he didn't vanish out of the door as soon as he'd got what he wanted. But now, slightly fuzzy around the edges, after a morning spent flirting with Ben, her worries were overwhelmed by her desire. Ben had encouraged her to live for the moment – and that was exactly what she intended to do.

'I did do a little pre-planning,' she murmured in his ear, reaching into her bag and handing him a condom. He looked at her, surprised but delighted.

'Here?' he said.

'If you don't mind being quick about it. It's pretty

quiet at this time of day – and if I do this, all you have to do is slide inside me.'

Lucy reached down and ripped a hole in her tights, easily tearing through the fishnet and using her fingernail to break through the sheer nylon below. Like Ben, she was going commando. She tore along the seam until she was exposed enough for Ben's needs – and her own – looked at him provocatively and then leaned against the door frame. 'I've been wet for most of the morning – you're so sexy when you talk about food. And now I'm hungry. You?'

'Hell, yes,' said Ben. 'You are the sexiest woman I have ever met.' He slid the condom on and turned her to face away from him, kissing her shoulder as he did, before pressing his cock against her, stroking her clit with it from behind, lubricating it with her juices. Lucy loved feeling his warmth against her skin but now wasn't the time for slow, sensual foreplay. She wanted to fuck. And she wanted it now.

'Please,' Lucy said, moving her hips in a way that left Ben in no doubt as to what she wanted.

He pressed the head of his cock to her entrance, groaning as Lucy rotated her pelvis in response. He gripped her hips as she slowly started pushing back, still circling, urging him to slide deeper inside her. She wanted him to move faster, but he stilled her pace with his strong hands, making it clear he wasn't going to rush, no matter where they were.

Lucy was moaning now, and Ben slipped his fingers

between her lips, helping her swallow back the scream she wanted to release. His other hand had moved from his cock round to her pussy and he rubbed her clit as he finally thrust into her, again and again and again, but slowly enough that she could feel the shape of his cock head as he opened her up and she welcomed him in.

Her body had been primed for him since the moment their date had been arranged. Although she'd masturbated about him, it was nothing compared to feeling his weight against her as he slid his perfect cock in and out of her, his trembling body making it clear he was holding himself back for her.

Lucy felt a rush of arousal, knowing that Ben was controlling himself for her pleasure: that he wanted her enough to shake with desire but respected her enough to put her needs first. But she didn't want sensitivity right now – she wanted pounding, hard and fast.

She put her hands on top of his and moved them to cup her breasts, starting to buck her hips back hard against him before he could slow her moves once more. She wanted him as deep as it was possible for him to go – and from the way his cock stiffened inside her, stretching her further, Ben wasn't objecting.

Lucy felt her orgasm rising, her muscles clamping hard around his cock, almost pushing him out of her. He groaned loudly, burying his face in her shoulder to try to muffle the animal noises he seemed unable to contain. As she exploded in orgasm around him, muscles gripping him tightly in rapid spasms, Ben started coming too, pulsing hard inside Lucy, again and again.

They drove each other's orgasm on: just as Lucy thought hers had stopped, Ben would spasm again and push his cock into her in a way that made her body jerk in response.

'Kiss me,' he muttered. 'I want you to kiss me while I'm coming.'

Lucy willingly stretched round as far as she could to feel Ben's lips on hers. She couldn't believe how hard she'd come, how amazing he'd felt inside her. She felt Ben's cock leap inside her again as their lips met and she knew this was just the beginning.

It was only when a car horn went off nearby, reminding them that they were in public, that Ben and Lucy returned to reality. As Ben gave her another kiss, after doing his clothes back up, Lucy wasn't sure she was going to stay there for long. She was on holiday, after all: why bother doing what she did for the rest of the year?

She kissed him back, hard, before taking him by the hand and leading him towards the river. She didn't know where she was taking him – but she was pretty sure he'd enjoy it when they got there.

CHAPTER 8

After a picnic lunch from Borough Market, eaten overlooking the Thames, Ben and Lucy spent the rest of the day laughing, kissing and fondling their way across London; in the dark corners – and the punishment chair at the Clink Museum; on the train from London Bridge to Surrey Quays; and in the floating pub that awaited them there, the Wibbley Wobbley. Lucy had read about it when searching for fun things to do in London and wanted to visit for the name alone. She was glad she had – they'd found a quiet corner where Ben had taken full advantage of its rocking motion.

He spent the night and the rest of the weekend at her flat, but she forced herself to send him away on Monday morning after a leisurely breakfast. He didn't make it easy for her.

First, he made her eggs Benedict with perfectly poached eggs – he'd effectively been Lucy's personal chef all weekend. He splashed hollandaise all over his T-shirt when he was beating it rather too vigorously and casually threw it into the washing basket, continuing to cook with his shirt off.

When he bent over to put the toast under the grill his

jeans slid down, revealing his lower back and hugging his delicious arse tightly. Lucy was tempted to go up behind him, slide her arms around him and run her hands down to his cock, but all too soon he was standing up again, now chopping herbs so effortlessly that he looked like he should be on TV.

Under a minute later he was buttering the muffins, carving off slices of the ham he'd cooked for dinner on Saturday night, sliding poached eggs off a slotted spoon and pouring creamy sauce over the top. Adding a sprinkling of chives, he passed Lucy her plate with a smile.

It smelled and tasted delicious but it was still hard to eat with Ben's body on display – all she wanted to do was touch him. Lucy could happily spend all day running her hands through the hair on his chest, and indeed for most of Sunday she had done. But she forced herself to focus on breakfast instead – it was too good to let it go cold.

They lingered over coffee, but when Ben suggested doing the crossword from Sunday's paper Lucy regretfully told him, 'I really need to get on with my week. I'm going to have to kick you out soon.'

'Do you really need me to go?' Ben asked. 'I could always stay for another day . . .' Appealing as the idea of more time with Ben was, Lucy needed thinking time without anyone else to influence her. That's why she'd taken the time off work. When he was around, there was only one thing she could think about.

'I've got too much to do – loads of life admin to sort. I'm meeting with STA Travel later too.'

'Going on holiday?'

The weekend hadn't really involved much talking: flirting, yes; and talking dirty but, for the main, communication had been kept at a more base level.

'Maybe,' she said. 'I thought I'd see what they had on offer – explore all my options. Even with accommodation, some of the trips look like they might be cheaper than London rent and I figured if Rachel can live on six grand a year and travel the world, why can't I? It's not like nine to five is the only way to live.'

'What's happened to the diligent Lucy I met?' Ben laughed.

'She realised life is for living,' said Lucy. 'Which is partly down to you.'

'And yet you don't want me to hang around . . .'

Ben had cleared away the plates, and stood behind Lucy's chair. He leaned over to kiss her neck, running his hands slowly down her body as he did so. Lucy felt her nipples stiffen under her sheer white oversized T-shirt.

'You are irresistible,' he whispered. His hands roamed further down, sliding between her thighs, before grabbing them and spreading them apart. A whimper caught in Lucy's throat.

'If I'm going, the least I can do is give you something to remember me by,' he said.

'You've already done that.' Lucy laughed.

But she didn't complain as he effortlessly lifted the

chair up, with her still in it, and turned it round so that she was sitting in front of him, thighs parted, ready for him to kneel in front of her.

Ben pushed up her T-shirt, though it was only just skimming the top of her thighs. He looked directly between her legs, his scrutiny making Lucy feel self-conscious – and horny.

'I can't wait to taste you,' he said, leaning forward, putting his hands underneath her bum and pulling her towards the edge of the chair.

'Thank you for this weekend.' He used the fingers of one hand to spread her labia, leaned in and softly kissed her clitoris, which twitched in response. Putting his lips to her entrance, he slid his tongue inside her. It felt as if he was French kissing her pussy rather than just going down on her. Lucy's muscles kissed him back, responding to his tongue's delicate touch.

Ben pulled away, slightly breathless.

'I love your pussy so much,' he said, looking her straight in the eye, pupils dilated and face wet, before returning to kiss her again.

By now, Lucy could feel her wetness starting to trickle over her labia and, as Ben dived in again, down her thighs. She abandoned herself to the soft touch of his tongue, let her pussy dance around it, just feeling, giving herself over to sensation.

Ben's hands wandered over her skin, worshipfully caressing her as he made love to her with his mouth. His hands circled her belly and her breasts, tracing concentric circles that got smaller and smaller until he was finally touching her nipples – which burned at his touch, so sensitised were the nerves. As he started to gently roll them between his fingers, running the underside of his tongue over the tip of her clit, Lucy couldn't fight the orgasm that rippled through her body – and she didn't want to. It started at her centre and spread through her stomach, chest and throat until finally her whole body was shaking and spasming as she came hard in Ben's face, lost in sensation as her orgasm shook her to her core.

Ben stayed where he was, stilling his movements as her orgasm peaked and then calmed. When he finally pulled away, he leaned down to give her clit another gentle kiss.

'You are amazing,' he said.

'Come here.' Lucy pulled him up her body to kiss her. Wanting to feel her skin against his while her orgasm still lingered, she ripped her T-shirt off over her head. When she felt Ben's cock running over her stomach, leaving a trail of pre-cum in its wake and scenting her with his desire, she wanted to taste him. She kissed him, hard, hungry, and shivered as his chest hair brushed against her nipples.

'Stand up,' she said.

Ben did as he was told. Where Lucy sat her head was now level with his cock, which was twitching in anticipation.

'I love your cock,' she said, deliberately echoing him as she leaned to kiss its tip. He groaned.

She slid her left hand under his balls and softly cupped and stroked them, feeling the skin tighten at her touch. Her right hand grasped the base of his cock and she held him in position as she bent to take the head in her mouth, keeping her mouth as wide open as she could and her lips soft so that Ben could feel her warmth but not the friction he must be craving.

Lucy looked up into Ben's eyes as she tilted her head back and gradually took more and more of his shaft in her mouth, allowing her tongue to play over it on occasion, but deliberately keeping the stimulation light and sensual. Her hand still stroked his balls and Ben's cock stiffened in her mouth.

Slowly she took Ben deep into her throat. When she tightened her muscles to swallow over the head of his cock, he gave three heavy breaths out.

'Fuck, Lucy, that's . . .' Ben's words trailed off as Lucy started to suck him, sliding her mouth right to the base of his cock. She was still looking up at him, keeping the line of her throat straight to take in as much of his cock as possible.

Now she sped up her movements, head bobbing up and down as one hand teased his balls and the other stroked and pulsed around his shaft, well lubricated by saliva. She smiled up at Ben as she slid her mouth to the base of his cock once more, sticking her tongue out to lick his balls, repeating the movement once, twice, three times.

She felt Ben's muscles tense and he gasped, 'Get

ready, I'm going to come.' He filled her mouth and she swallowed fast, but there was still too much for her and it trickled between her lips and down her neck. His cock spasmed again and again, encouraged by the finger Lucy was pressing into him, just behind his balls.

She gently sucked his cock until it started to soften in her mouth, and then pulled away, looking into Ben's eyes.

'I love the taste of your come,' she said.

'I love you tasting it.'

He sat down and patted his lap. 'Come here.' She sat and they cuddled for a while, basking in a post-orgasmic glow.

After making a cup of tea, Lucy regretfully said, 'I really need to get dressed and make a start on my day.'

'I think you've made a pretty good start already. Are you sure you really want me to go?' Ben said.

'I do, and don't start any of that nonsense again,' she replied, as he started kissing her neck.

'Go on, drink your tea and get out of here before I change my mind. I've got a lot of stuff to sort – on my own. And I know what will happen if I try to take a shower while you're still here.'

It was still half an hour before Lucy could bring herself to stop kissing Ben and finally get him out of the door.

Once he'd gone, she did feel a sense of relief. Even though it had been hard to ignore her animal urges, it was nice to be the one pushing him away, rather than vice versa. She felt more in control of the situation: he'd held all the cards until now, through his absence. Now he was waiting for her to fit him in.

Lucy rubbed at her thighs, which were aching a bit after the weekend's exertion. She needed a long soak in a salt bath – she was aching in ways that sent pleasant visuals flickering through her mind but made her grateful for a little respite. Sex made it so much harder to focus on anything else, even when her body was exhausted and spent.

She needed to work out what she was going to do for the rest of her life – or at least the near future. That wasn't going to happen with Ben wafting his pheromones at her and wandering around the place with those arms, that chest . . .

This thought made Lucy feel horny again, but she was too exhausted even to use her toy. Instead, she distracted herself from Ben's body by thinking about all the sweet things he'd said to her. Now that he'd stopped treating her as if she was his little sister, telling her what to do, he was becoming more romantic by the day. She wasn't sure if she could think of an inch of her body he hadn't praised; he had been exploring pretty thoroughly.

It was no good: she simply couldn't think about Ben without thinking about sex. She busied herself with running a bath, turning the radio on to distract her.

* * *

Distraction was a technique she relied on increasingly as the week progressed. On Wednesday Ben called, saying he had a spare ticket to a Correspondents gig. 'I think you'll like them. They're great to dance to – you haven't seen me dance yet, have you? It's my secret weapon.' His voice was jovial.

'Dance like nobody's watching?' asked Lucy.

'Hell, no – dance like everyone's watching because you know they're going to want to steal your moves. So, you fancy it?'

Lucy did, but she already had plans.

'Sorry, I'm going to a lecture about mythic women – Rosie's taking me. She's doing research for a new collection she's planning based on goddesses, and I thought it sounded interesting.'

'Choosing goddesses over me? Well, if you're already booked up, I guess I'll have to wait. Until . . . ?'

'After Monday,' she said firmly. 'I'll know what's going on one way or another by then. And I definitely want to see you as soon as possible.'

She was no longer insecure about telling Ben how she felt – not now he was so openly appreciative of her.

'Oh, you will,' said Ben. 'As much of me as you want to . . .'

Lucy decided the best way to figure out her passion – aside from Ben – was to start with things she'd always wanted to do. It had worked when she went to Brighton with him, after all. She made a list of places she'd wanted to visit and set out, Oyster card in hand, to visit them: Highgate Cemetery, the Peace Garden in Holland Park, Neasden Temple, the Magic Circle Museum. She didn't have any particular focus – just searched for 'interesting things to do in London' online and jumped down the rabbit hole.

As she gave herself over to leisure and searched for inspiration, she found there were so many beautiful and fascinating places to explore that she wondered why she'd wasted so many of her weekends working. Now, she needed as much time as possible just to fit everything she wanted to into her life – while allowing time to have lie-ins, of course. Exploring took a lot of energy.

She spent the next few days eating and drinking with friends, having long phone catch-ups and making plans with her family, ticking off places on her list, going to exhibitions and cabaret shows, and simply wandering round London, deliberately getting lost and enjoying being alone. She'd got so used to being surrounded by other people that she'd forgotten how much she liked her own company.

She spent hours on Pinterest, searching for pictures of new places to go, new things to do and new recipes to try. Even when her internet went down on Sunday she had lots to keep her busy: reading, drawing, flicking through a craft magazine looking for ideas and simply daydreaming. She'd missed solitude: and to think, she'd wasted so much time being scared of being alone.

She stocked up on luxurious but affordable food: a

packet of smoked salmon scraps, tinned crab, dark chocolate and pots of fresh herbs. She was impressed at how well the latter lasted – almost a week after buying them they weren't just alive, they were thriving. Perhaps she wasn't so bad at gardening after all? She felt a quiet satisfaction using herbs she had grown herself – or at least kept alive. Ben had told her to buy herbs from a plant shop rather than a supermarket and, when she'd seen a herb planter outside a florist, she'd followed his advice.

Lucy enjoyed cooking for herself, making it into a ritual that she was determined to turn into a habit. Breakfast was a drawn-out affair. She began each morning with a glass of juice and coffee, helping her wake up enough to cook: scrambled eggs with smoked salmon, potato rosti with chorizo, baked mushrooms in rosemary butter, bagels with cream cheese and chives – it was a pretty luxurious week.

She explored the internet looking for easy but enjoyable meals and watched some tutorials on YouTube to help hone her cooking skills. She'd tried to turn herself into the perfect housewife to please David; now she was putting her effort into pleasing herself. Within a week she was chopping as effortlessly as Ben had been – though she suspected that was in part down to the knife he'd bought her after realising she only had a paring knife and a bread knife. It felt very different chopping with a good knife – almost meditative, once she'd got the knack of it.

* * *

Lucy felt so much more alive when she was out and about, getting exercise through exploration, and decided she wanted to feel that way more often. She pored over a map of London, looking at how the places she wanted to go connected, and then working out what was feasible on foot. Not only was she getting fitter, but it also helped her see a new side of the city, exploring places she'd never been before. She deliberately left her phone at home on a few occasions, and enjoyed being out of contact with anyone but herself.

She'd spent so much time thinking, and listening to other people. Now it was time for her to start *doing* – as soon as she'd figured out what her next step should be.

Although she still hadn't worked out what she wanted to do with her life, by Friday Lucy felt happier in herself – something that grew with every day that passed. She was having fun, and looked forward to the days ahead, appreciating the small things: being able to wear her snuggliest pyjamas for as long as she wanted, people-watching over a coffee, seeing the trees colouring London with their blossom.

Spring really was in the air. When she'd been aiming for the top at BAM!, she'd felt anxious and guilty all the time. Now Lucy felt light, and free – as if she faced a new beginning. But how long would it last, she wondered? When did freedom become free-fall – and a crash landing? She couldn't put off the future forever.

In the end it was a letter from her landlord that gave Lucy the push she needed. After spending Saturday at

Kew Gardens, she felt more relaxed than she had for years. She came home ready to enjoy another evening of pampering herself, to find a formal-looking envelope on the doormat.

It contained the news that her rent was going to increase by £75 per week. She'd gaped at it in shock. That was a large chunk of her disposable income. She started mentally calculating the things she'd have to cut out from her life, doing a quick sum on the back of an envelope to see how much money would be required just to cover her daily expenditure. By the time she'd added in bills, the figure in front of her had horrified her. It was only marginally less than her wages – even if she got the pay rise she was now certain was on the cards. She'd be working all hours just to exist – and for what?

She'd looked around the flat. It was cosy enough – her fairy lights, candles and disco ball added frivolity to the room and she had a couple of nice pictures. But really, the room itself wasn't all that special. It smelled of damp and she couldn't even have a bath after nine o'clock. On which note – Lucy had checked the time – if she was going to have a decent wallow, she needed to run it now. She didn't want the neighbours to complain, and the bath was one of her favourite places to think.

Lucy didn't get to indulge her 'home spa' fantasies often, or at least she hadn't until this week. Although she was being careful with money, she had allowed herself some small indulgences along with the luxury food to help her make the most of her week off.

She poured her favourite aromatherapy oil into the bath and lit a delicately scented Jo Malone travel candle before she tentatively stepped into the water. It was perfectly hot – which meant she needed to take her time getting in.

Lucy buffed her skin with an exfoliating glove, feeling as though she was getting rid of the past, literally shedding a skin, enjoying the scent of her neroli body wash. She moved on to shaving, though she only gave her bikini line a quick tidy. She'd waxed for David for years, but now she'd decided she liked a more natural look – it made her feel more herself. She wasn't going to waste money on having a stranger pour hot wax over her and rip her hair out any more.

Only when Lucy had enjoyed an indulgent wallow in the flickering candle light, and felt satisfied that her body was exactly as she wanted it, did she let herself think about the issues at hand.

What was she going to do? Where was she going to go? What did she really want? She lay back, closed her eyes and relaxed, letting her mind work its way through her options at a leisurely pace.

By the time she'd finished her bath, she knew what she had to do.

After spending the rest of the weekend thinking about her decision, Lucy was certain she'd made the right choice. It was raining when she left to get the Tube on Monday, but she still smiled. Nothing was going to taint her good mood. She'd woken up feeling refreshed, had sung loudly in the shower, feeling joyful as she slipped into the outfit she'd laid out the night before: a black pencil skirt, cream jumper with vintage collar detailing, jacket with a nipped-in waist and mid-heeled black-and-white two-toned heeled brogues. They were designed for dancing, which perfectly summed up her mood.

Underneath, she wore a present that had arrived in the post from Jo after their chat: a pair of brightly coloured Wonder Woman knickers, with a note reading, 'Put on your Wonder Woman pants and know you're an amazing woman underneath it all, no matter what.' Lucy had laughed out loud – her friend knew how to make her feel good.

The train started moving and Lucy dodged as a woman stumbled into her, coffee in hand. She noticed foam splashing out onto the woman's jacket – thankfully missing her own – and reached into her bag for a tissue. She'd seen a pack covered in bright pink flamingoes when she was wandering around the shops and hadn't been able to resist buying them, because they reminded her of the first time she met Ben. The woman shot her a grateful smile and managed to clean the jacket before the mark took hold.

As Lucy put the tissues back into her bag, her fingers grazed the letter. She'd decided that handing her notice in was the only choice she could make. She didn't want to waste her life doing a job she hated for one moment longer. Her week off had taught her that. It was time to break free.

Anna seemed surprised when Lucy made her announcement.

'I can't say I'm not disappointed,' she said. 'I've invested a lot of time in you. And I thought you were really starting to find your feet. I'd appreciate it if you could work out your month's notice – hand over what you're working on before you go.'

Lucy nodded. 'Of course – I don't want to leave you in the lurch. I just don't think marketing is for me.'

'I understand – it happens. Is there anyone you've been working with who you think could be worth considering for your position? I've been spending a lot on recruitment recently and I'd rather handle it internally if I can. It doesn't look good to have too many job adverts out at the same time.'

'Annabel would be brilliant,' said Lucy. 'I've been working with her closely on Dogsbody and she's really smart.'

'Thank you. That's good to know,' Anna had said. 'Go to HR and ask them for the forms to fill in – your notice period can start today. And tell Annabel I'd like to see her – around three, ideally.'

As Lucy left Anna's office, she couldn't believe she'd actually done it. She felt nervous but excited. And most of all, she felt like anything could happen now.

* * *

Once she had told Anna she was leaving BAM!, it was on to stage two of the plan. Lucy handed in her notice on the flat that lunchtime, and started thinking about how she could reduce her possessions to the bare minimum. The less she had to carry around, the easier things would be.

Jo was shocked when Lucy called to share her news on Monday night, but immediately offered to help, as did Rosie, who she'd told over a drink after work. But Lucy turned them both down. Spending her nights sifting through everything methodically, alone, was exactly what she needed. Her week off work had made her realise how little time she usually spent on her own. Her thoughts were so much calmer when they were allowed time to breathe and work themselves out away from other people's influence.

She missed Ben, though. On Thursday, the day after he'd invited her to see The Correspondents, he'd been called to Cornwall by Clare. She was in therapy now, and apparently had been sober since her night in the cells.

'When she said she wanted to talk to me, she sounded different. She even thanked me for coming to her rescue so many times – and apologised. I want to be there for her – but it's not like before. I'd just like to see my sister again,' Ben told her.

Lucy agreed it was the right thing to do, much as her body told her otherwise. He called her every few days, getting updates on what she was up to, but it soon became clear it wasn't going to be a brief trip. Still, while phone sex might not be quite as good as feeling Ben's body against hers, he certainly had a way with words.

At first Lucy felt daunted at the idea of getting rid of her belongings, but as she quietly contemplated them over the course of the week, she recognised most were from a different life. She didn't need them any more – they didn't fit her.

The first weekend after resigning, she decided to get rid of the big stuff: a few pieces of furniture she'd collected over the years. They were full of memories but none so precious they merited the price of storage: she'd investigated, and it was the same price as a month's rent had been at university, even if that was a few years ago now.

Actually she'd had most of the furniture since then: the chipped chest of drawers, the wonky wardrobe, the battered futon with green and white stripes that she'd thought looked so sophisticated when she'd picked it out with her mum as a moving-in present for her first student house. Now it was wine-stained from too many student parties, no matter how much she'd scrubbed the covers. It was lumpy too – unsurprisingly as it had seen her through most of her lovers: the stories it could tell.

As Lucy stripped the futon cover off to wash it, she found a pair of stockings still knotted to the frame from a long-forgotten encounter. She smiled wistfully as she thought back to the night it had happened, back in her final year of university.

She'd decided to have a one-night stand: she'd never had one before and, after reading Fear of Flying on the recommendation of the leader of the Women's Association, she'd decided she was curious about the 'zipless fuck' – sex for its own sake, without even exchanging names.

She decided a fetish night would be the best place to meet someone up for no-strings fun – she didn't want to pick someone from her usual circle of friends and get a reputation – and had found a night at Rock City. It had felt odd getting dressed up for it – she'd had to ask her flatmate to help her get into the cheap rubber dress she'd bought – but when she saw her reflection in the mirror, as she buffed the latex up to a perfect shine, she felt a burst of confidence from the way she was dressed. Tonight, she wasn't normal Lucy: she was sexually confident, slutty Lucy – and she wanted to get laid.

From the moment Lucy saw the stranger, she wanted him. He was dressed in a red military jacket, deep in conversation with two stunning women, one elfin, the other with a cleavage so mesmerising that Lucy couldn't help but stare at it. But they were just scenery to her – she knew at first glance that she wanted her guilt-free fuck to be with him. She wasn't sure if he was wearing eyeliner or just had particularly striking eyes, but she was hypnotised. He had a rare quality: once your eyes settled on him, you couldn't look away.

He was slim but clearly toned, with no shirt underneath his jacket – which suited Lucy. Hiding that six-pack would be a crime. He was wearing tight jodhpurs that outlined his strong legs and prominent package, teamed with riding boots and a crop dangling from his belt.

His desirability teamed with Lucy's determination gave her courage, and she hovered at the edge of the group until a chance to interject presented itself. Which it did when one of the women suddenly started looking around, panicking.

'Have you seen my bag?' she asked her friends. When they said no she began searching under tables, to no avail. She became more and more panicked, turning it into a drama that she wanted as many people involved with as possible. She set off around the club with the other woman, stopping to ask Lucy if she'd seen it. Lucy shook her head apologetically, and used it as an opportunity to make eye contact with the man, who was half-heartedly helping in the search.

He looked at Lucy appraisingly as the other women headed off. 'I was supposed to be going back with those two for a threesome,' he said, 'but now Sophie's had her bag nicked it appears to have somewhat ruined the mood. Shame. So, you are . . . ?'

Something about being in a fetish club and knowing she only wanted sex made Lucy feel confident – different from her usual self. Or perhaps it was the three tequila shots she'd downed in rapid succession for Dutch courage.

'Looking for fun,' she replied. 'I can't offer you a threesome, but I might be able to help alleviate your frustration.'

She felt exhilarated as she waited for his response.

'I'm a total stranger, and you're offering yourself to me without even introducing yourself,' he said. 'Interesting. I think you and I are going to get on.'

Again, he insolently looked her up and down, and then walked around her in a circle. Lucy felt like an object being considered for purchase – but it turned her on rather than offending her.

'You do have a particularly spankable bottom. And I like the idea of seeing those pretty lips stretched around my cock.' He reached out and leisurely traced his thumb over her lower lip, smudging her lip gloss.

Lucy knew she ought to have been shocked at him speaking to her like that, but she had set the pace, and was instead thrilled by his blatant appraisal. She wondered what his cock was like. The word 'stretched' sounded promising.

'Well, three's a crowd but two's company,' he said. 'I'm an adaptable man. What are your plans for the rest of the night?'

His voice was dangerous, thought Lucy. It was deep, slightly sarcastic, with an underlying laugh. He reminded her of every bad boy she had ever met. But that was exactly what she needed: a partner in crime.

'My plans mostly involve fucking you,' she said. The man breathed in, clearly surprised but willing to give the matter some thought.

'I have to admit, the idea of defiling that delectable body of yours is rather tempting,' he drawled.

Without another word, he took her hand, pulled her into the ladies' loos and pushed her into a cubicle, locking it behind them. One hand slid straight between her legs, where she knew he could feel how wet his words had made her.

'You filthy little slut,' he said as he ran his other hand speculatively over her bum and up her back, before gathering her hair into a ponytail and pulling her head back sharply. 'So, you want to get fucked?' His voice and attitude had plunged Lucy into a fantasy state and she said, 'Yes,' in the most obedient tone she could muster.

'What made your pussy so wet?'

'The way you look. And what you said – the spanking.' Lucy blushed as she spoke, knowing what was sure to follow. She wasn't disappointed.

'Get your coat. I'm coming back to your place, tying you up and doing exactly what I want to you. Which will most certainly include a spanking – you obviously need bringing in line.'

Lucy knew what she was doing was risky, but the lewd images he conjured in her mind were too tempting to resist.

She sent Jo a quick message on the way back home,

and Jo wrote back promising to check in on her by text in an hour. They'd had the same system since their first year. She surreptitiously took a picture of the stranger and texted it to Jo – which got a reply saying 'Hot!'. Lucy couldn't agree more.

Things started almost as soon as they'd got through the door. After she'd poured him a glass of wine, he outlined his desires.

'What I want to do is tie you down and make you squirm like you've never squirmed before. I want to stroke, lick and nibble you all over, breathe over your pussy until you're begging me to bury my face in you, give you my little finger inside you but no more, so you're hungry for me and begging me for my cock. Does that work for you?'

Lucy nodded. She got the impression he liked to be the one doing the talking.

He moved over to where she was sitting, standing over her as he grabbed her hair and pulled her head back to look up at him.

'I want to get you to the point where you're so desperate to come that you'll agree to anything I ask – and, trust me, I have a very vivid imagination. I won't make you do anything against your will, of course. But I will make you want to do things you've never considered before.'

Lucy could feel her face burning from the graphic description – and her pussy getting even wetter.

'So,' he said, giving her hair another tug. 'Do you

want to play? It doesn't have to be this way, of course. I'm happy to take a more conventional approach.' When she said nothing, he narrowed his eyes. 'Spread your legs.'

Lucy did as she was told.

'Your obedience suggests that's the way you like it, though. Do you?'

He was looking at her intently with those hypnotic eyes. Lucy looked back at him.

'I do.'

He thrust his hand between her legs and slid a finger straight inside her, slipping in easily.

'It would appear that you do. Tell me anything you don't want to do. Then take off your stockings, give them to me and we'll begin.'

Lucy had learned more in one night than she had done in the rest of her time at university. But she was pretty sure she'd surprised him too. He'd made her hornier than she'd ever been, but once he'd awoken the passion within her, she'd been too hungry for orgasm to feel embarrassed and had let her filthiest fantasies come spilling out. It made her feel safer that he didn't even know her name: she could indulge her darkest desires without anyone ever knowing what she'd done.

She told him all the things she'd seen in the porn clips she'd furtively watched, feeling ashamed of watching women tied up, being spanked, teased and humiliated, but also wishing she was in the starring role. She only watched films on a site that had interviews with all the performers after the films, explaining that the pain shown on screen was something they enjoyed, but still, she felt a little embarrassed about admitting her need to be dominated to a man she had only just met. But she was never going to see him again so she took advantage of the anonymity to make some of her dirtiest dreams come true. She had never had so many orgasms in one night – even though he refused to fuck her, instead making her watch as he stroked his shaft and sprayed his come over her skin. It was his punishment for not letting him take her anally; Lucy had been too scared of the pain to try it, and he'd told her that denial went two ways.

In the morning, when he left, she'd been happy to see him go. The night had been more fun than she'd imagined sex with a stranger could be. But she was pretty sure that if they'd spent another night together, it would have gone too far – their darkest fantasies intersected so well that they had pushed each other to the edge. It had been an intense experience and something she was grateful she'd tried – but she'd never realised how far she could go sexually. It scared her a little – and formed the basis for fantasies that she still had to this day. She guessed she'd always had a thing for control.

The futon went to the charity shop on Sunday afternoon, but Lucy kept the memories. Looking back, she couldn't believe how free she'd been back then – far more so than now. David had knocked her confidence on a deeper level than she'd ever suspected. But, since Ben, she was beginning to feel much more like her old self.

The next week at work went quickly, now she was just going through the motions and tying up loose ends. She spent a few long lunches with Rosie brainstorming marketing ideas for her business but, friendship aside, she had already moved on mentally from BAM!. Instead, she focussed on preparing herself for her move.

As Lucy worked out what else she could get rid of, each night after work, she was surprised by how sentimental she felt about inanimate objects: a mug that reminded her of an old flatmate; a bunch of glittery grapes she'd bought at a festival. Every item, no matter how trivial, represented a part of her life. The Edinburgh Crystal glasses, an engagement gift from David's mum, went into the eBay pile.

Different days brought different memories, reminding her of all the people she'd been. On Saturday afternoon, a bag of incense plunged her straight back to her final year at university, living with a stoner and having to mask the constant fug. She lit a cone of it, and the memories came flooding back even more vividly. She put on a playlist from her student days that she'd found on an old memory stick to indulge herself further – but put the bag of incense into a pile of things she was setting aside for friends – along with five sets of worry dolls she'd somehow accumulated as gifts over the years She'd got three on one birthday, she remembered – and wondered if she should have paid more attention to her friends' jokey gifts.

The more her flat emptied, the more content she felt. It was as if she had room to simply *be*, without reminders of who she had been everywhere she looked. She learned a lot about herself as she decided what she loved enough to want to take with her to the next stage of her life, and what she no longer required.

After two weeks of slowly packing and sorting, she was increasingly ruthless about ridding herself of all but her favourite things. She'd cut her belongings by at least a third and her flat looked spacious now she'd got rid of most of her furniture.

Once she'd cleared her wardrobe, taking four stuffed bin-liners to the charity shop on Sunday afternoon, Lucy was surprised by how many classic basics she'd got. She decided these suited her much better than trying to be fashionable and honed her capsule wardrobe down until it was easy for her to carry in a backpack and small case. Everything could be worn with everything else, and Lucy knew she looked great in all of it. She tested out her newly streamlined wardrobe at work that week and garnered a lot more respect. She didn't think it was just because she was leaving imminently: she knew she felt more confident than she ever had before – and looked it too.

After getting her clothes sorted, Lucy devoted the

next weekend to the rest of her things: it was down to the last few odds and ends. She'd checked a couple of websites for tips on de-cluttering that week at work and they all seemed to recommend tackling it in 'zones'.

From her bookshelves, she kept a couple of childhood favourites – *A Little Princess* and *The Secret Garden* – along with a few textbooks she wanted to re-read and some novels that held a special place in her heart. The rest she divided into piles for friends and for the charity shop. She put all her DVDs and CDs aside to be sold, having transferred everything she wanted onto her laptop.

Clearing out her baggage had been good for her, Lucy thought the following Friday, as she faced her final night of sorting and packing. She felt a little tipsy after her leaving drinks, which had been thankfully short and sweet, though Rosie had given her a beautiful pendant in the shape of a winged woman, and Anna had bought a bottle of champagne, which had made it feel like a special occasion.

By the time she fell into bed at 2 a.m., there was only one small bag of items she hadn't managed to sort, with lighters, tealight candles, receipts, unclaimed scratch-cards, charms for a bracelet she hadn't been able to find and single stockings and socks whose partners might yet turn up in the wash – the only chore she had left to do tomorrow.

She put it in the top of a box to deal with later. One

bag of rubbish was manageable enough: she could deal with it when she was settled in her next place. But for now, she was done. Her mum was coming to help her finish moving out on Monday – and there was only one place she wanted to be this weekend.

As the train pulled into Brighton station on Saturday morning, Lucy glanced to her right to see the ivy-covered arches where the dragons lived. Ben's story had tickled her imagination.

She wore a backpack, had a red satchel slung over her shoulder and pulled a wheeled suitcase behind her. She'd decided the trip to Ben's was a good way to test out if she'd kept too much and needed to lighten her load – and even though it was only a short journey, she was now confident she'd reduced her belongings down to perfection. It was almost everything she owned: she'd only got a few boxes for her mum to take back and store for her in Andoversford. Rather than feeling a sense of loss, she was excited. Now she could go wherever she wanted, carrying her world on her back without needing anyone else's help.

But that didn't mean she didn't want anyone else around, she thought as she pushed through the barrier and Ben came into view.

'Hello stranger.' Ben's smile lit up his eyes.

Lucy felt a surge of excitement at seeing him – and feeling him against her as he pulled her into a hug, despite the constraints her baggage presented.

'You didn't have to meet me at the station,' she said. 'I could have made my own way to yours.'

'With those bags? What kind of a gentleman do you think I am – actually, don't answer that,' he said as Lucy opened her mouth to tease him. 'Anyway, I wanted to meet you here – see that smile of yours as soon as I could. How you doing? Tired after your last week at work?'

'Not at all. Tired after your trip back from Cornwall?'

Ben had returned on Thursday night and had immediately called to invite Lucy to visit.

'I feel great – particularly now you're here. I've got plans for you later. But before anything else, I'd really like it if you can put those down and give me a proper hug.'

Lucy was more than willing to oblige – and not entirely surprised when the hug turned into a kiss that made her stomach flip. He hardened as she pressed herself against him, and it was clear he'd missed Lucy every bit as much as she'd missed him.

'So how are things shaping up for you?' Ben asked later. They hadn't spent much of the day talking – he'd dragged her to bed almost as soon as they were through the door, and they'd only headed out into town to go shopping once hunger was too strong an urge to resist.

Now he was preparing a salad to go with dinner, in between taking trips to the roof terrace with plates loaded with food, while Lucy sat sipping a glass of elderflower champagne. He'd insisted he didn't need any help, and she was glad of the opportunity to take a closer look at his flat. Since she'd last been there the seedlings he'd planted had grown dramatically, and now it felt even more like she was sitting in a garden than a living room, with plants bursting out from every wall.

'I haven't made any definite plans,' she told him. 'I've decided to couch surf for a while. Mum's said I'm welcome to move back but I don't want to stay there for more than a few weeks – I've outgrown it, really. Or it's outgrown me – either way, it doesn't feel like home.'

Ben nodded. 'I know what you mean – Cornwall's a bit like that for me.'

'I might be going there too. Hope's well up for the idea of a free babysitter. There's a residential art course she wants to go on so I'm going to stay to help Ant with the kids for a bit.'

'Where do you think you'll end up then?' Ben asked. He was clearly trying to keep his tone nonchalant but Lucy thought she could hear a concerned note in his voice.

'I'm not sure,' she said truthfully. 'Rosie's looking for a new flat she can use as a studio too, and we've talked about maybe getting somewhere together – sharing seems the only way to live in London on a normal wage. But she's not sure when she'll have the money – and I don't know if I want to be in the city any more. Plus I can't imagine passing the reference for any housing agencies without a job.'

'So if you don't like Andoversford and you don't like London, where . . . ?' Ben stopped midway through the question, as if worried that finishing it might make him seem needy.

'I might go travelling – it was a lot cheaper than I thought it would be and I got a load of brochures to look through at STA. I spoke to Rach and it sounds like she's got some exciting stuff coming up – she said she'd be happy for me to tag along with her in her van so I wouldn't need to pay for accommodation.'

'So you do have a Bear Grylls side,' Ben laughed. 'I always knew it.'

'That's just one thing I'm thinking about – nothing's set in stone. I might look at finding somewhere cheap to live and work on setting up my own business. If I'm not tied to London, I can get a place somewhere cheaper with a minimum wage job to tide me over if I need to – work to cover my costs and spend the rest of the time doing who-knows-what.'

'Brighton's cheaper than London,' said Ben. 'If you like it here. I mean, I fell in love with the place within a week of living here but I know it's not for everyone.'

'I've fallen a bit in love too,' said Lucy, giving Ben a sideways glance. 'It's not just the seaside. Everyone's so friendly here – happy to stand out rather than fit in. I don't feel judged like I do in London.'

'Well, you certainly wouldn't get any complaints from

me if you moved here. I'd love to spend more time with you. So, are you ready for dinner?'

'Absolutely,' she said. She picked up the bottle of champagne and Ben's glass before following him out to the roof terrace.

The terrace looked even more beautiful than it had before. Since her last trip, Ben had done more work on the garden – most notably, adding a shimmery paint that lit up the roof like fairyland. He noticed her looking in wonder at the light it was casting over the roof.

'It's solar-powered paint – got some from a mate in environmental science at the university – they're doing some research on it. Like it?'

'It's magical,' said Lucy.

'Follow the path of light,' said Ben, and Lucy did as she was told, rounding the corner to find a small table, complete with white tablecloth and nightlights flickering in glasses. In the centre of the table was a whole roast chicken, and around it were bowls of coleslaw and potato salad, along with the vibrant mixed salad he'd been making and a small white jug of dressing. Another bottle of elderflower champagne sat chilling in a terracotta flowerpot he'd lined with a carrier bag and filled with ice. Although she'd seen him take it all outside, she hadn't been prepared for how beautifully he'd set it up – complete with a hamper bursting with flowers in the centre of the table.

'I know how much you like picnics,' said Ben.

'I do,' said Lucy. 'Although I'm not sure I'm quite ready for dinner, now I come to think of it.'

'Neither am I,' said Ben. 'I just didn't want to spoil the mood later, once we've worked up an appetite.'

'And how do you propose doing that?'

Ben took her by the hand and led her towards a grassy area he'd planted towards the edge of the roof.

'Do you want a blanket or would you rather feel the grass under your back?'

Lucy smiled.

'Great minds think alike,' she said. 'You see, I've been fighting the urge to do this.' She pulled her dress over her head, slipped off her shoes and stood in the moonlight wearing nothing but a tiny lingerie set made from white broderie anglaise with straps covered in embroidered ivy. She'd fallen in love with it and bought it on her week off.

'I'm glad you gave in to temptation,' said Ben, hurriedly pulling off his T-shirt, kicking off his shoes and socks and sliding out of his jeans before stepping forward to take Lucy into his arms.

His lips met hers and Lucy melted into him as she had from their very first kiss. His skin felt hot against hers, despite the spring breeze that gave a chill to the warm night, and there was something exciting about being near-naked outdoors. As she got used to her state of undress, the air against Lucy's skin felt like the stroke of a lover and she shivered, prompting Ben to hold her all the more closely as he rained kisses over her face, her neck, her chest.

When he reached her breasts he cupped them lovingly, holding them up as he slowly kissed and licked them where they rose out of the delicate lace, building her anticipation until she had to grab his hair and force her nipple into his mouth through her bra, she was so desperate to be touched.

'You want more?' Ben said, his hands sliding down her body, tongue close behind, running over her stomach, her thighs and, finally, inside her knickers to her pussy.

'I want *you*,' said Lucy.

'I know,' he said, as his fingers teased her entrance.

Lucy trembled at the touch of his fingertips against her hot, wet skin, and felt her juices trickling down. The flirtatious conversation, Ben's romantic plans and her rooftop striptease had all fed her desire and now that he was touching her, Lucy's lust was rising fast.

She knew what she wanted to do. She'd been thinking about it for a while; it was one thing she'd never done sexually but had always wondered about. She'd played around the edges of her curiosity but never felt ready to go all the way. But now, she wanted Ben to understand that he was different – special: and wanted to feel him in a way she'd never felt anyone before, for herself as much as for him.

'You don't know how much,' said Lucy, pushing his fingers down even lower and pressing them against her tight hole, making her intentions all too clear.

He breathed in sharply. 'Are you sure?'

'I've never done it before,' she replied. 'But I've been

thinking about it and I'd like to. With you. If you want to, of course.'

'I'd love to,' said Ben. 'I've never done it before either.'

'Don't worry,' said Lucy. 'I've read up on it a lot and I've got everything we need in my bag. And I've been warming up over the last few weeks on my own.'

Ben pulled her into a passionate kiss; then drew away to mutter, 'That might be the hottest thing you've ever said to me.' He squeezed her bum, his fingers sliding between her legs, and gave another moan as he felt her juices were now coating her thighs.

Lucy pushed him away gently and went to the table, where she'd left her bag. She produced a bottle of lube and a condom.

'These are for you,' she said. 'Lube's the magic ingredient, apparently.'

'You say the sweetest things,' said Ben, as he slipped the condom on and massaged the lube into his cock. 'Don't worry, I'll be gentle with you.'

He said it jokingly but when Lucy looked at him, his eyes were kind – and clearly appreciative.

Lucy lay on her side on the grassy bed, her lubed fingers circling her hole and sliding inside to stretch herself. It felt a little tender but also sensitive – her pussy was getting wetter as she made her nerves tingle with her caresses.

Ben groaned at the sight of her playing with herself, and began stroking his cock with more intent. Lucy slowly slid her finger in and out, feeling herself relax.

She enjoyed taking her time, knowing Ben had no desire to stop the show. After a while, she could feel herself opening up, and the unfamiliar sensation of feeling a finger *there* was becoming more comfortable – sexy even. She gradually slid her finger deeper but it was only when she added more lube and realised she could slip two fingers inside – and wanted to – that she felt ready for Ben.

'Care to join me?' She looked up at him.

He moved behind her, spooning her, arms wrapped around her and cock pressing against her. Lucy reached behind and moved him into position, first pressing just the head of his cock against her tight entrance. She felt a little pain as he pressed forwards, and steadied his hips with her hand.

'Let me set the pace – it'll be easier that way,'

She dripped more lube from the bottle over the point where their bodies joined, and massaged it into herself with Ben's hard cock. The idea was as intoxicating as the sensation – using him for her pleasure in preparation for giving herself to him in a whole new way.

Ben kissed Lucy's neck and back, one hand massaging her buttocks, the other arm wrapped snugly around her ribcage. Lucy felt ready, and though it took some wriggling it wasn't long before the first inch of him was inside her, and she could feel her muscles starting to ease around him. She flexed them and felt his cock stiffen in return, making her cry out – in pleasure rather than pain.

She circled her hips cautiously, getting used to the sensation of being stretched. After pouring over more lube, she felt an urge she'd never had before – a need to be filled – and felt herself relax and open up to let him slide deeper inside her.

Ben couldn't hold back a thrust, apologising instantly, but Lucy felt pleasure after the brief flash of pain. She started rocking back and forth, slowly at first, but speeding up as her body relaxed to welcome Ben in.

'Oh God, that's amazing,' he said. Lucy revelled in the thrill of Ben's cock sliding in and out of her. It was a darker feeling than she was used to – intense but so hot. She'd played with butt plugs with David *that* night but even in the state she was in, she had drawn the line at anal sex: the idea of him ramming into her in the way he usually did was just too painful to consider there. But this was different.

'Rub my pussy,' she said.

When Ben reached down and felt how aroused she was, he groaned. 'You like this?'

'I love it,' she replied. Now she was moving faster, urging him to climax – she wasn't sure how much longer she could take this level of sensation – but she didn't have long to wait. As her hips pushed back, and Ben's fingers played across her clit, Lucy felt her orgasm building, making her arse grip Ben's cock all the tighter.

'Come for me,' she begged him, and whether it was the words or the feeling of her pushing back against him while he was buried inside her tightness, it was enough to trigger his climax.

Lucy's own orgasm had taken over her body now, the combined movements of Ben's fingers and cock too much to resist. When he carefully pulled out of her a couple of minutes later, she felt a sense of loss. Her muscles seemed to reach for him, and she felt a tingle that made her feel alive – still horny despite her intense orgasm.

She curled up on Ben's chest, reaching out to hold his hand, and the pair of them lay in contented silence, looking at the stars.

'So do you think you might be tempted to move to Brighton, then?' asked Ben a while later.

Lucy thought for a moment before replying. She felt content and more peaceful than she had in years – but she wanted to be honest with him.

'I'm not sure it's right for me to settle anywhere at the moment,' she said. 'I've spent my whole life settling. Now I want to explore – although there's definitely a lot I want to explore in Brighton.' She ran her hand over Ben's chest to emphasise her point. 'And I do love it here. But I need more time to decide what I really want. It feels like I've only just started living my life – I don't want to rush into any big decisions yet.'

The disappointment was obvious in Ben's voice as he said, 'I understand – but I'm glad that Brighton's on your list. So what are you going to do next?'

Lucy smiled, and trailed her hand over Ben's belly, teasingly following the line of hair downwards.

'I'm going to make my dreams come true.'

She sat up and straddled Ben's body, looking down at him as her thighs squeezed his. 'And I'm hoping I'll make a few of yours come true too. Anywhere in particular you'd like to start?'

'Right here seems pretty good to me,' said Ben.

Lucy leaned forwards to kiss him and, as her breasts brushed his skin, she felt his cock start to rise once more.